THE HAUNTING OF TANA GRANT

ROBERT BATY

For Gail

CHAPTER 1

Tana was on deadline the day the ghost crept out of the grave. Lifeless skies hung over the city. Shadows filled the streets. The living, it seemed, were nowhere to be found. A good day to write about the dead, Tana Grant thought, as she turned away from the window and resumed working on an obituary for a woman she never heard of. Most of the people whose lives she memorialized for *The Bay Area Bugle* were famous in one way or another. But Helen Mayfield wasn't famous. She was just dead.

A shadow fell across Tana's cubicle. She looked up and saw Jack Donahue, aka JD, taking up space. He was a stocky white man in his fifties, with a barrel chest, graying red hair and glasses. He was wearing his managing editor uniform of white shirt and tie, khaki Dockers, and suspenders.

"How's it going with the Mayfield obit, Montana?" JD said.

Tana sighed.

Montana.

What kind of name was that for a girl? She blamed it on her parents. They thought it was cute to name her after the state where she was born, and mom and dad had a ranch. They had hoped that Tana, a rangy brunette who looked good in the

1

saddle, would stay on, and grow up to be a cowgirl. Instead, she fled to San Francisco and became a reporter.

"Fine, no problem," Tana said. "I mean it's just really sad she never saw her kid again."

Donahue shrugged, as if to say that they were all sad stories. "Maybe they'll find each other in the afterlife."

Tana looked at the photos that had been selected to run with Mayfield's obituary. One was a news photo of a woman in her thirties trying to fend off the media crowding in around her as she walked out of a courthouse. The other was a snapshot taken at a playground of a little girl coming down the slide with her arms in the air and a smile on her face.

"Her name was Emma," Tana said.

"So what's the lede?" JD said, his voice edgy with impatience.

Tana flashed a nervous smile. "You know what, Jack? I'm still working on it."

"I didn't ask you whether you were still working on it."

Tana felt the heat rush into her face. "Right, sorry," she said.

"Read me what you got."

Tana turned to her computer and read the copy on the screen. "Helen Mayfield, a juror whose lone vote to convict an alleged killer resulted in a hung jury and may have led to her daughter's disappearance, died Tuesday in San Mateo. She was 46."

JD nodded, impressed. "Not bad, Montana."

"Thanks, Jack, but it's Tana, okay?"

JD grinned. "Yeah, I know. Send me the rest when you're done."

"Sure, no problem," Tana said as JD turned and walked away.

Tana had just resumed working on the Mayfield obit when

a black woman in her late thirties with a tight afro, nose ring, and lacquered nails swung by her cubicle. Her name was Sheila, and when she wasn't swiping right or left on Tinder she worked on the online edition of *The Bugle*.

"What'd JD want?" Sheila said, nodding at Donahue, who was making his way across the newsroom toward his office.

"The usual. What was the lede."

"Then he asked you to read it to him, right?"

Tana nodded.

"Did he like it?"

"Yeah, he did."

"So you're done."

Tana rolled her eyes. "Sheila, I am so not done."

Sheila dismissed it with a wave of her hand. Her hot pink nails caught the light.

"You got the hook, baby." She glanced at the Apple Watch on her wrist. "I'd say that calls for a drink. And you know what? Happy hour's on the horizon." She looked up at Tana. "What do you say?"

"I gotta finish this."

"Do it later, girl. You got time, right?"

Tana gave herself a moment to be tempted, then looked up at Sheila and said, "You're on."

Sheila flashed a smile. "First round's on me."

An hour later, just before it started raining, Tana and Sheila grabbed a table by the window at a downtown dive bar. They ordered lemon drop martinis and snacked on beer nuts while they waited for their drinks.

"This is the part I hate," Sheila said, glancing at the bartender.

"What do you mean?"

"The waiting."

"What, for our drinks?"

Sheila nodded.

Tana smiled to herself. That was Sheila. Always in a hurry to get the party started.

Sheila threw another glance at the bartender, then turned to Tana. "So how do you like the obits desk? You've been there, what, a couple years now?"

Tana gave a disappointed shrug. "I don't know. Not exactly what I had in mind."

"What do you mean?"

"Duh, they're dead, okay?"

"Yeah, but they weren't always dead."

"Well, they sure are now," Tana said. "You know what JD told me when he hired me? Do a good job on the dead and we'll give you a shot at the living. That was two years ago."

"Give it time, girl, he'll come around."

Tana shrugged. "He keeps calling me 'Montana.' It's so annoying."

Sheila grinned. "I think it means he likes you."

"Yeah, right."

The barmaid returned with their drinks. "Here you go, ladies," she said, and set their drinks on the table. "This'll take the edge off."

She moved away from the table. Tana and Sheila raised their glasses in a toast, then sipped their drinks.

"Ooh, that's good," Sheila said, smacking her lips.

"You happy now?" Tana said with a teasing smile.

"And getting happier by the minute." Sheila took another sip, then set her glass down and looked at Tana. "So whose obit you working on?"

"Some woman named Helen Mayfield."

Sheila's eyes widened. "*The* Helen Mayfield?"

"Yeah. You know who she was?"

"Honey, back in the day everybody knew who Helen

Mayfield was. It was all over the news. You read about how she never saw her daughter again, right?"

Tana nodded. "I wonder if she's still alive?"

"The kid?"

Sheila made a face. "Can we change the subject?"

"You brought it up."

"Yeah, and now it's bringing me down."

"JD said maybe they'll be reunited in the afterlife."

Sheila shuddered. "The man's been spending way too much time around dead people."

"Yeah, I know. But what if it's true?"

"You're kidding me, right?"

Tana sipped her drink. "Sounds crazy, huh? Maybe I'm the one who's spending too much time around dead people."

It was raining hard, coming down in sheets that blurred the streetlights when Tana and Sheila came out of the bar.

"Hang on a sec," Tana said, opening her umbrella.

Lightning streaked across a starless sky. Tana tried to shield herself from a sudden, blinding flash that seemed to envelop her. She could feel herself losing her balance as the light swirled around her. Then a clap of thunder detonated in her ears. The umbrella fell out of her hands and she collapsed by the door.

Sheila froze. "Oh my God! Tana!" She crouched down beside her. "Are you okay? She looked around as the pouring rain drenched both of them. "Help! Somebody help!"

"It's okay, Sheila, I'm okay," Tana said, starting to come around.

"What happened?"

"I don't know," Tana said, feeling woozy. "I guess it was the lightning or something. It was like all of a sudden I went blind. There was just this flash of light and then everything went dark." She looked at Sheila. "But it was weird...I saw something."

"What do you mean, you saw something?" Sheila said as she helped Tana to her feet.

"I don't know...I can't explain it."

Sheila's face tensed with worry. "Are you sure you're okay? Maybe you should go to the ER."

Tana shook her head. "I'm okay, seriously."

A Toyota Camry with an Uber sticker in the lower right corner of the windshield pulled up in front of the bar. The driver, a Latino in his forties with an Oakland Athletics baseball cap and a salt-and-pepper beard, looked out at Tana and waved as the wipers swept the rain across the windshield.

"Here's my ride," Tana said.

"You want me to come with you, make sure you get home okay?"

Tana smiled and shook her head. "I'm okay. See you tomorrow." They embraced in the rain, then Tana climbed into the Camry and the car pulled away.

Fifteen minutes later, the driver double-parked in front of Tana's building on Nob Hill. She still felt woozy, but she wasn't sure if it was the lemon drop martinis or the lightning. What Tana did know was that she was soaked to the bone and couldn't wait to get out of her clothes.

"Thanks," she said, and pulled on the handle. But the door failed to open. She glanced at the driver, whose face was hidden in the shadows. "Could you open the door? It's locked."

A flash of lightning lit up the car. The driver turned and looked at Tana. But what she saw was no longer an Uber driver wearing an Oakland A's ball cap.

What she saw was the late Helen Mayfield.

CHAPTER 2

TANA STARED AT THE APPARITION AS FEAR SUCKED THE AIR out of her lungs and nearly suffocated her. Helen was wrapped in a translucent shroud that was flecked with soil, as if she'd just emerged from a fresh grave. Tana could see through her to the rainswept streets, but it was as if she was peering through a veil that separated the living from the dead. A heart-shaped pendant with a photo of a child was slung around her neck.

Emma.

Tana wanted to run, scream, anything. But all she could do was wait and see what the dead wanted. It was freezing in the car and when she gasped for air her breath came out in clouds.

Could this be real? Am I hallucinating?

Then the ghost removed the pendant from around her neck and held it out to Tana. She drew back from the dead hand coming toward her. But there was nowhere to go and the door was locked. The pendant dropped into the palm of her hand. Was it the look in the ghost's eyes that compelled Tana to take the pendant? But how could the dead see?

Tana looked down at Emma's photo. As she did so, the pendant began to glow, and suddenly Tana found herself standing outside a daycare center somewhere in the suburbs. A colorful sign was mounted above the entrance:

PICTURE DAY TODAY! SAY CHEESE!

It was the middle of the day. The sun was shining and kids were playing outside. Emma was one of them. She had curly blonde hair and blue eyes, just like in her photo, and she wore a pink top and gray pants with pink stripes. Tana felt strangely calm, as if in a dream. As if being transported from the back seat of a Toyota Camry on a rainy night in the city to a daycare center on a sunny afternoon was perfectly normal.

A teacher's aide emerged from the building and called the kids back inside. Most of them ran toward her, but Emma wanted to stay outside and play. Then someone inside apparently summoned the aide. She glanced at Emma, then turned and went back into the building.

A black SUV braked to a stop in front of the playground. A man jumped out and ran toward Emma. She looked up, saw him coming.

Run! Go back inside! Tana shouted.

But Emma couldn't hear her. The man grabbed her and dragged her screaming to the car. He shoved her into the back seat, then climbed in after her and pulled the door shut. Tana glanced at the license plate as the SUV drove off, tires screeching. She ran toward the building and was about to go inside when the door flew open, and the aide rushed outside. She scanned the yard, a frantic look in her eyes.

They took her! I saw them! Call the police!

Suddenly Tana was back in the Camry. The pendant was in her hand and her eyes were filled with tears. Then she heard the door unlock.

"Sorry about that," the driver said.

Tana stared at him. "Where is she? Where did she go?"

The driver glanced at her in the rearview. "Where'd who go?" he said, confused.

Tana looked down at the pendant and shook her head. "I don't know...I don't know."

"You okay, lady?"

Tana looked up at him. She was anything but okay.

"I saw her..."

"Saw who?"

"She was in the car..."

"What are you talking about?"

"She was behind the wheel...she was you."

The driver scoffed. "She was me, huh? No offense, but maybe you need to sleep it off."

"You don't understand," Tana said. "She gave it to me," She held up the pendant so the driver could see the photo.

He smiled warmly at the sight of the child. "Bonita niña, eh!"

"They took her...I saw them take her..."

Tana could see the driver watching her with a puzzled expression. She flung open the door and ran through the rain to her building, then shivered as she rode the elevator up to her floor. Water dripping from her clothes puddled at her feet. She imagined the elevator filling with water and drowning her before she even reached her floor.

But she was already drowning in the terrors that swam through her as she struggled to make sense of something that would never make sense. Why had the late Helen Mayfield appeared to her? Why was she able to see her? How could she have been transported to the daycare center so that she could witness Emma's abduction? Or was the whole thing just a hallucination, a waking dream that vanished in an instant? And yet, how could she explain the pendant she was clutching tightly in her fist, as if to protect it from the evil that had abducted Emma?

In the space of a moment, everything had changed. Nothing would ever be the same again. She would never be the same again. Who could I tell, she thought. No one. She could tell no one what happened. She was alone with it, this thing that happened to her, and it made her feel alone. How in the world could she ever explain it to anyone? What would she say? Ghost of the deceased visits obituary writer?

The elevator clanked to a stop on her floor, jolting Tana out of her thoughts. She stepped out and headed to her apartment. The muffled sounds of conversations, TV shows and music accompanied her as she walked down the corridor. The smell of dinner on the table seeped through the walls. People still alive, Tana thought, as she unlocked the door to her apartment and went inside.

She paused for a moment before turning on the lights, as if expecting to find another apparition waiting for her. But all Tana found was a chilly apartment that seemed colder than usual. She dropped her keys and the pendant on the coffee table, then turned up the thermostat and went into the bedroom and took off her clothes. She left them in a heap on the floor and pulled on a pair of gray sweats and a red Montana State University hoodie.

Then her iPhone rang. Tana looked at the screen and frowned. "Great. Just what I need," she muttered to herself.

"I've been calling you, babe, you get my messages?" a man said.

"We broke up, Justin, remember?"

"Yeah, I know, but I'm downstairs. Can I come up?"

"What's the problem? Aren't your other girlfriends available tonight?"

"What other girlfriends?"

"The ones you forgot tell me about."

"You got it all wrong, babe—"

"I gotta go, Justin."

"You sound different. Are you okay?"

"Yeah, never better," Tana said, and ended the call.

She knew that if she let him in, he would do his best to persuade her that the fact that he was seeing two other women besides her was just her imagination. And she might even believe him, if only for one night, because he was cute, and she still liked him. But not tonight. Not after what happened. She dropped the phone on the nightstand and went into the bathroom to towel-dry her hair.

That was when she saw it. The message scrawled on the mirror in bright red crayon, as if by a child.

Find me.

CHAPTER 3

EMMA.

Tana's hand flew to her mouth. She wanted to scream, but it was as if fear had frozen her voice. The dread in the pit of her stomach climbed into her throat. A chill rushed through her. She sank to the tile floor, which felt clammy and cold as a grave.

This isn't happening, she told herself, shaking her head. *It can't be. No way.* And yet when she looked up at the mirror the message was still there.

Find me.

Tana wrapped her arms around herself and rocked back and forth like a child. As if hugging herself would be enough to protect her from the forces that had crossed over from another world and now seemed to be closing in on her. She closed her eyes and hoped that when she opened them the nightmare would be over, and her life would be back to normal. But even in the dark behind her eyes she still saw it all—Helen, Emma, the pendant, the abduction at the daycare center—unspooling like an endless loop. She ran her hand through her hair and realized that it was still wet, then stood and walked out of the bathroom and closed the door behind her.

She glanced at the pendant on the coffee table for a

moment, afraid of what might happen if she touched it, then reached for her iPhone and punched in a number.

"Can you come over?" she said when a woman answered.

"Now?"

"Yeah, like right now."

"Are you okay?"

Just come over, okay, Mimi?"

"What's wrong?"

"I'll tell you when you get here."

Twenty minutes later Tana's intercom buzzed.

"Are you here?"

"I'm here."

Tana buzzed her in, then took a deep breath. What would Mimi think when she told her what happened? What would anyone think? Tana had no idea. She had thought she could face it alone, keep it inside like some dark secret that could never be revealed to anyone. But she was wrong. She had to tell somebody what happened, or her head would explode. She decided that her best friend was a good place to start, as long as it didn't scare her off. At least Mimi wouldn't try and have her committed for psychiatric observation. Then again, Tana thought, Mimi hadn't yet heard her story.

The doorbell rang. Tana opened the door and saw a short, chubby woman around her age with a round face, curly brown hair, tortoise shell glasses and a nose ring. She had a Tupperware container in one hand and a wine carrier in the other.

"Hi Mimi, thanks for coming over."

"Hey, what are friends for?" Mimi said as she walked into the apartment. She held out the Tupperware and the wine carrier. "I brought you some paella. It was the house special tonight. Everybody loved it."

Mimi was a line cook at *Falseta*, an upscale Spanish restaurant in the city, and liked to bring entrees with her when she hung out with her friends. Tana figured it was her way of taking her friends out to dinner at a restaurant they could barely afford on their own.

"Thanks, but I'm not hungry," Tana said as she closed the door.

"You sure? It's seriously good."

"I'm sure."

"That serious, huh?"

Tana nodded.

"Okay, well, why don't I open the wine and you can tell me what I'm doing here."

"Sure, sounds good."

Tana sat on the sofa, her eyes glued to the pendant. She could hear Mimi in the kitchen taking glasses down from the cupboard and opening the wine. They were familiar sounds, and for a moment Tana almost felt normal.

"Here you go, this'll fix anything," Mimi said, emerging from the kitchen with two glasses of Rioja. She handed Tana a glass, then sat down beside her.

Tana managed a weak smile. "Thanks."

Mimi nodded at Tana's wet hair. "You get caught in the rain?"

"Yeah, forgot my umbrella."

Mimi sipped her wine, then looked at Tana. "So what's the big deal?"

Tana paused, then said, "Could you do me a favor?"

"Sure, what?"

"Could you just go to the bathroom?"

Mimi looked at her with a puzzled expression. "Excuse me? I went at the restaurant."

"Just go to the bathroom and look at the mirror and tell me what you see, okay?"

"Seriously?"

"Seriously."

"What's going on, Tana?"

"Please?" Tana said, a pleading look in her eyes.

"Okay, no problem." Mimi leaned forward to set her wine glass on the coffee table and saw the pendant. "Oh, that's pretty," she said, reaching for it.

"Don't touch it!"

Mimi jumped back and looked at Tana, her eyes wide with alarm. "Now you're scaring me, okay?"

"That makes two of us. I'm already scared."

"You gonna tell me why?"

"Just go in the bathroom and look at the mirror."

Mimi shrugged. "Okay, okay. I'll go look at the mirror."

Tana buried her face in her hands. A siren wailed somewhere in the dark, then faded like a sigh. Mortality was everywhere, she thought. Maybe immortality, too. A moment later, Mimi emerged from the bathroom. Tana looked up at her.

"Did you see it?"

See what? The mirror? Yeah, I saw it. No offense, but it could use a little Windex."

"You can't see it, can you?"

"See what? What was I supposed to see?"

"Find me."

"Find me?"

Tana nodded.

"What's that supposed to mean?"

"Emma wants me to find her."

"Who's Emma?"

Tana sighed. "I don't know where to start or how to explain it."

"Try starting at the beginning."

"I could start at the beginning or the middle or the end and you still wouldn't believe me."

"Try me."

Tana paused to sip her wine. "Do you believe in ghosts, Mimi? The afterlife, stuff like that?"

Mimi shuddered. "That shit's too scary for me."

"Yeah, too scary for me too...until now."

"What do you mean, until now? Where you going with this, Tana?"

Tana didn't want to scare her, but there no other way to explain it. "You have to promise me something."

"Okay..."

"Promise me you'll just listen to what I tell you."

"Okay, I promise, but what are you going to tell me?"

With her eyes on the pendant, Tana said, "A ghost story."

CHAPTER 4

BUT THE SETTING WAS ALL WRONG FOR A GHOST STORY, Tana thought. She and Mimi should've been sitting around a campfire deep in the woods in the dead of night. Wasn't that how you were supposed to tell stories that made everybody shiver with the pleasures of being scared? Tana had no idea. She'd never told anyone a ghost story before, and yet here she was, living through her own ghost story.

But from the look in Mimi's eyes as she sipped her wine, Tana knew that she didn't believe a word of what she was telling her. How could she? Tana wasn't sure she believed it herself. And if it hadn't happened to her, she probably wouldn't have believed it. But that was the thing—it did happen to her. Every word of it.

"Seriously? You saw a ghost?" Mimi said.

"Yeah, I saw a ghost. I mean, what else could she have been? It's not Halloween or anything."

"And she wants you to find her kid."

Tana nodded. "I know it sounds crazy…"

"No shit, girlfriend."

"She wants me to find out what happened to Emma."

"What difference does it make, Tana? I mean, listen to

yourself. She's dead, okay? Maybe the kid's dead too. Did you ever think that maybe the whole thing is just one big hallucination, that's maybe you're just imagining it?"

Tana grabbed the pendant and dangled it in front of Mimi. "Am I imagining this?"

Mimi shrugged, unimpressed, and drained her glass. She stood and walked into the kitchen, then returned with the bottle of Rioja. "Maybe somebody left it behind in the Uber," she said as she refilled their glasses. "Stuff like that happens all the time."

Tana scoffed. "Right. Why can't you believe me?"

Mimi took a sip of wine, then looked at her friend. "Maybe you should talk to somebody, Tana."

"I'm talking to you, aren't I?"

"I mean like somebody professional."

"Yeah, right. Maybe I can have myself committed for observation."

"I'm just trying to help, okay?"

Tana nodded. "I know, I'm sorry."

"What if you call the police? Maybe they could help."

Tana was dismayed. "What am I gonna tell 'em, Mimi? That my Uber driver turned into a ghost who showed me how her daughter was kidnapped ten years ago? And now I'm supposed to find her?"

Mimi lowered her eyes, a chastened look on her face. "I'm not helping you much, am I?"

Tana took Mimi's hand and gave a grateful smile. "You're here, Mimi, and that helps."

"Yeah, but what are you gonna do?"

Tana shook her head. "I don't know. Maybe you're right, maybe I am going crazy."

"Maybe you shouldn't stay here tonight," Mimi said. "Maybe you should get a room or something." She paused. "I'd have you stay with me, but I don't know I'd explain it to Heather." She gave an embarrassed look. "You know how she is."

It's okay, Mimi. I understand."

Mimi glanced at her Apple Watch. "Speaking of which, I better go. Heather's gonna wonder what's going on."

Tana nodded, then looked at Mimi. "Don't tell her about this, okay?"

"Sure, no problem. I don't tell her everything, you know."

Tana's eyes fell on the pendant. "It happened, Mimi, it really happened, and now I don't know what to do."

The room fell silent. Tana knew that Mimi didn't know what to say. Tana didn't either. But she knew that her ghost story had made Mimi uncomfortable, and she wanted to leave. Tana decided to make it easy for her.

"Thanks for coming over, girlfriend."

Mimi finished her wine, then threw arms around Tana. "Call me tomorrow. I want to know you're okay."

"I promise," Tana said.

"And eat the paella. It's really good."

Tana walked her to the door. They embraced again, then Mimi was gone. Tana closed the door behind her. Is it still there, she wondered. She went into the bathroom and saw that the message was still on the mirror.

"I can't live like this," she said to no one in particular.

She walked out of the bathroom, then returned moments later with her iPhone, a roll of paper towels and a bottle of Windex. She took a pic of the message on the mirror, then checked Photos to see if it was there. But it wasn't. All she saw was her reflection of herself in the mirror taking a selfie. Tana caught her breath, then backed away from the mirror, as if it were possessed.

She shoved the phone in her pocket, then grabbed the

Windex and sprayed the mirror until the message disappeared in the mist. But when she tried to wipe it clean with a paper towel, Tana saw that the message was still there.

Find me.

She shook her head, as if to deny what she was seeing.

"This isn't happening," she said out loud. "Tell me this isn't happening."

But there was no answer. Just the message on the mirror.

"Go away!" she shouted. "Just get the fuck away from me!"

Then Tana remembered that she was on deadline. In all the otherworldly excitement that had engulfed her life, she had forgotten that she had to finish Helen's obituary and send it to Donahue. But how could she focus on it now, after all that had happened? She had to find a way. She had to make it appear as if her life was normal, even though it wasn't. The last thing JD or anyone else at *The Bugle* needed to know was that the ghost of the woman whose obituary she was writing had made an appearance.

Tana went back into the living room. She threw a glance across the room at her MacBook, which sat on a desk by the windows. The screen was dark, and the laptop was off. She was about to go into the kitchen and make a pot of coffee when the MacBook's screen suddenly lit up, startling her. How did that happen, she wondered

Tana walked over to her desk, pulled out a chair and sat down. She turned on the desk lamp she had bought at *Design Within Reach* and saw that Helen's obituary was on the screen. But as she scrolled through the Word doc Tana realized that there was nothing left for her to do. The unfinished obituary she had emailed to herself before she left the office had been completed. Who finished it?

And then she knew.

CHAPTER 5

Tana jumped up from her desk. Stared wide-eyed at her laptop as if it were alive. Her legs felt rubbery and for a moment she thought she would collapse.

"You're here, aren't you?" she shouted as she looked around the room. "I can't see you, but I know you're here. Why can't you find her yourself? What do you need me for?"

But the only answer she got was a damp breeze that washed across her face as she sat on the sofa and ran her hands through her hair. Her heart was pounding as she gasped for breath. Tana glanced at her MacBook then stood and pulled on the coat she had slung over a chair and stepped to the door.

Where are you going? I don't know. What if it's still raining? I don't care, I have to get out of here.

Tana walked out of the apartment, closing the door behind her, then took the stairs and went outside. It felt good to be out among the living, and it reminded Tana that she too was still alive. The storm had passed, but the air still smelled like rain and Tana could feel the mist on her face. The streets were slick black mirrors, reflecting the lights of passing cars.

She walked for blocks, her thoughts swimming between two worlds, then noticed that St. Mary's, the old Catholic church on the edge of Chinatown, was open for evening services. She'd walked past the church before, but usually the doors were closed and homeless were slumped on the steps next to their shopping carts. She'd never been inside—never been inside any church, really. Her parents weren't religious and as a result neither was Tana. In fact, her father had taught her that religion was a con that lured people into believing that there was some reward waiting for them on the other side, a bonus for having been alive, when in reality there was nothing.

But now Tana wasn't so sure. Not after what happened. Perhaps that was why she decided to walk up the steps and go inside. She stood in the vestibule and looked around. A handful of parishioners, mostly older women, were kneeling in pews, heads bowed and hands clasped in prayer, or lighting candles to the Virgin Mary and their favorite saints. A tall, thin priest with a ruddy complexion, beak nose and white hair emerged from one of the confessionals. He noticed Tana and walked over to her.

"Welcome to Saint Mary's," he said with a kindly smile. "I'm Father Collins."

Tana smiled politely. "Hi." Up close she could see the dandruff on his black cassock.

"Your first time?"

Tana looked at him. "That obvious, huh?"

"You get to know faces after a while. Most of my parishioners attend services regularly."

"Can I ask you a question, Father?"

"Of course. What would you like to know?"

"Do you believe in ghosts?"

Father Collins gave an avuncular smile. "I believe in the Holy Ghost, my child."

"What makes a ghost holy?"

The priest looked at Tana, as if taken by surprise. "The love of Our Lord, the giver of life."

Tana said nothing. She looked toward the sanctuary. A crucifix hung over the altar. Why do people like looking at a half-naked man nailed to a cross, she wondered. Was it because he was supposedly the son of God? Was that enough reason? And what kind of God would let his son be nailed to a cross? Maybe her father was right, Tana thought. She turned to Father Collins.

"Can other ghosts be holy too, or just the Holy Ghost?"

Father Collins chuckled. "What an amusing question. There are no other ghosts. There is only the Holy Ghost, and he dwells in the hearts of the faithful."

Tana noticed that more and more parishioners were walking into the church, stepping past Tana and Father Collins and filling the pews.

"I'm about to say evening Mass," Father Collins said. "Would you like to join us?"

Tana thought about it for a moment, then shook her head. "Not tonight, Father, but thanks."

"Well, perhaps another time. God is always available, my child."

"I'll keep that in mind."

Tana turned and walked out of the vestibule and went down the steps, making her way through the faithful, who were heading in the opposite direction, toward salvation.

When she reached the sidewalk Tana stopped and looked up at the church. Father Collins wanted her to believe, she thought. But would he believe her if she told him about what happened? It occurred to Tana that maybe she knew more about the other side than he did. She'd been there. He hadn't. She turned and headed back to her apartment, and to what she knew was waiting for her.

The MacBook screen was glowing in the darkened room when Tana opened the door. It beckoned to her, drawing her toward it as if it were a magic lantern that would show her what she had not seen.

Send the obit to JD, she told herself. You can't make sense of what's happening, so stop trying and just send it. Pretend that everything's fine, business as usual, just another day at the office.

She took off her coat and slung it over a chair, then walked over to her desk and sat down. She would read the obituary again, edit the copy to conform to the *Bugle's* guidelines, then send it off.

But as she scrolled through the copy, Tana noticed something she had missed the first time around. The discovery that the obituary had been completed without her had blown her away and left her so disoriented that she failed to notice that a child's drawing had been attached to the document. It was a portrait of a mother and daughter, as seen through a child's eyes, and it was drawn in bright red crayon, just like the message that appeared on Tana's bathroom mirror. But their faces were streaked with blood-red tears.

CHAPTER 6

HELEN MAYFIELD'S OBITUARY RAN THE NEXT MORNING under Tana's byline in the print edition of *The Bugle*. The online version had gone live at midnight. But the drawing didn't appear in either version. Tana had deleted it before she sent the doc to JD. She understood that the drawing, like the message on the mirror, was meant for her eyes only. She also understood that she didn't want to have to explain JD how the drawing happened to come into her possession.

But a chill came over her as she sat at her desk and read the obit. It was as if the living and dead had worked together, and it marked the first time she had collaborated with the deceased on their own obituary. How was that even possible, Tana thought. And yet, somehow, it was. I hope this doesn't catch on, Tana thought. Because if the dead start writing their own obits I'm out of a job. She tried to laugh, but the joke died in her throat.

"Hey, Montana!"

The voice jolted Tana out of her thoughts. She looked up and saw JD and rolled her eyes. Would he never stop calling her "Montana?" The morning edition of *The Bugle* was tucked under his arm and he was carrying a manila folder. He came up to Tana and swatted her playfully with the newspaper.

"Nice job on the Mayfield piece," he said.

"Thanks, JD, but do you think you could like call me Tana?"

Donahue feigned innocent surprise. "Why? Montana's your name, isn't it?"

Tana sighed. "Yeah, but I like Tana better, okay?"

Donahue shrugged, then changed the subject. "How'd you find out so much about Mayfield and her daughter? I don't remember seeing a lot of that material in the research or the interview transcripts."

Tana shrugged. How could she ever possible explain it? "I just kept digging," she said.

Donahue nodded. "Seems like you took a personal interest in this one."

"I guess maybe I did."

Donahue paused. "I guess I'm wondering why."

Tana felt her face get hot. Was it that obvious?

"Guess I'm a sucker for sad stories," she said.

"They're all sad stories, Montana. You want to know why? Because they're dead."

That's not all they are, JD, Tana thought. But all she did was smile, nod in agreement, and hope that would be enough.

"Here's the next one," he said, and dropped the manila folder on her desk.

"Thanks," Tana said.

Donahue nodded and walked away. Tana opened the manila folder and quickly skimmed the cover sheet. A faded seventies metal star named Gary Dunham, who, with his band Gary and the Gladiators, liked to perform in Roman gladiator outfits, had dropped dead onstage at some casino in Florida during an oldies tour. Tana had never heard of him. Then again, she had never heard of Helen Mayfield either. And now she would never forget her. She closed the manila folder and turned back to Helen's obit.

And as she stared at her screen the obit pixelated, then disappeared and was replaced by a message scrawled in bright red crayon that Tana had seen before:

Find me.

"I know," Tana said, softly, as if she was speaking to Emma. "I know."

Or was she talking to herself? Had she accepted what she could not have imagined and yet had somehow become real? Or was she simply losing her mind and descending into madness at a young and tender age? Would this have happened if she'd never become an obituary writer? Was there something about the job that connected the living and the dead? Or was it just her? Too late now. A mother's love had reached out to her beyond the grave, and there was nothing Tana could do except answer the call.

How old was she when she lost her child? Twenty-two. A guy she met on Craigslist. A quickie at his place in the Mission on her lunch hour. Tana sucked in her breath when it suddenly occurred to her that had she lived, her nameless child would be the same age that Emma was when she disappeared. Was that why Helen Mayfield had reached out to her? The symmetry of their children's lives? Tana's eyes filled with tears. She had let her child go even before she was born, and here was Helen, still seeking her child, even from the grave. Tana reached for a tissue and wiped her eyes before anyone could notice the tears rolling down her cheeks.

Then the phone rang. Tana quickly composed herself, then answered it.

"Obituaries, Tana Grant."

"Hey, ghost girl, what up?"

Tana sighed. "Not funny, Mimi."

"Sorry. How you doing? Are you okay?"

Not really, Tana thought. But all she said was, "Yeah, I'm fine."

"I was worried about you after last night...I mean it wasn't like I didn't believe you; it was just weird, you know—"

"It's okay, Mimi. You don't need to worry about me."

"You want to meet up for lunch? There's this great new sushi place I heard about. I'm dying to try it."

"I can't, I'm on deadline," Tana said.

She had other plans for lunch, and they didn't include being grilled by Mimi about what she had seen or not seen. If she was to find out what happened to Emma, Tana needed to know more about her disappearance. Spending some time in the morgue reviewing the Vargas case and the police investigation into Emma's abduction would be a good place to start.

All she knew was that ten years ago, Helen was a juror in the murder trial of some lowlife named Hector Vargas. The DA's star eyewitness was a supermarket checker named Carmen Flowers, who claimed she saw Vargas gun down two clerks when she went into the Lucky Star MiniStop to buy cigarettes.

But on the stand, Flowers developed a sudden case of amnesia and recanted her testimony. The word around the courthouse was that she took a bribe. Helen's fellow jurors decided that the prosecution failed to meet the burden of proof and voted to acquit. But Helen refused to join them. She was convinced that Vargas was guilty and voted to convict. Her vote hung the jury and freed the defendant. A week after Vargas walked, Emma disappeared.

But the Vargas case and its connection to Emma's abduction wasn't the only reason Tana begged off lunch. More than anything, she wanted Mimi to believe her. And yet she didn't want to have to try and persuade Mimi to believe her. She didn't need Mimi telling her that she was seeing things. She was seeing things—that was the problem.

"Deadline with the dead, huh?" Mimi said, chuckling.

"Yeah, something like that."

"Okay, then I'll let you go. Love you."

"Love you too," Tana said, and hung up.

The phone rang again a moment later.

"Saw Helen Mayfield's obit in the paper this morning," a man said. He sounded middle-aged or older, and his voice was rough with cigarettes and whiskey.

"Yes?"

"You wrote it, right?"

"Yes, that's right."

The call surprised Tana. Readers didn't often contact her directly about the obituaries that appeared under her byline. If they did have comments, they usually posted them online or wrote letters to the editor. She wondered if the caller might be a friend or family member, but decided that was unlikely, as she had interviewed Helen's survivors. Who was he, then?

"Montana Grant, right?"

"Tana Grant. What can I do for you?"

"You left something out," the man said.

"What's that?" Tana said, reaching for a pen and a notepad.

"Me."

CHAPTER 7

Twenty minutes later Tana walked into a bar down the street from *The Bugle* called The Ruby Room. It was the middle of the day, lunchtime anywhere else. But the place was dead quiet, and the barflies hanging out in the shadows all looked like they'd been there since breakfast. A rugged, middle-age man wearing a gray work shirt and faded jeans was hunched over a drink in a booth by the window. He had a narrow face, long hair going gray at the temples and salt and pepper stubble. A double shot of bourbon was on the table in front of him. The man saw Tana and motioned to her.

"Frank Aiken?" Tana said as she came up to him.

Aiken nodded.

"Have a seat."

Tana slid into the booth, then looked at Aiken with a puzzled expression. "How'd you know it was me?"

"You don't look like the type," Aiken said.

"The type?"

"The type who drinks their lunch in a place like this." He sipped his bourbon. "You wouldn't be here if I hadn't called you, right?"

"Why did you call me?"

"Didn't want to be left out."

"Left out of what? I don't understand."

Aiken knocked back the rest of his drink. He paused, then said, "I'm Emma's father."

The news startled Tana. Her eyes widened. She stared at Aiken. "Her father?"

Aiken nodded. "They didn't tell you about me, did they?"

"They?"

"Her family. You interviewed them, didn't you?"

"Yes, of course—"

"But they didn't tell you about me, did they?"

Aiken motioned to the barmaid, and when he got her attention, he pointed to his empty glass. Then he turned to Tana.

"You want something?"

Tana shook her head. "I'm good."

"So what'd they tell you when you asked about Emma's father?"

Tana shrugged. "They didn't say much, really. They just said you and Helen didn't get along and that you weren't part of her life. When I told them I wanted to interview you for the obituary nobody knew where you were or how to get in touch with you."

"Like I didn't exist, right?"

Tana nodded. "Something like that," she said quietly.

Aiken's craggy face hardened. "Bastards."

The barmaid came up to them and set Aiken's drink on the table.

"Thanks," he said. He looked at Tana. "You sure you don't want anything?"

Tana nodded. The barmaid moved away.

"Was it true what they said about not knowing where to find you?"

Aiken shrugged. "I was gone a lot, sometimes for months at a time."

"Why?" Tana said, wondering if Aiken had been in prison.

"I was workin' offshore oil rigs. Texas, Louisiana, Gulf of Mexico. It's not the right kind of work for a family man, but the money was good and Helen didn't want me around anyway. But it wasn't just the work. I wasn't part of Emma's life because Helen kept me out. I tried...tried for years to be part of that kid's life." Aiken paused to sip his drink. "And then she disappeared." He gave a cold smile. "I guess what goes around comes around, huh?"

"Excuse me?" Tana said. "I don't understand."

"Helen took her away from me, and then somebody took Emma away from her."

Who smiles when their kid is kidnapped, Tana wondered.

"Were you here when it happened?"

Aiken shook his head. "I was in Texas."

"Did you talk to the police?"

"Yeah, they wanted to know if I had an alibi."

"Did you?"

"Like I said, I was in Texas."

"Did you know about the trial before Emma went missing?"

Aiken shook his head. "Just what I heard on the news."

"Her relatives said Helen was afraid of you...they said she got a restraining order."

Aiken sipped his drink. "Yeah, so what? You married?

Tana shook her head.

"Shit happens when you're married, okay? Don't mean I'm not Emma's father."

They fell silent. Aiken stared into his drink. Tana wondered if Aiken knew more about Emma's disappearance than he was letting on.

"You said your name was Aiken," she said. "But Helen's name was Mayfield."

Aiken nodded.

"She went back to her maiden name after we split up. Didn't want nothin' to do with me, didn't even want my name." He sipped his drink, then looked up at Tana. "Then I saw your obit in the paper and that's when I found out Helen had passed. That's how come I called you. Didn't want to be left out no more."

"Got any idea what happened to her?"

"Emma?"

Tana nodded.

Aiken shrugged like it wasn't worth thinking about. "She's gone, that all I know."

"But somebody took her."

"Yeah, somebody took her." Aiken knocked back the rest of his drink. "I guess I wasn't the only one who got pissed at Helen."

"Pissed enough to kidnap her daughter?"

"Looks that way. Like I said, what goes around comes around."

Tana shuddered. Was she sitting across from the man who a decade ago had kidnapped his own daughter? She glanced at her watch.

"I better get back. I'm on deadline."

Aiken chuckled. "I'll bet you're on deadline every day."

Tana gave a rueful smile. "People die every day."

"Yeah, so I hear."

Aiken looked down into what was left of his drink. Maybe into what was left of his life. He motioned to the barmaid for another round, then turned to Tana as stood and prepared to leave.

"A word of advice."

Tana looked down at him. "Excuse me?"

"I'd let Emma be if I were you."

"Is that a threat, Mr. Aiken?"

Aiken coughed up a smile filled with tobacco-stained teeth. "You have a nice day, hear?"

CHAPTER 8

TANA'S INTERVIEW WITH FRANK AIKEN WAS ON HER MIND as she headed back to the office. No one had ever threatened her before, and she worried about what lay behind it. Did he mean it, she wondered, or was he just trying to scare her? But why? Was it because he had something to do with Emma's disappearance? Her involvement with the subjects of her obituaries ended the moment she filed the copy. They were dead and she was done. But with Helen Mayfield, she knew it was far from over. And Aiken's threat seemed to confirm that her work had only just begun.

Then a text from JD jolted her back to her day job.

"Where are we on the Gary Dunham obit?" he said, referring to the front man for Gary and the Gladiators.

"Working on it," Tana replied.

"Good. Get it done. We need to run it as soon as possible."

"What's the rush?"

"Our publisher was a fan back in the day, saw the Gladiators on tour, got his autograph, even bought one of his gladiator outfits off eBay. Wants to see his obit in print sooner rather than later."

"On it," Tana texted.

Get started on the Dunham obit, she told herself, before JD throws a shadow across your cubicle and asks you to read him the lede. She opened Dunham's folder and began reviewing the materials.

"Hola, chica, why'd you stand me up?"

Tana looked up at saw Ricky standing by her cubicle with a hurt expression on his face. Ricky was slender, Puerto Rican and gay, and he covered celebrities, gossip, and the social scene for *The Bugle*. He loved to dish, and Tana loved to listen, which made it easy to be friends with him. That was the thing about gay men, Tana thought. You could actually be friends with them in a way that was never possible with straight men, who always assumed that if you wanted to be friends it meant you wanted to fuck. She had shared much of her life with Ricky, but he never read the obituaries she wrote because he was superstitious and thought if he read about the dead he would be next to die. As a result, he didn't know about Helen Mayfield or her daughter. And he never would.

"Sorry, JD was on my case about an obit."

"I came by, you weren't here," Ricky said.

"I was having trouble concentrating, so I went for a walk."

She hated lying about why she'd blown off their lunch date, and she figured he probably knew she was lying to him. But what else could she do? She was beginning to feel as if she was leading a double life and wasn't quite sure which one was real. Maybe they both were. But how could she live that way?

"I would've gone with you, you know," Ricky said.

"I know, I'm sorry, honey."

Ricky offered a diva shrug. "That's okay, I'll survive...somehow."

Tana grinned. "I'll make it up to you."

"How about tonight? Matt and I are doing Queens on Mars Night at Oasis," Ricky said, referring to his white, blond, All-

American boyfriend, who did hair and color at a trendy down-town salon.

Just what she did not need, Tana thought. Drag queens at a gay bar in the Castro.

"Not tonight, Ricky. But you girls have fun."

"Okay, mi amor, but if you change your mind, you know where to find us..."

Tana nodded at her computer. "I better get back to work. JD's on my case about it."

Ricky nodded. "No problem. I can tell when I'm not want-ed." Then he grinned. "See you later, girlfriend," he said and walked away.

Tana turned back to Dunham's obituary. She had lied to Ricky about why she stood him up. But she wasn't lying when she told him she was having trouble concentrating. That was the truth. Emma and Helen Mayfield had become a part of her, and it frightened her. She had seen Helen's ghost, she had seen Emma's message on the mirror, she had seen the drawing on her MacBook, and now she couldn't not see them, much as she might want to.

Tana spent the rest of the day on Dunham's obit. It turned out to be the most difficult obituary she had ever written. But not because of anything having to do with its subject. She had always been able to focus. That ability had served her well in college and helped her land the job at *The Bugle*. But that was before Helen and Emma had turned her life upside down. Finally, after four drafts, the last of which included edits from the publisher, who had his own fanboy ideas about how Gary Dunham should be remembered, she was done.

She rubbed her eyes, then shut down her computer and packed up her things. It was almost six, and she'd had enough of dead people for one day. She glanced at the stack of manila folders on her desk. The recently departed, trapped between two worlds and waiting for their fifteen minutes in the morning edition. They would have to wait. Tana looked up and saw JD staring at his cellphone as he headed towards the elevator, his coat slung over his shoulder. Time to go. She pulled on her coat and went to pee before she left the office.

When she came out of the stall Tana found Brianna primping in the mirror. Better known as Bree, Brianna was one of the interns at the paper, and spent most of her time tweeting and retweeting on Twitter. She glanced at Vivian's reflection as she traced Amy Winehouse cat eyes with her eyeliner.

"Did you read @Gossip_Gal today on Twitter?" Brianna said.

Tana shook her head. "Sorry, way too busy."

"Oh my God, it was total dish. She knows everything. I guess that's why she has a ton of followers."

Tana smiled politely but left it at that. She had often wondered what Brianna was doing at *The Bugle* in the first place, and assumed it had something to do with using social media to attract younger readers to the paper.

Brianna gave her a curious look. "You like write about dead people, right?"

"Something like that," Tana said.

"Must be really boring, huh?"

Tana looked at her. "Excuse me?"

"I mean like duh, they're dead." Brianna unbuttoned a button on her blouse to reveal more cleavage. "Is this better?"

Only if you want everybody staring at your boobs, Tana thought. Which of course was exactly what Brianna wanted.

She finished doing her eyes and offered Tana her eyeliner.

"No offense, but you could use a little touch-up."

"I'm good," Tana said with a tight smile.

"K," Brianna said. "See you tomorrow."

Can't wait, Tana thought, as Brianna walked out, and the

ladies room fell silent. Tana glanced at herself in the mirror and wondered if Brianna was right. Did she need a little touch-up?

Then she saw it.

The message scrawled in bright red crayon on the mirror, as if by a child.

Hurry

CHAPTER 9

Tana felt a chill rush down her back. Her spine turned to ice. She stared, transfixed, at the word scrawled on the mirror.

Hurry

"Hurry where?" she said out loud. "Where am I supposed to go? Why do I have to find you? Why me?"

Just then Sheila entered the ladies' room. She saw Tana and smiled. "Hey, girlfriend, you down for our double date tonight?"

Tana ignored Sheila, as if she hadn't heard her or was unaware of her presence. As if all that mattered was the message on the mirror.

"I don't know where to find you," Tana continued. "I don't know where to look for you, I don't know anything, okay?" Her eyes filled with tears.

Sheila stopped, startled. To her it seemed as if Tana was talking to herself while staring at her reflection in the mirror. She appeared to be in some kind of trance, and the sight of it frightened Sheila. She watched Tana for a moment as if unsure of what to do next, her face clouded with fear and confusion.

"Tell me where, okay? Give me a sign. Show me what I'm supposed to do," Tana said.

"Tana..." Sheila said in a cautious tone of voice. "You okay?"

Tana turned and looked at Sheila with a wild, helpless expression. Her face was pale and her cheeks were streaked with tears.

"What is it, honey?" She came up to Tana, her face creased with worry. "What's wrong?"

Tana wiped her tears. She nodded at the mirror. "Look," she said.

"Look at what?"

"Can't you see it?"

"See what, girl?"

"She wrote it on the mirror."

Sheila glanced at the mirror. "Wrote what? There's nothing there."

"They won't leave me alone until I find her."

'Who won't leave you alone? What you talking about?"

"I can't explain it...I just can't...you wouldn't understand anyway..."

"Try me."

Tana shook her head, then ran out of the ladies' room.

CHAPTER 10

TANA PUSHED OPEN THE DOORS AND CAME OUT OF THE building, then stopped cold in the middle of the street. It was rush hour in downtown San Francisco, and the streets were filled with cubicle drones wearing backpacks and shoulder bags who jostled Tana as they tried to make their way around her. They were done for the day, and in no mood to have their evening commute blocked by a woman who apparently had no idea what she was doing, or why.

Where was she going? Tana had no idea. But she decided to get out of the way before somebody ran over her. She crossed to a Muni bus shelter at the end of the block, then sat on the bench and buried her face in her hands. Maybe Mimi was right, she thought. Maybe she did need professional help. Somebody who could come up a perfectly rational explanation for what was happening and then make it all go away. But she knew that was impossible. How could they help her? She had seen what they would never see. And in her heart, she knew that it would never go away until she found Emma. The wail of a siren sliced into her thoughts. She looked up and saw an ambulance with flashing red lights trying to push its way through rush-hour traffic. Then, as the ambulance moved out of her field of vision and the siren faded, Tana saw Sheila come out of the building and scan the street for her.

Not now, Tana thought as she watched Sheila. What if she told everybody at the paper about what she saw in the ladies' room? What if everybody knew that Tana was talking to a mirror like some raving lunatic?

Then Sheila saw her. "Tana!" she shouted, waving her arms and trying to get her attention.

Tana looked up and saw Sheila start down the block toward the bus shelter. I can't deal with this now, Tana thought. She looked around, as if for an escape route. Then a bus pulled up and the doors hissed open. Tana glanced at Sheila, a helpless glance that would tell her nothing, then boarded the bus. The doors closed and Sheila watched the bus pull away with a puzzled expression on her face.

Tana made her way down the aisle and found an empty row near the back of the bus. She slid over to the window seat and looked out at the nighttime streets flashing past her. Lost in her thoughts, she had no idea which bus she'd boarded or where it would take her, but it didn't matter to her. If she went missing somewhere in the city it would be just as well. Perhaps then Helen and Emma wouldn't be able to find her. Perhaps then no one could find her.

The bus pulled up at a stop at McAllister and Jones in the heart of Mid-Market, south of the Tenderloin. Tana spotted the Art Deco Hibernia Bank building on the corner and suddenly realized that she had boarded a 5R bus. If she was right, it could take her all the way to Ocean Beach, the western edge of the city and the end of the line. Where would she go from there, she wondered. Maybe she could swim to Treasure Island. Wash up on shore at dawn. Grab a bite at MerSea and take in the views of the city. She and Justin had gone there for lunch just after it opened, Tana remembered. They had sat at one of the outdoor tables and talked about the future, back when it seemed they might have a future, before the future went south, along with everything else.

Tana looked around at the other passengers on the bus. A teenage blonde sitting in an aisle seat staring at her cellphone caught her eye. She was about fourteen years old, Tana guessed, and seemed to be traveling alone. As if aware of Tana's gaze, the girl looked up from her phone and flashed an enigmatic smile. Why is she smiling at me, Tana wondered. Then it occurred to her that the girl was around the same age Emma would be now if she was still alive.

Tana felt her face get hot. Was this the sign she had been waiting for? Had Helen and Emma heard her plea when she tried to talk to them? Or was she just tipping over into madness? The bus rolled on for a few more blocks, then slowed as approached the intersection of McAllister and Divisadero. Tana looked out the window and saw that they were in NoPa, which stood for North of the Panhandle, the narrow, eastern strip of Golden Gate Park. The girl slipped the cellphone into her pocket, then leaned over and pulled the cord. The "Stop Requested" sign lit up. The girl stood and walked to the front exit. Tana hesitated for a moment, then stood and walked to the rear exit. The bus pulled over and the doors hissed open. Tana and the teenage girl stepped off the bus at the same time.

Tana stood by the bus shelter for a moment and watched the girl as she waited for the light to change. Then, with her heart pounding, hammering in her chest as if it was about to burst through her ribcage, she followed her.

CHAPTER 11

THE GIRL WALKED HALFWAY DOWN THE BLOCK ON Divisadero, then went into a pizza joint called Pizza Pup, which was sandwiched between a nail salon and a Chinese restaurant. There was a sign out front of a happy puppy wolfing down a slice of pepperoni pizza like there was no tomorrow. Below the sign, through big picture windows that looked out onto the street, Tana could see a few red, Formica-topped tables and chairs, a counter and the ovens. Kids in their twenties wearing red Pizza Pup T-shirts were working the counter and sliding pizzas in and out of the ovens.

Tana watched as the girl fist-bumped with the Pizza Pup kids, then disappeared through swinging doors in the back of the restaurant. Tana paused. Now what, she asked herself. She'd stalked a total stranger to a pizza joint. The thought it made her feel self-conscious, as if everyone who was brushing past her to go into the restaurant knew why she was there. She was still debating whether to stay or go when the girl reappeared wearing a Pizza-Pup T-shirt, and Tana realized that she worked there.

She couldn't leave now, Tana decided. Not yet. She needed to know more about the girl, though what exactly she needed to know wasn't clear to her. She wanted to know her name, of course, but did she really expect that if she asked the girl her name she would say "Emma?" She no longer knew what to expect. The boundary between the living and the dead had been erased. She was no longer just writing about the dead— she was also doing their bidding. She went inside and joined the line of customers waiting to place their orders.

The pungent smells of melting cheese, peperoni and sausage took Tana back to her college days, pulling all-nighters and surviving on pizza and sodas. How long ago that seemed to her now. Back then her biggest challenge was maintaining a grade-point average that could help her land a job at a metropolitan daily. She got the job she wanted, but never could have imagined that it would lead her into another world from which she feared she might not return.

The line slowly shuffled forward and when Tana reached the counter the girl smiled at her, the same smile she had flashed on the bus.

"Hi, welcome to Pizza Pup. What can I get you?"

"Just a slice of cheese, I guess."

"You got it. Here or to go?"

"Here."

"Order up, Charlotte!" the red-faced pizza cook standing by the ovens shouted.

The girl threw a look over her shoulder. "On it," she said.

So that was her name, Tana thought. Charlotte.

Charlotte turned back to Tana. "Sorry about that," she said.

"No problem," Tana said.

"You were on the bus," Charlotte said as she rang up Tana's order.

Tana nodded. "Yeah, I was."

"Thought I recognized you."

Tana smiled politely.

"You're not like stalking me or anything, are you?" Charlotte said with a teasing smile.

Tana caught her breath. How could she know, she wondered. Dread stirred in the pit of her stomach. She felt herself break out in a cold sweat.

"Just kidding," Charlotte said. "That'll be five-twenty with the tax."

Tana fumbled in her wallet for the cash, then handed Charlotte a ten-dollar bill.

"My mom says I'm too nosy and I should mind my own business," Charlotte said as she handed Tana her change.

"What's her name?"

Charlotte looked at Tana. "My mom?"

"Umm hmm."

"Renee. Why?"

Tana shrugged. "Sorry, I'm a reporter. I guess I'm just used to asking questions."

Charlotte grinned. "See, you're nosy too."

Tana felt her face flush. Charlotte slid a slice of cheese pizza onto a paper plate and handed it to Tana.

"Enjoy."

"Thanks," Tana said, and moved away from the counter.

She walked over to a table by the window and sat down. But she let her pizza get cold as she watched Charlotte work the counter. She wasn't Emma, and Tana knew it was crazy of her to think so. But it wasn't much crazier than anything else she was thinking. She'd followed what she thought was a lead and it had led her to a slice of cheese pizza. Not exactly what she was looking for. But she had only imagined that it was a lead. What else was she imagining? Had she reached the point where she could no longer tell the difference between what was real and what was not?

Her iPhone pinged with a text. Tana glanced at the screen and saw it was Sheila.

"Where the fuck are you? I thought we had a date."

Tana sighed. Sheila had swiped right on Tinder and met a cute guy who wanted to have a drink with her. When cute guy mentioned he had a friend, also cute, Sheila begged Tana to join them for a double date. Tana had agreed, but not because she was looking. She was still getting over Justin, and nowhere near ready to rebound into something new with somebody else. But Sheila was long past ready. She wanted a boyfriend she could turn into a husband and a family and maybe a house in the suburbs.

Tana had stood her up, which was bad enough. But that wasn't the worst part. How could she face Sheila after what she saw in the ladies' room?

Her phone pinged with another text:

"Hello? U there?"

There was no way out. Either she faced Sheila at the bar or she faced her at the office tomorrow morning. The bar would be way better, Tana decided. At least she could have a drink. Maybe more than one.

"Sorry," Tana texted. "On my way."

She stood and walked to the door. She glanced at Charlotte, who was busy taking orders. They would never see each other again, Tana thought, even if for a moment she could have been Emma.

CHAPTER 12

Tana hailed a cab outside a convenience store on Divisadero. The store had a sign out front that said PLENTY GROCERIES + LIQUOR in big red letters, as if that was all you needed to get by. The cab driver was a Sikh in a pink turban, and he was listening to Indian music on the radio. He had it turned down low so that none of his fares would be disturbed by it. Tana could barely hear it, but during the time to took to drive across town, she closed her eyes and pretended she was in another country where everything would be different, including her.

Twenty minutes later she walked into Hi Dive, an Embarcadero watering hole in the shadow of the Bay Bridge. The music was loud and the place was crowded with couples and singles around her age. Happy Hour was history but that was no excuse to stop drinking. Tana spotted Sheila at a table near the windows that looked out at the lights on the bay. Two guys, maybe in their thirties, were sitting across from her, their backs to the door. Sheila looked up, saw Tana, and her face brightened with relief. She leaned forward and said something to the two guys, then stood and walked over to Tana.

"Hey you," Sheila said. "Where you been? Are you okay? I was worried about you."

Anybody would've been worried, Tana thought, if they'd seen what Sheila saw. She wondered if maybe Sheila was also worried that she might start talking to herself again and wreck her date night plans. But the part that Sheila didn't know about was that Tana wasn't talking to herself at all. She just couldn't explain who was on the other side of her conversation.

"Sorry," Tana said. She paused. "Look, about what happened—"

Sheila cut her off with an awkward smile. "Not now, okay?" She glanced at the two guys, who had swiveled in their chairs and were watching Tana and Sheila. "They're waiting for us." She took Tana by the hand and led her to the table, then announced, "Yay! She made it!"

Tana gave a self-conscious smile. She felt as if Sheila had announced her arrival with a bit too much enthusiasm. But then she knew that underneath it all Sheila was desperate not to stay single.

"Todd, Lester, this is my friend Tana."

Todd and Lester looked up at Tana and checked her out.

"Glad you could join us," Lester said with a smile. He was black with a tight afro, trendy glasses, and a soul patch.

"Yeah, for real," Todd said. He was blond and up close he looked like a surfer pushing forty who hadn't seen a wave in years. He nodded at an empty seat. "Have a seat, babe, let's get this party started."

"Thanks," Tana said. She pulled out the chair and sat down.

"So what's your pleasure?" Todd said.

"Lemon drop martini," Tana said.

"Comin' right up."

Todd motioned to a barmaid, and when she came up to the table he ordered Tana's martini.

"Thanks," Tana said.

"Sure thing," Todd said, with a leering smile that made Tana feel as if he was already coming on to her.

You don't waste time, do you, Tana thought. She had just arrived, and Todd was already looking ahead to some quality time. Out of the corner of her eye Tana saw Sheila's face tighten, and figured that Todd was the one she was interested in. She remembered that Sheila always liked to date outside her race. For some reason, she seemed to think that when it came to landing a husband, she would have better luck with white guys. So far, though, she hadn't had much luck with either race. Black guys were too street for her, and the white guys she dated thought she was too exotic. But Sheila didn't want to be exotic. She just wanted to be somebody's wife.

"So you guys work together at the paper?" Lester said.

Sheila nodded. "Tana's a reporter and I work on the online edition."

"A reporter, huh?" Lester said, looking at Tana with interest. "What's your beat?"

"Dead people."

Lester and Todd flashed nervous smiles.

"I write obituaries," Tana said.

"Must be kinda quiet," Lester said. Then he and Todd did high-fives and broke up laughing like frat boys.

"Obits, huh?" Todd said. "You give 'em a final sendoff, right?"

"Who says it's final?" Tana said with a teasing smile, suddenly feeling the need to shake things up. Or maybe it was because the afterlife was the only thing on her mind, and she couldn't help talking about it.

"Whoa," Todd said, "what, like vampires and zombies and shit?"

"Maybe. I guess you won't know for sure until you're dead, right, Todd?"

Todd's face flushed. He flashed a tight smile, then gulps his drink. "Who the fuck says I'm gonna die, bitch?" he said. "Maybe I'm gonna live forever. You ever think of that?"

"Yeah, right," Tana said, wondering what Sheila saw in this jerk other than the color of his skin.

Sheila frowned. "Why we all got to be talking about dead people? We're supposed to be having fun, aren't we? Dead people don't have no fun."

"Yeah, and they don't get to drink, either," Lester said, knocking back the rest of his drink. "Everybody ready for another round?"

Talking about the dead always seemed to make people nervous, Tana thought. It used to make her nervous too. But then she found out that dying wasn't always the end Sometimes it was just the beginning. Everybody ordered another round, then Sheila pushed her chair back and stood up.

"I'll be right back," she said.

"Yeah, me too," Tana said.

"Can I come too?" Todd said.

Tana stood, then turned and looked at him.

"I thought guys peed standing up, Todd," she said with mock-surprise. "But if you sit down to pee, you can come too."

Todd's face flared bright red as Lester roared. Tana could still hear him laughing as she and Sheila made their way through the crowd to the ladies' room. They waited their turn, then went into empty stalls to pee.

That was when Tana heard Sheila say, "So what do you think?"

"About what?" Tana said, as she finished up and came out of the stall.

She heard a toilet flush and then Sheila joined her. "You know what, the guy."

"The white guy, Todd."

"Yeah, white guy Todd."

Tana shrugged as she washed her hands. "He's a jerk. He was coming on to me the minute I sat down."

"Yeah, I know," Sheila said, sounding discouraged.

"What about Lester? He seems nice."

"I don't know. Me and the brothers, it don't always work out."

"You should give it a try."

"Yeah, maybe."

Tana looked at herself in the mirror, then turned to Sheila. "Listen, about what happened—"

"It ain't no thing," Sheila said. "You were just talking to the mirror, right?" She grinned

"Please don't tell anybody, like at the office or anything."

"No worries, girl, I got you. But what happened? You gonna tell me what's going on?"

"I can't tell you."

"Can't or won't?"

"Maybe both."

"Am I gonna have to be worried about you?"

Tana shook her head. "I'm okay," she said, wishing she could believe it.

Todd and Lester looked up at Tana and Sheila when they came back to the table.

"You ladies ready for more?" Todd said, holding up his empty glass.

"No thanks, I have to get up in the morning," Tana said.

"On deadline, right?" Lester said. "Can't keep the dead waiting, huh?"

Tana nodded. "You got it."

"Call in sick," Todd said.

"I gotta go," Tana said, and pulled on her coat.

"I'll walk you out," Todd said.

"It's okay. I know the way."

Todd leered at her. "Yeah, me too."

"See you, Lester," Tana said.

Lester waved. "Later."

Tana and Sheila embraced. See you tomorrow," Tana said.

"See you there," Sheila said. "Thanks for coming."

Tana headed for the door. As she feared, Todd was right behind her. There was a cool breeze blowing in from the bay and she pulled her coat tightly around her as they stepped out of the bar.

"You need a ride?" Todd said

"I'm just gonna get an Uber," Tana said, pulling out her cellphone.

"So am I gonna see you again?"

Tana locked eyes with Todd. "I'm not really looking for anything, right now, okay?"

"Sure, no rush, we can ease on into it."

He held his arm out and pushed it forward for emphasis. The way he did it made Tana think that he was talking about his dick, and she had a pretty good idea of what he meant by *it*.

She paused, then says, "We're not gonna ease on into anything, okay, Todd?"

Todd's face, red from the alcohol, darkened. He scowled at Tana.

"Bitch."

Tana gave a weary smile. Another great date. She turned and walked away. As she headed down the Embarcadero, she could almost feel Todd staring bullet holes into her back. She thought of Justin, and suddenly missed him. But there was no way back with him, not now anyway. Maybe not ever. If she couldn't explain it to Sheila, and if Mimi didn't believe her, how could she ever explain it to him? She ordered up an Uber, then waited for her ride to arrive. And hoped that Helen Mayfield wasn't behind the wheel.

CHAPTER 13

IT WAS A PERFECT DAY AT THE BEACH. SOMEBODY WAS sure to post it on Instagram. Fat yellow sun riding a sea blue sky, waves churning surf into whipped cream, kids building castles in the sand. Tana was there too, along with Helen and Emma. They all wore bathing suits and sunglasses. Emma's bathing suit was pink, and she wore matching pink sunglasses. Tana and Helen lay on red-and-white striped beach towels while Emma used a little yellow shovel to fill a blue bucket with sand.

Tana smiled as she watched Emma, then closed her eyes. She could hear the soft roar of the sea rolling in from somewhere else. She knew they were at the beach, but she wasn't sure which beach. Whose idea was it to go the beach, anyway? And how did they get there? She couldn't remember. All she knew was that Ocean Beach, the beach in San Francisco, wasn't anything like what you thought of when you thought about the beach.

It was gray and cold, and nobody went there to work on their tan.

You had to go south for that kind of beach. Venice, Malibu, Zuma, Santa Monica. So they had to be somewhere else. But where? Tana had no idea. It really didn't matter, though, because she could lay in the sand and let the sun hypnotize her so she could forget about everything. Maybe that was why people went to the beach, Tana thought. So they could forget about everything, at least for a while.

Tana was still in the kind of trance that came from way too much time in the sun when she heard Helen shout, "Emma! Where are you going? Come back here!"

She sat up and saw that Emma had abandoned her bucket and was running full speed toward the water. Helen kept shouting at her to stop but Emma ignored her or maybe couldn't hear her over the sounds of the roaring surf and the seagulls calling one to another as they swooped over the sand, riding the wind no one could see. Helen jumped up and ran after Emma. But for some reason she couldn't catch up to her, and Emma remained out of reach as she raced toward the shore. Helen screamed for help, but none of the other people on the beach or even the lifeguard, shiny and tanned on his perch, paid any attention to her. Tana didn't jump up to help her either. She just sat on the blanket and watched, as if she was a spectator gazing at something happening somewhere outside of her.

The roar of the surf kept getting louder and louder, thundering from one end of the beach to the other. Then Tana saw Emma rush into the water. The waves crashed over her, and she disappeared in the roaring surf. Helen dove in after her. But there was no sign of Emma. Helen kept calling Emma's name as she looked around for her, a desperate, stricken look on her face. But there was no sign of her. She was there one moment and gone the next, as if she had never existed. Helen kept screaming as the waves crashed over her, then finally sank to her knees and sobbed.

Tana woke suddenly in a cold sweat. She sat up in bed,

gasping for air. She looked around her still and darkened bedroom, then realized it was only a dream. But if it was a dream, why was it so vivid? Why did it seem as if she was on the beach with Helen and Emma? She could still hear the seagulls, the waves crashing, and see the smile on Emma's face as she poured hot golden sand into her blue plastic bucket.

Tana rubbed her eyes, then threw back the comforter and climbed out of bed. As her bare feet hit the hardwood floor, she felt something gritty between her toes. She switched on the lamp on the nightstand next to her bed and looked down at the floor. There was a trail of sand leading from the bedroom into the living room. Tana caught her breath at the sight of it. She stared at the sand as if it too was a dream. She could feel her heart start beating faster. Fear uncoiled in the pit of her stomach and snaked into her throat. She followed the trail into the living room and turned on a light.

That was when she saw it. The blue plastic bucket on the floor by the coffee table. The bucket was overturned, and sand had spilled out of it. The little yellow shovel lay beside it, along with Emma's pink sunglasses.

Tana stared at the bucket. The shovel. The sand. Stared as if time had stopped.

Then her cellphone rang.

CHAPTER 14

Tana jumped at the sound. As if she'd never heard her phone ring before. She looked around the room, then spotted her phone on the coffee table. She stared at it for a moment, frightened that someone was calling her in the middle of the night. Good news never rang in the middle of the night. Only bad news. She thought of her parents and wondered if something terrible had happened. But she was already frightened by the bucket, the sand, the shovel. Was that was the call was about? Were Helen or Emma calling in from the other side? She realized she was afraid to answer the phone. She let it ring a few more times, then grabbed the phone and took the call just before it went to voicemail, which was unlike her.

"Sally?" a man said.

"Who?" Tana said, confused and still disoriented by what she had discovered on the living room floor.

"I want to talk to Sally. Is she there?"

Tana lost it. "There's no Sally here, okay? No fucking Sally!"

"Sorry, guess I got the wrong number."

"Yeah, no shit," Tana said angrily as she ended the call.

Tana dropped the phone on the sofa, then plopped down beside it and ran her hand through her hair. The dream and what had followed her from the dream into real life was on the floor in front of her. She was strung-out and sleep-deprived, but sleep was the last thing she wanted, and she knew why. For the first time in her life Tana was afraid to go to sleep, afraid of what might lie in wait for her if she closed her eyes.

Three hours later Tana was sitting at a table by the window at the Peets on Mission Street, not far from the paper. She was working on her second cup of French Roast black no cream no sugar when Mimi walked in the door. She scanned the crowd, saw Tana, then pointed to the coffee bar. Tana nodded, took another sip, and waited for her.

"You look terrible," Mimi said as she sat down with her coffee.

"Thanks," Tana said.

It was true and she knew it. She did look terrible.

"So what happened?" Mimi said.

"I was up all night," Tana said.

"Because of work?"

"I have to find Emma."

Mimi looked at her with a puzzled expression. "In the middle of the night?"

Tana said nothing. She looked down into her coffee and let the silence speak for itself.

Mimi reached across the table and took Tana's hand. "I'm worried about you, girlfriend. Where are you going with all this?"

Tana shrugged. "Wherever it takes me, I guess."

"Yeah, that's what scares me," Mimi said.

"Something else happened..." Tana looked up at Mimi. "You won't believe it."

"I already don't believe it and you haven't even told me what happened."

"I wanted to show you pics, but they wouldn't come out," Tana said, holding up her iPhone.

"Pics of what? What are you talking about?"

"I had this dream last night...I went to the beach with Helen and Emma."

"You went to the beach with a ghost?"

"Two ghosts," Tana said with a weary smile.

She ran her hand through her hair. And then she told Mimi about the dream.

"When I woke up Emma's bucket was on the floor, the one she was playing with in my dream. And there was sand on the floor, too."

"But that's not possible, Tana. It was just a dream, right?"

"I don't know anymore. Then this morning the sand and the bucket were gone."

"See? There you go," Mimi said. "You were still dreaming when you saw it. You thought it was real, but it wasn't."

Tana shook her head. "I think it was real. I think Helen wanted me to see her and Emma happy together...I think that's what the dream was about. She wanted me to see a mother's love. And then when Emma ran into the water Helen wanted me to see the pain she felt when Emma disappeared."

Mimi gave a skeptical frown. "You know how you sound?"

"Why can't you believe me, Mimi?"

"Would you believe me, if it was me?"

Tana looked up at her friend. Their eyes met, then Tana looked down into her coffee. "I would now, yeah."

Mimi didn't want to believe her because if she believed her then it would mean it was real, and if it was real, then there was reason to be scared. Tana didn't much like the idea of scaring

Mimi, but she had to tell somebody. Somebody had to know what was happening to her.

"I want to believe you, Tana..."

"I know. I don't want to believe it either."

"You know what I believe, Tana? I believe she's dead. You know about dead people, right? You write about 'em every day."

Tana shook her head. "Helen's not dead. Not yet anyway."

Mimi's jaw dropped. She stared at Tana. "Excuse me? What is she, some kind of zombie?"

"She's a mother who won't rest until I find her daughter."

"Why you? Why is it your job to find her?"

"I don't know. It just is, I guess. Maybe because I wrote her obituary."

"What's that got to do with it?"

Tana shrugged. "I told her life story."

"So what? Her life's over."

Tana shook her head. "Not until she knows what happened to Emma."

Mimi shook her head in disbelief. She looked around the coffee shop as if searching for what to say, then turned to Tana. "You know what's really crazy, Tana? We're sitting here at eight o' clock in the morning talking about dead people who aren't dead. Not only are they not dead, they're taking you to the beach."

Tana flinched. "You know what, Mimi? It's okay if you don't believe me, but you don't have to make fun of me."

"I'm not making fun of you, honey," Mimi said in a softer tone of voice. "I'm just trying to get my head around it."

"Yeah, well, me too."

"What are you gonna do? You can't go on like this..."

Tana gave a helpless shrug. Mimi sipped her coffee, then looked at Tana.

"Does anybody else know about this?"

Tana shook her head. "Just you. But it's starting to show."

"What do you mean?"

"Sheila from the paper, I think maybe you met her once..."

"The black chick?"

"Yeah."

"What about her?"

"She caught me in the ladies room talking to the mirror."

"Talking to the mirror?"

"It was on the mirror."

"What was on the mirror?"

"Hurry."

"Hurry?" Mimi said with a puzzled expression.

Tana smiled bitterly. "It was from Emma. She was telling me to hurry up and find her. Don't you see? I can't escape it." Tana felt herself tearing up. She reached for a napkin and wiped her eyes. "Sorry."

Mimi reached out and took Tana's hand. "It's okay, honey." She pulled a business card out of her wallet and handed it to Tana.

"What's this?"

"Somebody I went to see when me and Heather were having problems."

"I don't need a marriage counselor, Mimi."

"I know, but she's really nice and she's easy to talk to... maybe she can help."

Tana knew Mimi meant well, but she wasn't quite sure how a therapist could help her find Emma. Then again, maybe it wasn't about finding Emma; maybe it was about Tana finding herself before she became totally lost.

"Thanks, I'll think about it." Tana glanced at her watch. "I gotta go, I'm on deadline."

Mimi locked eyes with Tana. "I think you should do more

than just think about it, girlfriend. I'm worried about you, okay? This isn't normal."

Tana nodded. But she had already decided that what she needed to do was stop talking to people who didn't believe her and start learning more about the case that led to Emma's abduction in the first place.

CHAPTER 15

THE LEAD DETECTIVE ON THE EMMA MAYFIELD CASE, Tana learned from contemporaneous reports in *The Bugle*'s morgue, was a homicide cop named Aloysius Powell. He had led the investigation until the case went cold and the search for Emma, or her remains, was abandoned. But that was ten years ago. Was he still on the force? Tana had no idea, but she figured that Road Runner, aka Phil Jacobs, might know. Jacobs was the police reporter for the paper and covered the crime beat. He had been at *The Bugle* for more than a decade, and much of the coverage of the Vargas case and Emma's subsequent abduction and disappearance appeared under his byline.

Jacobs was at hunched over his keyboard in the rear of the newsroom when Tana came up to him. He was tall, lean, and built like a runner, and snapshots of Jacobs running in local marathons were taped to the walls of his cubicle, along with cartoon images from the Road Runner and Wile E. Coyote cartoons.

The word around the newsroom was that at first Jacobs didn't much like being called Road Runner, but over time he had given up trying to fight it and had finally embraced it as a sign of affection, rather than ridicule. Tana wasn't so sure, but the nickname had stuck and there wasn't much he could do about it. Tana guessed Jacobs was in his late forties, but never knew for sure. He had a long, narrow face and wore black Clark Kent glasses that always looked as if they were about to fall off of his face.

"Hey Phil, got a minute?" Tana said.

Jacobs looked up and squinted at Tana. "Sure, what's up?" he said.

"Got a question about the Emma Mayfield case."

"Oh yeah. I saw your obit for her mother. Kind of brought it all back again." Jacobs took off his glasses and rubbed his eyes. "Sad story." He put his glasses back on. "So what's your interest? That was a long time ago, Tana."

"You remember a cop named Aloysius Powell?"

"You mean Bud Powell, don't you?"

Tana looked at him with a puzzled expression. "I just read the coverage. They said his name was Aloysius."

Jacobs grinned. "It was. His mother was a devout Catholic. Named him after some saint."

"Where'd Bud come from?"

"From what I hear, his dad hated the name from day one. Plus, he was a Bud Powell fan back in the day, so he started calling him Bud and it stuck."

"Oh, like the piano player, right?" Tana said.

Jacobs reacted with surprise. "You know about Bud Powell?"

"Yeah, sure. He played bebop with Monk, Bird, Dizzy, all those guys."

"Could've fooled me," Jacobs said.

"Yeah, I can tell," Tana said with a smile. "So Powell worked the Vargas case and then led the search for Emma Mayfield after she was kidnapped, right?"

Jacobs nodded. "Right. What about him?"

Tana gave a shrug she hoped looked casual. "Just curious about what happened, I guess. Working on the obit made me want to follow up. It's the tenth anniversary of Emma's abduction. Thought I'd talk to him and see if maybe there's a story there."

"Yeah, but you're on the obituary desk, not features."

Tana stiffened. She didn't appreciate Jacobs or anyone else telling her what her place was. But she masked her feelings with a smile. "I'll run it past JD, see what he says."

"Well, Powell retired five years ago. I heard he was working part-time as a PI but that was awhile back. Not sure if he's still around. I guess you could Google him."

"Just thought you might know."

Jacobs shrugged. "About the only thing I know for sure about Bud Powell is that he liked to go bowling. Probably still does."

"Bowling?"

"Yeah, big time."

"Thanks, Phil. I'll check it out."

Tana turned and went back to her cubicle. She was about to tap a key on her keyboard to wake her computer when she suddenly stopped herself, afraid of what appear on her screen. She smiled wearily and shook her head. This is ridiculous, she thought.

What are you afraid of, girl? A ghost in the machine?

She held her breath, tapped a key, and a moment later her screen lit up. A quick Google search turned up a Facebook page for a bowling league called *The Bowling Stones* that met at the Albany Bowl. There was even a picture of Powell and his fellow bowlers, all wearing league bowling shirts embroidered with their names. According to the bowling alley's website, the Albany Bowl was located on San Pablo Avenue, two blocks south of the El Cerrito BART station. Tana decided to head over there after work and see if she might get lucky and run into Bud Powell.

"Bowling on company time, Montana?" a familiar voice said, jolting Tana out of her thoughts.

Tana swiveled and saw JD looking over her shoulder at the Albany Bowl home page on her screen. A thick manila folder was in his hand.

"Hey JD," Tana said flashing a nervous smile as she scrambled to come up with a story. She glanced at the screen, then turned back to Donahue. "It's for my mom and dad."

"Your mom and dad?"

Tana nodded. "They're thinking of coming out for a visit and they like to bowl," she lied. "I told them I'd look for a place."

"Well, now that you found it, maybe you can get back to work." He dropped the manila folder on Tana's desk.

"Sure, on it, Jack."

Donahue threw a suspicious glance at the screen, then at Tana, then turned and walked away. Tana took a deep breath. That was close, she thought. Next time it could be even closer. Two hours later, Tana closed her files, shut down her computer and walked to the elevator. Ricky was already there.

"Hey girlfriend, what's up?" he said. "Fancy meeting you here."

Tana smiled.

"Done for the day?"

"Totally."

"Me too."

"Got plans?"

Ricky rolled his eyes. "Matt's found some new Vietnamese restaurant that he said we just have to try. Everybody's raving about it. Between us girls, chica, I'd rather order in and watch Netflix." He shrugged. "Oh well. What about you?"

"Got plans too."

"What kind of plans?"

"Just plans."

"Won't say, huh? Must be hush-hush. Wouldn't be a boy, would it?" He leaned in closer to Tana. His voice dropped to a stage whisper. "Or maybe a girl."

Tana grinned. Let him believe it was about a boy, or even a girl. It was easier than telling him the truth. They said good-night outside the building and Tana headed to the BART station at 16th and Mission.

CHAPTER 16

THE TRAIN HOWLED INTO THE STATION. SARDINE SPECIAL, Tana thought, as the doors slid open and she pushed her way into the hot, overcrowded car. It was packed with rush hour commuters who endured the ride because they had to, and because they knew that fighting traffic on the Bay Bridge during commute times would be far worse and take even longer. The riders who were lucky enough to score seats either stared at their cellphones and tablets or closed their eyes and pretended to be somewhere else. Tana spent the hour it took to get there crammed in by the doors as more and more riders squeezed in around her. By the time she disembarked at the El Cerrito station, night had swept across the city, and Tana was grateful for the cool bay breeze blowing down San Pablo Avenue as she walked alone to the bowling alley.

The big neon sign out front blared "ALBANY BOWL" in hot pink letters against a blazing red background. Another sign announced Happy Hour on Wednesdays, Thursdays, and Fridays from noon to 6pm. So even if you kept losing one game after another there was plenty of time to get happy. Tana noticed that the bowling alley was across the street from a

Goodwill store, and she wondered if the two had anything to do with each other.

As she approached the entrance, the door swung open and a black guy wearing a San Francisco Giants cap and carrying a ball bag stepped out onto the sidewalk. He saw Tana and held the door for her. She smiled and took him up on his offer. The smell hit her first—the greasy stink of fast-food burgers and fries, chili dogs, and nachos and cheese that seemed to stick to the walls. Then came everything else. The video arcades and pool tables. The pounding beats and slashing guitars of arena rock and hip-hop on the soundtrack. Music videos flashing on multiple screens. Strobe lights washing across the lanes in primary colors. The thump and hum of bowling balls hitting the planks and rolling inexorably toward the pins. The hollow, knocking sounds of the pins as the balls crashed into them with fatal inevitability. Tana could see bowlers waiting in suspense after they'd released their balls, then clenching their fists and doing high fives when they scored a strike. Or giving a sheepish grin and shrugging if the ball rolled into the gutter.

The scene took her back to when she'd gone bowling with her Phys Ed class when she was in high school. It was okay, but she liked it better later on when she had a boyfriend who liked to bowl, and they could make out in the parking lot after dark. Then one night they got caught half-naked in the back of his car by security, and never saw each other again. She never went bowling again either.

Tana looked around, then noticed a man standing at a concession counter in front of a glass case filled with bowling memorabilia. He was round and in his sixties, and reminded Tana of a bowling ball. He wore a button-down Albany Bowl shirt that rolled over his stomach. He looked as if he was waiting for customers to belly up to the counter and buy something.

"Excuse me," Tana said as she came up to him.

"What for?" the man said. "Did you do something wrong?"

He laughed at his own joke, a raspy smoker's laugh that sounded like cancer. Tana smiled politely.

"Now that you're excused, what can I do for you?" the man said.

"I'm looking for somebody—"

"Got lots of somebodies out there," the man said, looking out at the bowlers filling the alley's sixteen lanes. "Any somebody in particular?"

"I'm looking for Bud Powell," Tana said. "I was just wondering if he was here tonight."

"Bud Powell, huh?"

Tana nodded.

"I saw him a while ago, not sure if he's still here," the man said as he scanned the bowling alley. "I don't see him bowlin', so I reckon he must be drinkin'." He looked over at the bar and his eyes lit up in recognition. He pointed at a man sitting at the end of the bar. "There he is, last stool on the left." Then he leaned in and stage-whispered, "Just don't call him 'Aloysius.'"

"Thanks," Tana said.

"Anytime."

Tana walked over to the crowded bar, passing the row of bowlers hunched over their drinks until she reached Powell. She could feel her stomach tighten as she approached him. How would he react to her, she wondered. What if he didn't want to talk about a case he failed to solve? She noticed that Powell was wearing a white bowling shirt that said "The Bowling Stones" in big red letters on the back. A beer and a bowl of nuts were on the bar in front of him.

"Excuse me," she said.

Bud Powell turned and looked at her. He was in his fifties, Tana guessed, with a weathered face that seemed to bear the weight of every case he worked on, thick salt-and-pepper hair and sharp eyes that even in the shadows seemed to look right through her.

"Bud Powell?" Tana said.

"Who's asking?"

"My name's Tana Grant. I work for *The Bay Area Bugle*."

Powell took a long look at Tana, long enough to make her uncomfortable.

"Your name rings a bell. Have we met?"

Tana shook her head. "I wrote Helen Mayfield's obituary."

Powell nodded. "Right. Now I remember. I saw your piece in the paper." He took a sip of his beer. "So what can I do for you?"

"I wanted to talk to you about Helen Mayfield...about the case. You were the lead detective—"

"Save your breath," Powell said. "I retired five years ago."

"Yes, but I was wondering if you could just walk me through what happened."

Powell scoffed. "Walk you through what happened? You wrote the obit. You know damn well what happened. Vargas walked, Emma was abducted, and Helen died without ever seeing her again." He took another sip of beer. "I leave anything out?"

"Yes, I know all that. But those are just the headlines."

"Isn't that enough?"

"I want the details, the story behind the headlines."

"Why? You think it's gonna make a difference?"

"It's the tenth anniversary. I was thinking it might be worth a feature story."

Tana had decided that this would be her cover story if anyone asked her why she was looking into the case.

"Some anniversary," Powell said with a bitter smile.

Tana glanced at the bar crowd that seemed to surround them.

"It won't take long," she said. She nodded at the cocktail tables across from the bar. "Maybe we could grab a table."

Powell gave himself some time to think about it, then glanced at his watch.

"You got ten minutes," he said. He looked at Tana. "You drinking?"

Tana shook her head. "I'm good."

Powell grabbed his beer, then slid off the stool. Tana followed him to an empty table and they both sat down.

"Thanks," Tana said, "I appreciate it."

She pulled out a pen and a notepad.

"Thanks for what? You seem to think I got something to say."

"How do you feel about not finding Emma?"

Powell scowled at Tana. "Stupid question. How the fuck do you think I feel?"

"Was that why you retired?"

"I put in my twenty, it was time."

Tana hesitated for a moment, then looked at Powell. "Why didn't you keep looking for her? You're kind of like a PI or something, aren't you?"

Powell's face tightened. He glared at Tana. "Who the fuck are you coming in here and asking me that? You don't even know me. Fuck you and your story."

He scraped back his chair, grabbed his beer, and stood.

Tana looked up at him. "Please, don't go. You're right, I don't know you and I shouldn't have said that. But I have this feeling that you wanted to keep looking for her."

Powell considered it for a moment, then settled back in his chair. He knocked back the rest of his beer and looked at Tana.

"You got a lot of fuckin' nerve, you know that?"

Tana locked eyes with Powell and held her ground.

"Am I right?"

Powell looked down into his beer, as if it held the answer. "The leads dry up, the case goes cold, you move on to other cases. You can't solve 'em all, but you never get over the ones you don't close. Is that what you wanted to hear?"

Tana nodded. "Yeah, that's what I wanted to hear."

"Good. We done here?"

"What about Hector Vargas?"

"What about him?"

"It all started with him, didn't it?"

"Ended with him too."

"Because of the witness, right?"

Powell nodded.

"Carmen Flowers," Tana said.

Yeah, Carmen fucking Flowers."

"So what happened?"

Powell shrugged. "You tell me. According to the D.A., she was in the store buying cigarettes when it happened and would I.D. Vargas as the shooter. But when she got on the stand, she recanted her testimony and claimed that she had heard shots and seen someone running from the store but hadn't actually witnessed the killings. Blindsided the D.A. and sank the case."

"I heard the rumor was she took a bribe."

Powell gave a cold smile. "Rumor my ass. She got paid to develop a sudden case of amnesia. Simple as that."

"Who bribed her? Vargas?"

Powell scoffed. "Who else? She was supposedly an eyewitness. Her testimony would've put Vargas on death row."

"Are you sure it was Vargas? I mean, could it have been somebody else? What about the jurors?"

Powell looked up at her. "What about the jurors?"

"Did you talk to them?"

"Of course we talked to 'em. Interviewed every one of 'em. But none of em was a person of interest and the interviews failed to provide any substantial leads."

"What did they say about Helen?"

Powell shrugged. "Who cares what they said, Tana? It was over and done with ten years ago."

"I want to know, okay?"

"You expect me to remember after all this time?"

"You must remember something."

Powell sighed. "Some of 'em were pissed at her for hanging the jury, others thought she was trying to do the right thing." He sipped his beer. "But we didn't know any more after we talked to 'em than we did before. Then the investigation got shut down."

"Why?"

"Limited resources."

"What's that supposed to mean?"

Powell shrugged and looked up at Tana. "What it always means. Too many cases and not enough cops to go around. Or so I was told. The fact of the matter was that the suits saw the case go cold and decided to cut their losses."

"Did you agree with that?"

"Hell no, I didn't agree with it. But it wasn't my call."

Tana smiled to herself. He hadn't been a cop in years, but he was still on duty. And she had a feeling that when it came to Emma Mayfield, he always would be.

"So maybe it wasn't Vargas, right?" Tana said. "Maybe it was somebody else."

Powell's eyes narrowed. "Who are you, fucking Nancy Drew?"

"Tana stiffened. "I'm just asking, okay?"

"Just asking, huh?"

"Yeah, just asking. I'm a reporter, remember? That's what we do."

Powell scoffed. "A reporter, huh? I thought you wrote obituaries."

"Well, yeah, I do," Tana said, suddenly flustered.

Powell gave a sly smile. "But you want to be a reporter, don't you?"

Tana locked eyes with Powell. "What if I do? You still haven't answered my question."

Powell paused to sip his beer. "Look, if you're asking did we have any evidence implicating Vargas—"

"Did you?"

Powell flashed mounting annoyance, then quenched it with a sip of beer. "No. But we didn't have any evidence implicating anybody else either."

"What about Frank Aiken? Did you talk to him?"

Powell looked up, surprised by the mention of Aiken's name. "What do you know about Frank Aiken?"

"He called me when he saw Helen's obit. Told me he was Emma's father."

Powell nodded. "Yeah, that made him a person of interest in the case. Especially since Helen had sought a restraining order against him."

"You think he might've kidnapped Emma to get back at her?"

"It's been known to happen. But he had an airtight alibi. Hard to snatch anybody when you're a hundred miles offshore."

"Yeah, he told me he was on an oil rig in the Gulf of Mexico at the time."

Powell nodded.

"But it was weird though, the way he talked about it."

Powell looked up at Tana. "How so?"

"I don't know to describe it exactly. He was smiling and it was almost like he was glad Emma was kidnapped. He was pissed that Helen never let him see Emma, and he said what goes around comes around."

"What do you mean, what goes around comes around?"

"Helen stole her from me and then somebody stole Emma from her."

"That's what he said?"

"Yeah. Weird, huh?"

Powell nodded. "You know where to find him?"

Tana shook her head. "I met him in a bar down the street from the office, but I jotted down his number when he told me he was Emma's father. So maybe he doesn't have an airtight alibi, and maybe it's not Hector Vargas, right?"

"Wrong. It was Vargas then and ten years later I still believe it was Vargas. I just couldn't prove it. And neither could the D.A."

"Okay, let's say it was Vargas. How'd he get to Carmen Flowers?"

"Hell if I know how he did it, but he did." His face hardened. "She should've been charged with perjury. And he should've been charged with witness tampering, on top of the double murder with special circumstances."

"But she wasn't, was she?"

Powell shook his head. "Neither was he. So she walked, just like Vargas."

"She still around?"

"Carmen?"

Tana nodded.

"No idea. She basically disappeared after the trial."

"Just like Emma."

"Yeah, just like Emma," Powell said quietly. "One minute

she's outside playing with the other kids, the next minute she's gone." He shrugged. "Nobody saw what happened."

They fell silent for a moment. Tana could hear the sounds of the bowling alley swirling all around her, but she was somewhere else. A place she'd seen before.

"I saw what happened," she said.

CHAPTER 17

Powell leaned in close and stared at Tana. No man had ever looked at her the way he did. Not Justin, not her father, not anyone. She felt as if he was looking straight through her. And she knew in her heart that you could never lie to a man like Bud Powell. But lying was the last thing Tana wanted to do. What she wanted more than anything was for Powell to believe her. And yet she feared he never would.

"You saw it? What the fuck do you mean, you saw it?"

The sounds of the bowling alley seemed to fade away. The bar crowd disappeared. There was just the two of them sitting across from each other. And Powell was staring holes in her. No way out, Tana thought. She had backed herself into a corner of her own making, and now she would have to explain herself. But did she really expect that a hardnosed street cop like Powell would believe her? Mimi didn't believe her; why would he? She had to take the chance, no matter what it cost her. Otherwise, she would never find Emma, dead or alive. And Helen would never rest. And if Helen never rested, neither would she.

"I saw it," Tana said. "I saw them take Emma."

Powell's jaw dropped. His eyes went wide. "You saw what happened ten years ago and you're just coming forward now?"

Tana shook her head. "You don't understand..."

"Yeah? Which part?"

Tana sighed. How could she ever tell anyone this story without sounding as if she'd lost her mind? She couldn't. It was a ghost story.

"You know what?" she said. "I think I'll take that drink now."

"What's your pleasure?"

Tana glanced at his empty beer mug. Keep it simple, she told herself.

"Beer's okay," she said.

Powell nodded, then motioned to the barmaid. When he got her attention, he held up two fingers and pointed at Tana and himself. The barmaid nodded like she got the message. Powell turned back to Tana.

"You need a drink first, huh?" he said with a sly smile. "Must be one helluva story."

Tana smiled to herself. Dude, you have no idea. The barmaid came up to the table with two beers and set them on the table.

"Thanks, Deanna," Powell said.

"Sure thing, Bud, anytime," Deanna said with a smile, then moved away.

Tana took a sip, then looked at Powell. "Can I ask you a question?"

Powell frowned. "I'm looking for answers, lady, not questions."

"Did anyone you talked to at the time see what happened?"

Powell shook his head. "We talked to the kids and the teachers, but they were all inside when it happened. All except Emma. They heard her scream, but when they ran outside she was gone without a trace. We never got a line on how many people were involved, what kind of car they were driving, nothing."

"Do you want me to tell you what happened, or are you just gonna blow me off?"

"I'm listening."

Tana paused. "There were two of them," she said quietly. "They were driving an SUV."

"Go on."

"They pulled up and a guy jumped out and grabbed Emma. He pushed her into the back seat and they drove away." Tana sipped her beer. "I got the license plate number."

"You did, huh?" Powell said, his voice dripping with sarcasm.

"You don't believe me?"

"I guess I'm just waiting for the part where you tell me how you saw what happened ten years ago and just now decided to come forward."

Tana shook her head. "I didn't see it ten years ago. I saw it last night." She paused. "Helen Mayfield showed me what happened."

CHAPTER 18

WHAT HAPPENED NEXT TOOK TANA BY SURPRISE. IT CAME after she took the plunge and told Powell about the strange turn of events her life had taken since the night she saw the ghost of Helen Mayfield and had a vision of Emma's abduction. He listened with more patience than she had expected, and as she went on it became easier to tell a story that even to her sounded like one long hallucination. Powell said nothing when she was finished and remained silent for what seemed like an eternity.

Finally, he looked up at Tana and said, "Want to take a ride?"

"Where?" Tana said, thrown off balance.

"Nowhere."

Tana felt her body tense. Was this the part where he assaulted her, then dropped her off at the nearest psycho ward? "I don't understand..."

"You will," Powell said. He drained his glass, then stood and looked at Tana. "You coming or you scared?"

Both, maybe, Tana thought. But there it was again, that look seemed to go right through her. How could she say no? She drained her glass then pushed back her chair. She stood and locked eyes with Powell.

"Yeah, I'm coming," she said.

They went out to the parking lot. The night had turned cold, but the fresh night air felt good on Tana's face after the bowling alley's canned AC.

"It's over there," Powell said, pointing to a 4x4 in the back of the lot.

"It's a Ford Bronco, right?" Tana said.

Powell nodded. "Yeah, it is." He looked at Tana. "You know about Broncos?"

"My dad had one. Back in Montana."

Powell unlocked the doors and they got in the car.

"Montana, huh? Is that where your name comes from?"

Tana rolled her eyes. "Yeah, my parents thought it was cute to call me 'Montana'."

Powell grinned and started the engine. "I guess you didn't like that much, huh?"

"Not much."

"So what are you doing here? You run away from home 'cause they called you 'Montana'?"

Tana shrugged. "I didn't want to be a cowgirl. I wanted to be a reporter."

"Fair enough," Powell said.

He gunned the engine and they pulled out of the lot.

This feels seriously weird, Tana thought as they rolled in silence down Pablo Avenue. He's acting like everything's normal when nothing about what I told him was normal.

"You didn't say anything," Tana said.

Powell glanced at her. "About what?"

"About what I told you. You're acting like everything's normal. What's up with that?"

"What were you expecting?"

"I don't know, I just didn't expect this. That's for sure."

Powell smiled but said nothing. He turned off San Pablo

and climbed into the East Bay Hills above El Cerrito. Tana felt a stab of dread in the pit of her stomach. She should never had agreed to go for a ride with him. A ride to nowhere, he had told her. Wasn't that enough of a warning? When they reached the top, Powell pulled off the road into a rest area, and as he swung around and parked the Bronco, Tana saw the San Francisco skyline, gleaming in the distance like a mirage. The view took her breath away.

"Wow, that is really cool," she said. She looked at Powell. "Is that why you brought me up here? So I could see the view?" Then a shadow fell across her face. Before Powell had a chance to respond, she said, "You're not gonna come on to me now, are you?"

Powell scoffed. "Is that why you think I brought you up here?"

"I don't know why you brought me up here."

"I figured it was a good place to talk."

"About what?"

Powell paused. "What you told me didn't come as a surprise," he said, looking out at the lights of the city.

"It didn't? You're kidding me. That's a first."

Powell turned to Tana. "You want to know why?"

"Yeah, I do."

"Because it happened to me too, more than once."

Tana was stunned. Her eyes widened. She stared at Powell. "You?"

"I know what it's like, and I know how hard it is to tell anybody what happened."

"I don't know what to say...I thought I was the only person in the world this happened to."

"You're not, but once it happens it's the kind of thing that sets you apart from everybody else."

Tana gave a knowing smile. "You got that right. I tried to

talk to my friend Mimi about it. She didn't believe a word of what I was telling her. Told me to go see a shrink."

Powell chuckled. "The only way a shrink is gonna help is if they've had the same thing happen to them. Otherwise, they're clueless. You gotta go through it too, and even then, you don't know what to do."

Tana looked at Powell. "So what happened to you?"

He paused and looked out the view, as if he was taking the time to collect his thoughts.

"I was married back then—"

"You were married?"

Powell nodded. "Been married five years when it happened. Me and my partner were working a drug bust in the Western Addition when I got the news. Her name was Nora. I loved her so much it hurt it sometimes." He smiled sadly. "I used to worry she was gonna wake up one day and ask herself what the hell she was doing married to a cop. But that never happened. She was happy being married to me, and God knows I was happy with her."

"What happened?" Tana said, as a foreboding grew inside her.

"Nora was in a supermarket parking lot when it happened. She was putting the bags in the trunk when this guy came up to her and tried to grab the keys. She pushed him away and he pulled out a gun and shot her. Then he took off in the car. She was dead by the time he rolled out of the lot."

Powell fell silent. Tana could feel the dark pouring into the car.

"My life fell apart after she died," he said. "It was like I was trying to kill myself any which way I could. Drinking too much, taking chances on the job that could've gotten me killed, roughing up suspects in ways that would sabotage a case and get me suspended. You name it, I was doing it." He paused.

"Then I saw her." He gave a sad smile. "Scared the shit out of me but made me happy too."

"What happened the first time you saw her?"

"I'd passed out dead drunk on the couch, and when I came to in the middle of the night she was there, watching me. I wanted to put my arms around her, but when I tried it was like I was hugging smoke. But it was the sad look on her face that went right through me."

"I've heard that a ghost is a soul that can't rest because something on earth remains unresolved," Tana said. "That's why Helen can't rest, she wants to know what happened to Emma." She looked at Powell. "What did Nora want?"

"She wanted me to find a way to go on living. Sometimes, when I was home alone, which was all the time after she died, I'd catch a whiff of her favorite perfume, and then I'd know she was there, with me, watching over me like some kind of guardian angel."

"When was the last time you saw her?"

"It was when I finally caught the perp who killed her. Fuckin' little street rat with a rap sheet as long as your arm. I didn't arrest him or call it in or take him to the station. Instead, I took him out to an empty field and forced him to dig his own grave. Then I made him kneel facing the grave, so that he could see himself falling into it when I shot him in the back of the head. I was about to cap him when I saw her, floating above the grave. I just froze, looking up at her. She was smiling at me and shaking her head and I just started crying. The perp of course had no idea what the fuck was going on. One minute I was gonna shoot him, and the next minute I was bawling like a baby. But I knew right then I couldn't do it. That was what she came to tell me. So instead of shooting him I cuffed him, read him his rights, and dragged him back to the car. And when I looked back to where she was, she was gone." Powell

87

paused as the memory lingered, then said, "Last time I saw her."

They fell silent. Tana looked out at the moonlit bay, the lights of the city glittering in the distance. She wanted to say something, but the usual things people said when they wanted to offer their condolences seemed empty and meaningless to her. She wrote about the dead every day, and yet she couldn't imagine what it was like to have a loved one torn away from her forever. Then she remembered the child cut out of her before she was born, and her eyes filled with tears.

Powell must have noticed, because he turned to Tana and said, "You okay?"

She wiped her eyes and looked at him. "I had an abortion when I was nineteen, some guy I met online. I went home afterwards like nothing had happened..."

"Not so simple, huh?"

Tana shook her head. "I don't even know if it was a boy or a girl. I keep wondering what it would've been like to be a mom. I never gave myself a chance to find out. Never gave my kid a chance either."

"Is that why you want to find Emma? So you can make up for it?"

Tana shrugged. "I don't know. Maybe that's why Helen chose me. Maybe that's why she showed me what happened. But we have to find her, Bud. We have to find Emma."

"We?"

Tana looked up at him and their eyes met.

"Is that why you looked me up?"

Tana held his gaze, then lowered her eyes. "I can't do this by myself, okay?"

"You're not writing a story about any ten-year anniversary, are you?"

Tana shook her head. "I was afraid you wouldn't talk to me if I told you the truth."

"Maybe you were just afraid, period."

"Maybe."

"How'd you know I'd want to help you?"

"I didn't. I just hoped you would. Her mother won't rest until we find her. Just like Nora couldn't rest until she knew you were okay."

Powell seemed to flinch at the mention of his late wife.

"Sorry," Tana said.

Powell dismissed it with a wave of his hand. "You said you got the plate."

Tana nodded. "It's on my phone."

She pulled out her cellphone and launched the Notes app, then showed Powell the license plate number.

He pulled out a notepad and jotted down the number.

"Can you trace it?" Tana said.

"Yeah, I can get a buddy of mine who's still on the force to trace it. Doesn't mean we'll find it. Car could've been crushed and recycled by now. Ten years is a long time."

"But you can find out who the registered owner was, right?"

Powell nodded. "I don't suppose the guy who grabbed Emma was Hector Vargas."

"I couldn't see his face...it all happened so fast."

"It usually does." Powell ran his hand through his hair. "No matter who it was, it's gonna be hard to track 'em ten years later. No way to track Emma either. Hell, we don't even know if she's still alive."

"So we just give up? Like you did five years ago?"

Powell's face hardened. He scowled at Tana. "I didn't give up, okay? The system gave up, but I didn't!"

Tana smiled. "That's what I figured. So can we get started?"

HELEN MAYFIELD SEES THE REPORTERS WAITING FOR HER to come out after her shift. They're crowding the sidewalk in front of the DMV. The one on Fell Street in San Francisco. She's dead tired after nine hours on her feet processing vehicle registrations, license applications, renewals and transfers of ownership. She still has to pick up Emma at daycare. They'll charge her if she's late. The last thing she wants to do is explain herself.

"I guess you're some kind of star now, huh, Helen?" the black security guard says, nodding at the press mob.

Helen looks at her. She's wearing a uniform and dreads that hang to her shoulders. "Can't you get rid of them?" Helen says.

The guard gives Helen a helpless shrug. "Honey, as long as they stay on the sidewalk there ain't a damn thing I can do about it."

Helen nods. The sidewalk is public property. Anyone can stand there. Even reporters who won't give her a moment's peace.

"You gonna go get your kid now?" the guard says.

"Yeah, if I can make it to my car in one piece."

Helen pauses at the door and takes a deep breath, then

walks out to the parking lot. The reporters rush over to her, hoping to get in a question and maybe an answer before the security guard herds them back to the sidewalk.

"Hey, Helen," a young woman says. She sticks a microphone in Helen's face. The cameraman behind her aims his video camera at her as if it were a weapon. "Got a minute to talk about the vote?"

"Excuse me," Helen says, pushing past her.

"Why'd you vote guilty when all the other jurors voted not guilty?" a heavyset woman calls out as she pushes her way to the front of the pack.

A black reporter in dreads yells at her. "Did you know something they didn't?"

"How do you feel about the case ending up with a hung jury?" a young reporter in glasses shouts.

Helen does her best to ignore the questions as she runs the gantlet to the silver Subaru Outback parked in the lot. Out of the corner of her eye, she can see the guard coming toward her, as if to rescue her. But then, just as she reaches the car, a middle-age man with swept-back silver hair who reminds Helen of the salesman who sold her the Subaru asks the question she's been asking herself.

"Are you worried about what Hector Vargas might do now that he's out?"

It's not the first time a reporter has asked her if she's scared. She'd faced another mob on the courthouse steps after the judge had declared a mistrial. But it doesn't scare her any less to hear it again. She turns and looks at the reporter. He's wearing an expectant expression, as if he's waiting for an answer. But Helen doesn't give him one. The look on her face should tell him all he needs to know, she decides, as she gets in the car and slams the door.

She glances in the rearview as she slowly backs out of the

parking space, careful not to run over a reporter, even though the idea has occurred to her. Then she pulls out of the lot and heads down Fell Street to Apple Pie Daycare. She's lucky and finds a space out front and turns off the engine. Cars are pulling up around her, doors are opening and closing and kids are streaming out of the center and running into the arms of waiting parents.

Helen pulls down the sun visor and looks at herself in the mirror, as if to make sure she's presentable for her daughter. She's in her mid-thirties, with a round face that's peppered with freckles, red hair that she wears in a ponytail and brown eyes. She's been told she's attractive, but she knows she could stand to lose a few pounds, and she worries that she never looks her best at the end of the day. She blames it on the canned air at the DMV, which she believes is ruining her complexion. Not that Emma would care. All that matters to her is that her mother is there for her, every day, forever.

But are those crow's feet around her eyes, or is she just tired? What about the lines on her neck? Where did those come from? She leans in closer to the mirror. Is it the lighting or has the glow begun to fade? What glow, she asks herself. She's a single mom raising a kid by herself.

But that's not all she is. She's also a juror who just last Friday voted to convict an accused murderer because she believed he was guilty. She still believed it even after the prosecution's eyewitness recanted her testimony and her fellow jurors turned against her. She had seen it in his eyes, watching him day after day as she sat in the jury box. Killer's eyes, she told herself. But now the tables have turned. The killer is free while Helen's imprisoned by the fear of what might happen next. She glances at her watch, then flips up the visor, pulls the keys out of the ignition and gets out of the car.

Emma's playing with other kids who are also waiting for

their parents to show up when Helen walks in the door. She's blonde and blue-eyed and four years old, and when she sees her mother her face lights up like Christmas.

"Mommy!" she yells as she runs to her mother.

Helen crouches down and sweeps Emma up in her arms. She's four years old and everything Helen wants in the world.

"Hi pumpkin face," Helen says.

Emma wrinkles her nose. "I'm not a pumpkin face. You're a pumpkin face."

Helen laughs and kisses her. "Want to go home?"

Emma shakes her head. "I want ice cream!"

Helen smiles. "Ice cream, huh?"

"Yeah!"

"What kind?"

"Chocolate!"

Helen looks up and sees one of the teachers, a tall, thin woman with short red hair, smiling as she watches Emma.

"I guess she knows what she wants," the teacher says.

Helen nods. "How's she doing?"

"Great. Happiest kid I know. You must be doing something right, Helen."

"I hope so." Helen looks down at Emma and smiles. "Ready for some ice cream?"

"Yeah!" Emma shouts and starts pulling Helen toward the door.

"See you tomorrow," Helen says over her shoulder.

They step outside. Helen notices a black sedan parked at the curb. What is it about black sedans that makes them seem so menacing, she wonders. Or is it just me? Two men are sitting in the car. They don't look like parents, she thinks. They don't look like reporters either. If they were reporters, they'd be running over to her and shoving microphones in her face. Helen unlocks the Subaru, then buckles Emma into the car seat. She walks around the car and climbs in behind the wheel. She tries not to look at the men in the black sedan, but she imagines they're looking at her. Isn't everybody now?

Then the driver gets out and starts across the street. He's in his forties, well-built, looks like he works out. Helen feels her stomach tighten. Is he coming toward me, she wonders. She throws a glance at Emma in the rearview, then watches the man as he walks past her into the daycare center. Moments later, he emerges with a young boy riding his shoulders and walks back to the car.

Helen sighs with relief, then smiles wearily and shakes her head. Lighten up, girl, she tells herself. Don't be so paranoid. Not everything's about you.

"Mommy, I want ice cream!" Emma shouts.

"Coming right up, pumpkin," Helen says with a mother's smile as she turns the key.

CHAPTER 20

IT WAS JUST AFTER MIDNIGHT WHEN POWELL WHEELED the Bronco into the red zone in front of Tana's building. She lowered the window and looked out at the dark. Empty streets, no one around, just the hum of the cables running beneath the tracks on the Hyde Street cable car line. The sound had kept her up at night when she first moved into the building, but over time she found it comforting, and soon fell asleep to the rhythms of the system's underground machinery.

Powell killed the engine and looked at her. "Here you go, home sweet home."

Tana smiled. "Thanks for the ride."

"My pleasure."

"You didn't have to do this, you know," Tana said.

"Yeah, I know."

"I mean, you live in the east bay and now you have to turn around and drive back to Oakland."

"Couldn't let you ride BART this late at night. Never know what might happen to you."

"Still protecting people, huh?" Tana said with a teasing smile.

Powell gave a wry smile. "Old habits die hard, I guess."

"So what do we do next?"

"Run the plate and see who crawls out. In the meantime, get some sleep. We'll talk tomorrow."

"Sounds good," Tana said, and opened the door.

She looked up at her building as she started to get out of the Bronco. The lights were out in all the windows and the building was plunged in darkness, as if the night had thrown a shroud over it. Suddenly, for reasons she couldn't explain, Tana felt afraid. She stopped and turned to Powell.

He could see it in her eyes. Something was wrong. "What is it?" he said.

Tana hesitated. She could feel Powell watching her. "I'm scared."

"You're scared?"

Tana nodded.

"Of what?"

"I don't know," Tana said with a shrug. "Everything I guess." She paused and looked up her building again. The dark stared back at her. She turned to Powell. "You mind coming up with me?"

"Sure, no problem."

They rode the elevator in silence. It occurred to Tana that she hadn't had a man in her apartment since she broke up with Justin. Especially a man twice her age. But this wasn't a date. Or a hookup. It was just fear. But fear of what, Tana asked herself. It was nameless, she thought, a nameless something that would be waiting for her when she opened the door and turned on the lights.

The apartment felt colder than usual. There was a chill in the air, as if fear itself could ever be anything but cold. Tana shivered as she turned on the lights, then stood by the door and looked around the living room. The sofa, the coffee table, the desk by the window—everything was in its place. Nothing she hadn't seen before, and nothing to be afraid of. And yet, she was scared.

"Nice place," Powell said as he stood behind her.

"Thanks. I'm just gonna look around, okay?"

"Sure, no problem," he said. "Take your time. You might want to turn up the heat while you're at it."

Powell waited by the door. He could hear Tana moving through the kitchen, the bathroom, the bedroom, as if searching for an intruder that wasn't there.

Then he heard her scream.

CHAPTER 21

Powell ran toward the sound, which seemed to come from the bedroom. He found Tana kneeling on the bed and staring up at something on the wall.

"What is it?" Powell said as he rushed to her side. "What's wrong?"

"Do you see it?" she said, eyes wide, staring at the wall, as if in a trance.

Powell followed her line of sight and saw what she saw. What appeared to be a video or a home movie, but could have just as easily been a hallucination, was playing on the bedroom wall in living color. A black SUV was rolling down a highway. A child was crying in the backseat. There was a man sitting next to her. Another man was behind the wheel. The child turned and looked at the camera as tears rolled down her cheeks.

Emma.

"It's her, isn't it? It's Emma."

"Yeah, it's her," Powell said quietly, too in awe to be scared.

A car carrier stacked with crushed cars passed the SUV. Emma watched it roll by then turned back to the camera.

"Was that the car you saw at the daycare center the day she got kidnapped?" Powell said.

Tana nodded.

"It's a Cadillac Escalade. Is that the license plate you saw?"

"Yeah, that's it."

Tana noticed that Emma was wearing the same pink top and gray pants with pink stripes that she was wearing the day she was abducted. A moment later, the image faded out and disappeared.

Tana looked up at Powell, who was standing by the bed. She was trembling and her face was pale and slick with sweat.

"It's not just me now, is it?" she said. "It's us, you and me. I thought I was in this alone...and then you saw it too."

Powell stared at the blank wall, as if Emma was still there, alive and real and four years old, and yet just out of reach. He slumped in a chair across from the bed and ran his hand through his hair as waves of emotion washed over him.

"I never thought this was gonna happen again...not after Nora."

Tana smiled. "Emma knew you weren't ready to stop looking for her."

"When the case went cold, I figured that was it. Never expected it was gonna come back to me...not like this anyway. But she's leading us to Emma."

"Helen?"

Powell nodded.

"So she knows where to find her?"

"Maybe, but she can't do anything about it."

"I don't understand."

"Helen's got unfinished business, Tana. But she's kind of helpless to do anything about it because she's caught between this life and the afterlife. All she can do is haunt the living."

"You mean haunt me, don't you?" Tana said. She glanced at

the wall, as if Emma's apparition was still there. "You too now, I guess."

"Right. So she's giving us the clues we need to find her. She let you see what happened when Emma was kidnapped, so you could see the plate. We didn't know that before. Now she's showing us what happened next."

"Okay, I get that. But what's the clue this time?"

"The car carrier. Has to be."

Tana looked at Powell with a puzzled expression.

"The car carrier? What, they put her on a truck? I don't understand."

"I don't either, not yet anyway. But it has to mean something, or she wouldn't have shown it to us."

Tana sighed. She stood and began pacing. Then she stopped and turned to Powell. "I don't know how to do this, okay?"

Powell looked up at her. "Do what?"

"This, what we're doing. It's crazy. How am I supposed to do this and do my job and pretend I have a life?"

Powell shrugged. "You don't have a normal life anymore, Tana." He gave a rueful smile. "Hell, neither do I now."

"What if I can't do it?"

"I don't think you have a choice."

Tana sat on the bed and buried her face in her hands. Then she looked at Powell. "Why me?"

"Does it matter?"

"I guess not. I just don't understand—"

"There's nothing to understand, Tana. Helen Mayfield reached out to you."

But why?"

"You were telling her life story. That's what an obituary is, right? But the story's not over until she knows what happened to Emma."

Tana shuddered. "It scares me when you say it like that."

Powell smiled. "Get some sleep. It's been a long night. I'm gonna head out."

He stood and started to walk out of the bedroom.

"Wait."

Powell stopped in the doorway and turned back to Tana. "What is it?"

Tana paused, then said, "I don't want to be alone."

"You still scared?"

"Aren't you?"

"Not yet."

"Why not?"

Powell shrugged. "I've been here before, remember?"

"Yeah, well, I haven't, okay? And right now, I don't feel like being alone." She nodded at the wall. "What if she comes back or something else happens?"

"Maybe you should call your boyfriend."

Tana scoffed. "Yeah, right. Maybe he can bring his new girlfriend with him."

"Is that what happened? He dump you for somebody else?"

Tana's eyes narrowed. She looked sharply at Powell. "Excuse me? I dumped him, okay? The asshole was cheating on me."

Powell paused. "So I guess you want me to stay, huh?"

Tana looked up at Powell. "Is that weird?"

Powell gave a wry smile, then nodded toward the living room. "I'll take the couch."

CHAPTER 22

POWELL WAS FOLDING THE COMFORTER HE'D USED FOR HIS restless night on the couch when Tana emerged from the bedroom. He wore a faded San Francisco P.D. T-shirt and jeans, and his forearms were splashed with tattoos. Tana saw him, saw the tattoos, and felt something stir inside her. She hadn't had a man stay over since Justin, and even though she and Powell hadn't shared a bed together, and he was old enough to be her father, he was still a man, and it was still the morning after.

"Morning," she said.

Powell looked up at her as he punched his pillow into shape and placed it on top of the folded comforter.

"Morning."

"You sleep okay?" Tana said.

Powell shrugged. "Off and on."

"Sorry, I should've taken the couch."

"No problem," Powell said. "I'm used to sleeping on a couch."

Tana looked at him. "Don't you have a bed?" she said, wanting to hear the rest of it.

"I spent a year on the couch after Nora was killed. Almost

sold the bed. Took me months before I could sleep in it again. I'd wake up half-asleep in the middle of the expecting to find her next to me. Then I'd remember she was dead, and every time it happened it was like I'd just found out she was gone."

Powell fell silent. He stared across the room like he was looking for Nora and she was a million miles away.

Tana paused, then said, "I'm sorry," which sounded like the dumb thing everybody said, because they couldn't think of anything else to say. But the fact was she couldn't think of anything else to say either. Even though she wrote about the dead every day.

Powell smiled sadly. "Yeah, me too," he said quietly.

"Thanks for staying over," Tana said.

"No problem."

"I just didn't know what to expect...still don't."

Powell nodded. "That makes two of us."

"You want some coffee?"

"Yeah, sure, that'd be great."

Tana went into the kitchen and took two mugs out of the cupboard. Powell watched her as she switched on the Keurig, then filled the tank with cold water. When it was ready, she popped in a pod and pressed "Brew."

"Easy, huh?" Powell said, nodding at the coffee maker.

Tana nodded. "Yeah, and the coffee's pretty good too." She handed Powell the mug of hot coffee. "Cream and sugar?"

Powell shook his head. "Not for me."

"Me either," Tana said, as she popped a pod into the coffee maker, then waited for the coffee to brew.

Powell sipped his coffee, then nodded like he was impressed.

"You're right, it is good."

Tana smiled. "Told you."

Powell took another sip, then looked at her.

"You get some sleep?"

Tana shrugged. "I kept waking up and looking at the wall, like something was gonna show up in the middle of the night and scare the shit out of me." She removed her mug from the coffee maker and took a sip. "It's weird, it's like I know something's going to happen now, but I don't know when."

Powell nodded. "That's how it gonna be until it's over."

"But what if it's never over? I mean, what if we've crossed over and we can't ever get back to how it was before?"

Powell locked eyes with Tana but said nothing.

"Is that how it was when you saw Nora?"

Powell nodded. "Yeah, I guess it was." He smiled sadly. "One minute you're living your life and the next minute...the next minute you don't know what you're living. I didn't mind though because I kept wanting her to come back. But after the last time I knew I'd never see her again."

They fell silent, then Tana said, "It's Helen's funeral today."

Powell looked up at her. "Today?"

Tana nodded.

"We should go and pay our respects," Powell said.

"You think?" Tana said.

"I got a feeling she'd want us to be there."

Tana gave herself a moment to think about it, then nodded and said, "I want to show you something."

She opened a drawer and took out the gold, heart-shaped pendant with Emma's photograph that Helen had given her the night she appeared to her.

"Look," she said, and held it out to Powell.

He took the pendant and looked at the photo, then looked up at Tana.

"Yes," she said, anticipating his question, "it's Emma."

"Where'd you get this?"

"Helen gave it to me."

"Why?"

"She wanted me to see what happened to Emma."

Powell looked down at Emma's photograph. "Cute kid, huh?"

Tana nodded. "I think she should be reunited with her mom."

CHAPTER 23

They laid Helen Mayfield to rest under sunny skies at Cypress Hills Memorial Park in Colma, a cemetery town south of San Francisco populated mostly by corpses and car dealers. A simple casket rested above a freshly dug grave, next to a mound of dirt covered with Astroturf.

Tana and Powell stood off to one side as a small, somber crowd composed mostly of older women huddled with their heads bowed and listened to the minister preach over the hum of nearby freeway traffic about eternal life. Was there such a thing, Tana wondered. Then again, maybe he was right. Maybe life did go on forever. They were burying Helen's body, but as she and Powell knew firsthand, the rest of her was very much alive.

The minster finished his homily and then the service was over. The crowd began to disperse. Mourners clutching funeral cards drifted away. As they did so, Tana saw a woman approach the grave. She was in her forties, Tana guessed, around the same Helen would be if she were still alive. She was dressed in black and carrying a long-stem red rose. She placed the rose on the casket, then clasped her hands and bowed her head, as if in prayer. Who was she, Tana wondered.

And what did Helen mean to her? She watched as the woman touched her fingers to her lips, then placed them on a casket. Moments later, she wiped her eyes and walked away from the grave.

Tana turned to Powell. "I'll be right back."

Powell nodded, as if he knew what Tana was about to do, then watched her as she walked over to the burial site. The cemetery workers were about to lower the casket and start filing the grave.

"Excuse me," Tana said, "could I have a moment?"

The workers exchanged glances, then nodded. Tana smiled, then stepped over to the casket. She took out the pendant and looked at Emma for one last time. She raised the pendant to her lips and gently kissed Emma's photo, then laid the pendant on the casket next to the rose. Her eyes filled with tears as she looked down at the image of Emma resting on her mother's coffin. Then she wiped her eyes and walked away.

As the mourners fanned out across the graves, one of them, a woman in her sixties, dressed in black with short silver hair, saw Powell. A look of surprise spread across her face, and she walked over to him as the other mourners headed back to the rest of their lives.

"Detective Powell," she said.

"Hello, Ann. Been a long time."

"Yes, quite a long time. What are you doing here?"

Powell shrugged. "Just seemed like the right thing to do."

"I wish we could have brought Emma home to her before it was too late," Ann said, glancing back at Helen's grave.

Just then, Tana came up to them. "I'm Tana Grant, Ann, we spoke on the phone," Tana said, feeling the need to introduce herself, even though she knew the woman was Ann Taylor, Helen's aunt on her mother's side.

"Oh yes, of course. You wrote her obituary for *The Bugle.*

Tell me, Tana, do you attend the funerals of all the subjects of your obituaries?"

Tana flushed. "No, not usually."

"So why Helen's funeral?"

Tana and Powell exchanged uneasy glances.

"It's hard to explain," Tana said. "I guess there was just something about Helen's story that made me want to be here."

"I know what you mean," Ann said. "All funerals are sad, but this one's especially so, isn't it?" She looked at Powell. "You're not back on the case, are you, Detective, after all these years?"

"Some cases never let go of you," Powell said.

Ann nodded. "It's never let go of me, that's for sure. You'll let me know if something turns up?"

"Of course," Powell said.

"Not that I expect anything after all this time." She shook her head. "Poor child." Ann shared a sad smile with Tana and Powell, then walked away from them, stepping past the graves of those who had gone before.

Tana watched Ann as she walked across the grass toward the parking lot. Then she felt Powell stiffen. She looked up at him and saw that his face had hardened.

"What's wrong?" she whispered.

Powell nodded at two men who were standing near the grave, and yet apart from the other mourners. Tana had no idea who they were, only that they looked out of place, as if they didn't belong. But who was she to say who belonged at a funeral and who didn't? One of them was a thick, stocky man with a broad, fleshy face, olive complexion and greasy, slicked-back hair that he wore in a ponytail. He wore a scuffed black leather jacket and appeared to be in his forties. His companion was a skinny white guy wearing a beige suit and wingtips. He had a sallow complexion, frizzy afro-style hair, and looked to be around fifty. Tana noticed that both men were smiling, as if Helen's funeral was a joke. Who laughs at a funeral, she wondered. Only someone who was happy that the guest of honor was dead. Was that why they were there?

"You know them?" Tana said.

Powell nodded. "The ponytail is Hector Vargas."

Tana's eyes widened. She stared at Vargas. "That's Hector Vargas? The guy who was on trial?"

Powell nodded. "The killer Helen voted to convict."

"Who's the guy in the afro?"

"His lawyer. Jimmy LaSalle," Powell said, his voice dripping with contempt.

"I guess you don't like him much, huh?"

Powell's eyes hardened. "Jimmy's not just a defense lawyer, he's a traitor."

"What do you mean?"

"He started out in the DA's office, got a rep as a tough prosecutor who pushed for guilty verdicts and long prison sentences. But then he found out that he could make a lot more money as a defense attorney. The cops who'd worked with him felt betrayed. Like one of their own had stabbed them in the back. Things came to a head when LaSalle defended a black kid who'd gunned down a cop. From then on LaSalle and SFPD weren't just on different sides, they were enemies. Jimmy shrugged it off and laughed all the way to the bank."

The case may have gone cold, but Tana could see that it still burned hot in Powell. As far as he was concerned, the Vargas acquittal was a miscarriage of justice that needed to be set right.

"So what are he and Vargas doing here?"

The crowd thinned. Tana noticed that Vargas had seen Powell. She watched as he turned to LaSalle, then pointed out Powell.

"I think we're about to find out," Powell said.

Tana felt her stomach tighten as Vargas and LaSalle walked toward them across the grass, past the gravestones.

She turned to Powell. "You know what? Maybe we should just leave. The funeral's over, right?"

But Powell wasn't listening. And as Vargas got closer, Tana realized there was nothing she could do but wait. The sight of the man whom Helen had voted to convict for murder frightened her, and yet she did want to know what Vargas was doing at Helen's funeral, and what he might know about Emma. Not that Tana expected him to tell her anything about her, but she had a feeling he knew plenty.

Vargas and LaSalle came up to them. Vargas stood with his feet apart, hands in the pockets of his leather jacket. He gave a mocking smile as he sized up Tana and Powell.

"Been a long time, detective," Vargas said in a Latino accent.

"Not long enough, Hector."

"You look soft, man. You put on a few pounds?"

Vargas grinned at LaSalle, who grinned back at him as he pulled out a pack of Marlboros and tapped out a cigarette. Tana felt Powell stiffen.

"There's no smoking on cemetery grounds, counselor," Powell said.

"You worried about their health, detective?" LaSalle said with a smirk, nodding at the graves around them.

He was about to light the cigarette when Powell stepped forward, snatched the cigarette out of his mouth and crushed it under his heel.

"Like I said, smoking is not allowed on cemetery grounds."

LaSalle glared at Powell, then sneered. "Still can't get over it, can you?" he said.

"What's that?" Powell said.

"Your side lost." He glanced at Vargas. "My client walked."

"There's still time, Jimmy," Powell said in a deadly tone of voice.

LaSalle scoffed, but Tana thought she saw a flicker of fear in his eyes.

Vargas nodded at Tana. "This your girlfriend?"

"Excuse me?" Tana said.

"She's a little too young for you, man. Not too young for me though, eh?" Vargas glanced at LaSalle and, as if on cue, they both leered at Tana.

"You wish," Tana said with a sneer.

"You got a mouth, eh," Vargas said, as if taken aback by her. "What else you got?"

"Nothing you're ever gonna see," she said.

Vargas gave Tana a sidelong glance, then looked at Powell. "You better manage your girl here, Powell, before somebody puts her down."

Tana scowled. "Seriously? You're threatening me at Helen's funeral?"

"Maybe I put you down myself, eh, puta?" Vargas said.

He grinned at LaSalle, who grinned back at him.

But Tana wasn't grinning, and she wasn't amused by Vargas's macho swagger. She stepped forward and slapped Vargas hard across the face, startling not just Vargas, but also Powell and LaSalle.

Vargas staggered, stunned by the blow. Tana didn't move. Stared hard at Vargas as he backed away from her and rubbed his cheek.

"Got yourself a volcan here, don't you, Bud?" he said.

Powell swiveled to Tana, blindsided by her sudden, unexpected move. She could feel him watching her.

"We done here?" she said, her eyes on Vargas.

"Not quite," Powell said. He looked at Vargas. "What are you doing here, Hector?"

Vargas threw a glance over his shoulder at Helen's grave. "We came to pay our respects, man." He turned to LaSalle. "Ain't that right, Jimmy?"

"Yeah, that's right."

"Yeah, you knew her, didn't you, Hector?"

Vargas shook his head. "Never met her."

"But she knew about you, didn't she? Knew a killer when she saw one. That's why she wouldn't change her vote." Powell nodded toward heaven. "I bet she's looking down at you right now and saying, 'Who invited a killer to my funeral?'"

Vargas threw a worried glance at the sky, then glared at Powell. "Fuck you, man. I didn't kill nobody."

"The prosecutor dropped the charges, remember?" LaSalle said.

"Yeah, I remember. I remember wondering why he dropped the charges. Wouldn't have had anything to do with Carmen Flowers, would it?"

Vargas gave a casual shrug. "Maybe you should ask him," Vargas said. "Ask her too if you can find her. Ten years is a long time. Bitches got a way of disappearing."

"Maybe you should disappear too, detective," LaSalle said.

Vargas nodded at Tana. "And take the bitch with you."

"Disappear like Emma?" Tana said. "Is that what you mean?"

Vargas glared at Tana, his eyes hard as marbles. But Tana didn't flinch. She held his gaze until he and LaSalle pushed past her and Powell and headed toward the parking lot.

Powell whipped around to Tana. "What the hell was that about? You want to tell me what you think you were doing?"

"He pissed me off. I hate guys like that."

"So you just slap 'em down, huh?"

Tana shrugged. "A girl's gotta stand up for herself. You got a problem with that?"

"No, but Hector Vargas might," Powell said. He watched as Hector and LaSalle walked across the lot toward a waiting SUV, then turned to Tana. "You ready?"

Suddenly, the sky darkened. A wind came up out of nowhere and howled across the graves. Lightning ripped the sky, followed seconds later by a deafening clap of thunder. Then torrential rain drenched the cemetery and the mourners rushing to their cars. Tana and Powell exchanged puzzled glances, then ran to the Bronco. They were about to climb in when Tana saw something.

"Look," she said, pointing.

Powell followed her line of sight and saw Vargas standing in the parking lot, lashed by wind and rain, a terrified look on his face. Suddenly, he pulled out a 9mm semiautomatic and began shooting at the sky. He squeezed off a few rounds as mourners scattered, screaming. Then LaSalle managed to drag him to the SUV and pushed him into the back seat.

Tana and Powell climbed into the Bronco and wiped the rain from their eyes.

"What was that?" Tana said as she closed the door.

"Fear," Powell said.

He turned the key, started the engine, and they drove away from the land of the dead.

An hour later, having fought rush-hour freeway traffic from Colma to the city, Powell double-parked the Bronco in front of Tana's building, then flipped on the emergency flashers.

Tana looked at him. "It was Helen, wasn't it?"

"The storm?"

Tana nodded.

"Who else?"

"We're the only ones who know that, aren't we? Everybody

else, all the people at Helen's funeral, they probably just thought it was a freak storm or something."

"I don't think Hector thought it was a freak storm. He was scared. I figure he's more afraid of Helen now than he was when she was alive."

"I can't believe he was there. It was like he was bragging that he got away with it."

"He got away with nothing. Just got to find a way to take him down."

"Can he be tried again on the same charges?"

Powell nodded. "The judge declared a mistrial, which means that the D.A. can retry him anytime he wants. Helen would've done Hector a favor if she'd gone along with the rest of the jurors and voted not guilty."

"Why?"

"Double jeopardy. He can't be tried twice for the same crime. But with a mistrial, there's always the chance he will be. Probably another reason he was pissed off at Helen."

"Doesn't look like the D.A.'s gonna retry him anytime soon," Tana said. "It's been ten years."

"There's no statute of limitations on murder and kidnapping, Tana."

"But there's no Carmen Flowers either, right?"

Powell nodded in acknowledgement.

The ride home had given Tana time to think, but things were no clearer to her now than when they left the cemetery. They had buried Helen's body, filled her grave with dirt, and yet she was alive in Tana's life in ways that had left her bewildered and confused. At least Powell understood. Were it not for him, she would have found herself utterly alone. And yet it was as if the life she knew had been torn away from her, replaced by another life that she could scarcely comprehend.

"Did you see that woman, the one with the rose?"

"At the funeral?"

Tana nodded. "She was dressed in black, and she put the rose on Helen's coffin."

"Guess I missed her."

"Just wondering who she was." She paused, then said, "So what do we do now?"

"I'll follow up on the plate. Let's see if we can find out who the registered owner was around the time Emma was snatched."

"What do you want me to do?"

"Just sit tight. I'll let you know what I turn up." Powell looked out at the building. "You want me to come up?"

Tana smiled and shook her head. "I'm a big girl."

But was she? Tana wasn't sure. But she did want Powell to believe that she was capable of more than just being scared.

Powell grinned. "Yeah, I know."

Tana nodded and climbed out of the Bronco. She stood on the sidewalk and watched Powell drive away, then turned to go into her building. She paused for a moment when she reached the door to her apartment, then decided she was ready for whatever or whoever was waiting for her. But what Tana saw when she opened the door was the last thing she expected.

CHAPTER 24

Her parents.

Ransom and Betty Grant.

The two of them sitting side by side on the sofa like they lived there. Suitcases with United Airlines luggage tags were parked by the door. Tana stared at her parents as if for a moment she wasn't sure who they were. Or was it that she never expected to find them waiting for her in her apartment?

Ransom, his wavy blond hair going gray at the temples, and dressed in jeans and cowboy boots, as if he'd just come straight from the stables, not SFO. Betty in jeans, a gray sweater, and a fleece vest. All that was missing were the cowboy hats and Ray-Bans they liked to wear when they were working on the ranch. Tana remembered teasing them once that if they ever got tired of ranching, they could model for Ralph Lauren Americana ads. But those ads were fake. Ransom and Betty, on the other hand, were the real thing.

"Surprise!" Betty said, a little too brightly.

She jumped up from the sofa, rushed over to Tana, and gave her a hug. She was smiling, but Tana thought she detected a trace of worry in her eyes.

Ransom looked up at her and smiled. "Hey Montana," he said in his radio-friendly baritone. He stood and walked over to Tana and embraced her. "How's my beauty queen?"

Tana rolled her eyes. "I was never a beauty queen, Dad."

"Sure you were. Shepherd Junior High. Don't you remember?"

"I was twelve years old. I was in junior high."

"You were the prettiest girl of all, and you'll always be my beauty queen."

"Oh, Dad," Tana said, touched and embarrassed at the same time.

"I'll bet you're wondering what we're doing here, huh?" Betty said.

"Yeah, I am," Tana said, still dazed by their presence. "What *are* you doing here? How'd you get in?" Questions tumbled through her brain faster than she could process them.

"The manager let us in," Ransom said and embraced her.

"Richie let you in?" Tana said, doing her best to follow along.

Ransom nodded. "Sure did. We ran into him downstairs, told him we were your mom and dad come to see their little girl and he just opened the door and told us to make ourselves at home."

"You don't mind, do you, honey?" Betty said.

"No, of course not. It's great to see you guys," Tana said. "I'm just surprised, is all."

"Well, we thought about calling you first, but then we decided we didn't want to wait to see you."

"Well, here I am," Tana said. "I guess we can all sit down now."

"I reckon we can," Ransom said, sitting back down on the sofa.

Betty tittered, then sat down next to him.

"Can I get you guys anything?"

Ransom shook his head. "We're good."

"Great," Tana said. "So how was the flight?"

"You know me and airplanes, Montana," Ransom said. "I'd rather have my feet on the ground, but trains take too long, and we wanted to see you."

"Don't listen to him, honey," Betty said. "The flight was fine. We were on the ground before we knew it."

"So how long are you gonna be in town? Maybe I can get some time off and we can go to dinner and I can show you the sights."

"Well, that depends."

"On what?"

Ransom took a deep breath, then let it out slowly and looked in earnest at his daughter. "On you."

Tana looked at her father with a puzzled expression. "On me? What are you talking about?"

"We miss you, honey, and we figured the only way we were gonna get to see you was to come to San Francisco, seeing as how you never want to come out our way."

"I'm sorry, dad...I'm busy, I have a job..."

"Yeah, I know. But you could have a job back home too."

Tana looked at her father. "Excuse me? I like my job, okay?"

"I know you do," Ransom said. "We were just wondering—"

"We were just wondering if you ever miss it." Betty said.

"The ranch?"

Betty nodded.

Tana shrugged. "I don't know, sometimes, maybe."

The question took her by surprise. She thought of the vast

Montana sky at dawn when she went out to feed the animals. The chestnut mare that threw her when she was twelve. The boy who broke her heart in high school. The first days in San Francisco, when she wandered the streets homesick and alone, struggling to acclimate herself to a damp city so different from the one she had left behind.

The wind had been hard to live with in the beginning. It was a city on the bay, the locals told her. The wind and fog just soak your bones. All you can do is get used to it. And after a while she did get used to it, the way people got used to anything, no matter where they were, or how bad their circumstances.

It was cold and windy in Montana too, the high winds knocking you off your feet as they roared across a big sky country that seemed to go on forever. But San Francisco wind was different. It came in off the bay, picked up the chill of the sea and propelled it ashore. You couldn't fight the wind in San Francisco. You had to learn how to let it rush through you. Otherwise it would blow you away.

"But I live here now."

"You could live there too. We could use the help. We're not getting any younger, you know, and it's all gonna be yours one day anyway."

Tana looked at her parents with growing suspicion. Had they flown halfway across the country to try and persuade her to move back home? It didn't make sense. Why now?

"You want me to quit my job and be a cowgirl? What's this about? Why are you guys really here?"

Ransom and Betty exchanged nervous glances, then Betty took hold of Tana's hands and said, "We were worried about you."

"Worried about me? Why?"

"We wanted to see you, see if you might want to come home for a while," Ransom said.

Tana pulled her hands away from her mother. "Cut the crap, Dad. Why are you here?"

Ransom paused to throw another glance at his wife, then said, "Mimi called us."

CHAPTER 25

TANA JUMPED TO HER FEET. THE HEAT RUSHING INTO HER face was hot enough to scald her. There was only one reason why Mimi would've called her parents. The last people who needed to know.

"She did what?" she said, shaking her head in disbelief. "She called you? She fucking called you?"

Ransom frowned. "Hold on now, Montana," he said. "There's no need for that kind of language."

"Like hell there isn't!"

"She was just trying to help."

"She was worried—" Betty chimed in.

"I can't believe this," Tana said. "What did she tell you?" As if she didn't know, Tana thought.

Ransom and Betty shifted on the sofa and traded uncomfortable glances, as if they would have preferred to be doing anything except having this conversation. That makes three of us, Tana thought, picking up on her parent's discomfort. She felt betrayed. She knew that Mimi didn't really believe her when she told her about the apparitions. But while she wanted Mimi to believe her, Tana never expected that she would breathe a word to anyone, let alone her parents. And yet she had turned around and done just that.

"What did she tell you?" Tana repeated. "You wouldn't be here if she hadn't told you something."

"She told us you were seeing things..." Betty said.

"Seeing things, huh? Like what things?"

"You know, scary things," Betty said, fumbling for words.

"Oh, for Christ's sake, Betty," Ransom said, glancing impatiently at his wife. He looked up at Tana, "She said you told her you were seeing ghosts and they were sending you messages or something."

"Ghosts?"

"That's what she said."

"More than one, huh?" Tana said.

Betty frowned. "It's not funny, Tana. She said you were seeing the people you were writing about."

"And you believed her."

Betty gave a helpless shrug. "Well, of course we believed her. That's why we're here."

"She's your friend, Tana," Ransom said. "Why would she go through the trouble of calling us if it wasn't true."

Because it was too delicious to keep to herself, Tana wanted to say. But instead, she decided that lying about it was her only way out.

"That's not what I told her," Tana said. "I told her I was having nightmares about the people I'm writing about. I guess she misunderstood me."

Betty nudged her husband, beaming with vindication. "See what did I tell you, Ransom?" She looked at Tana. "I told Mimi that it was probably an occupational..." She turned to Ransom. "Hon, what is it they call it?"

"Occupational hazard."

Betty's face lit up. "That's it. Occupational hazard. Maybe it's because of the job."

"Maybe you need a different job, Montana."

"Right," Tana said. "In Montana."

"We just hoped you might want to come home for a while."

"Whether I want to or not, is that it?" Tana could feel tears coming but crying in front of her parents was the last thing she wanted to do. "Mimi calls you and tells you to stage an intervention, is that it? I'm surprised she's not here too. So what's the plan? You gonna drag me back to Montana and have me committed or something?"

Ransom stood. "Hold on now, Montana. Nobody's talking about anything like that."

"So what then, dad? What are you talking about?"

"Don't be upset with us, honey," Betty said. "She scared us, that's all."

"I think what your mom is trying to say is that we'd feel better if you lived closer," Ransom said. "Maybe you would too."

"Yeah, right. I'd feel great," Tana said in a sarcastic tone of voice. "Totally great." She looked around for her coat, saw it slung over a chair and grabbed it. "You know what? I gotta go." She headed for the door.

"Where you going?" Betty said.

Tana pulled the door open.

"Montana!" Ransom shouted.

The door slammed shut behind her.

CHAPTER 26

T̲HE̲ ̲LINE̲ ̲OUTSIDE̲ F̲ALSETA̲, ̲THE̲ ̲HOT̲ S̲PANISH̲ restaurant where Mimi worked as a line cook, stretched down the block. They didn't take reservations, so even on a weeknight scoring a table for two could mean waiting for hours to get seated. Nobody seemed to mind, though, as night after night patient diners killed time by staring at their smartphones, chatting with their dinner dates and shuffling slowly toward the door.

But Tana wasn't there for dinner. And she wasn't feeling especially patient either. Her stomach was in a knot and food was the last thing on her mind, even though, according to *The Bugle*'s restaurant critic, *Falseta* served some of the best Iberian cuisine this side of Madrid. The quality was high, but so were the prices. If it wasn't for Mimi bringing Tupperware specials and entrees with her whenever she came by to visit, Tana would've never had a chance to sample firsthand what everyone was raving about. Now she wondered if she ever would again. She paid the cabbie and climbed out of his Prius, then pushed her way through the crowd milling around the sidewalk tables in front of the restaurant and went inside.

The place was packed with a noisy crowd and the air was

thick with the mouth-watering smells of paella, gazpacho, tapas, gambas al ajillo and more. A hostess with long black hair, gypsy eyes and the body of a flamenco dancer smiled at Tana, her pen poised to jot down her name on the waiting list.

"Buenas noches, señorita, party of one for the counter?" she said with a Spanish accent.

Tana smiled politely. "Not tonight," she said, as she pushed past her and headed across the dining room toward the kitchen.

The hostess rushed after Tana and tried to grab her shoulder. "Excuse me, señorita, you can't go back there..."

Tana shook her off and kept walking, dodging waiters and servers as she moved inexorably toward the swinging kitchen doors. She burst through the doors and into the heat and noise and chaos of a busy restaurant kitchen. Chefs, line cooks, porters and dishwashers were at their stations, working amid the fire and clang and hiss and sizzle of kitchen life.

Tana looked around and spotted Mimi at a stove. She was wearing a chef's jacket and a cap and assembling the ingredients for paella.

"What the fuck, Mimi!" Tana shouted at her. "I thought you were my friend!"

The kitchen fell silent as everyone stopped what they were doing. They traded glances, then looked over at Tana, puzzled and surprised by her outburst. Mimi looked over at her as well, and though her face was red from the heat of the stove, it seemed as if the color drained out of it when she saw her friend.

"I am your friend," Mimi said. "I was just worried..."

Tana came up to her. "So you called my parents? Seriously?"

Mimi glanced nervously at her coworkers, a mortified expression on her face. "Can we talk about this later please?"

"Why?" Tana said. She looked around the kitchen. "Don't you want everybody to know how you stabbed me in the back?"

"I didn't stab you—"

"You think that's why I told you? So you could blab to my parents about it?"

"I wanted to help you—"

"They're here, okay? They want to drag me back to fucking Montana. Is that what you want, Mimi? Was that how you were gonna help me?"

"Please, Tana, not now."

Tana shook her head. "Yes, now. Yes, right fucking now."

"I can't now..."

The head chef, a beefy, bearded man in a toque and kitchen whites came up to them.

"What's going on here?" he said.

"I'm sorry, chef—"

"Get back to work," he said, glaring at Mimi. He turned to Tana. "What are you doing in my kitchen?"

"I needed to talk to Mimi."

"Get out."

"I'm not finished," Tana said, standing her ground.

The head chef's eyes narrowed. "Excuse me?"

Please, chef, it's not her fault," Mimi said.

The head chef whipped around to her. "I said get back to work! Now!"

"Yes, chef," Mimi said with a nod, and resumed working on the paella.

"All of you get back to work!" the head chef said, scowling at the kitchen staff. Then he snapped his fingers and two men came up to him. "Get her out of here," the chef said.

The two men nodded and took Tana by the arms.

"Bitch!" she shouted over her shoulder at Mimi as the men escorted her out of the kitchen.

"I'll call you later, okay?" Mimi shouted.

"Don't bother," Tana said as the two men pushed her through the swinging doors.

"I know the way, thanks," Tana said as they approached the front door. She shook off the two men and stepped out of the restaurant.

Then, with her coat zipped up and her hands thrust in her pockets, she walked for what seemed like blocks down cold, dark streets, As if she wanted to put as much distance between herself and Mimi as possible. But as her anger and resentment began to subside, Tana realized that she already missed Mimi. She was one of her dearest friends, dear enough that Tana had confided in her about the most terrifying, profound and unexplainable thing that had ever happened to her—the apparitions of Helen and Emma Mayfield. How could she have betrayed that trust? And how could they ever begin to repair their friendship? Tana had no idea. All she felt now, as her anger cooled, was loss, and the feeling of it made her lonely.

She sat on a Muni bench and watched the lights of passing cars flashing past her. Everybody going somewhere, she thought. Or maybe nowhere. Maybe just killing time like she was killing time.

That was when she saw the bus. The destination sign read NOT IN SERVICE, but Tana noticed that there was a passenger onboard. A four-year-old girl with blonde hair. Her face was pressed against the window as the bus rolled past the stop.

Tana had seen her before.

Her name was Emma.

Tana felt a sudden chill, an icy current that ran down her spine and made her shiver. She stood and watched as the bus disappeared in a sea of night filled with headlights and taillights that seemed to float in the darkness.

"Find me," Tana said softly to herself. "I know. I will."

She thought of Helen sleeping underground on a satin pillow. Emma riding a bus to nowhere. Her own child, lost before she was born. She pulled out her iPhone and punched in a number she knew by heart. Seconds later, she smiled and said, "Hi, Mom."

CHAPTER 27

POWELL PARKED THE BRONCO ON A CEMETERY LANE NOT far from Nora's grave. He turned off the engine, then climbed out of the Bronco and opened the tailgate. He took out the folding chair he'd picked up at Target, then closed the tailgate and walked across the grass with the folding chair under his arm. The gravesite was near the top of a hill and shaded by oak trees. When he got there Powell unfolded the chair and set it on the grass a few feet from her grave. Then he sat down and looked at the headstone. It was nothing special, just a simple marker that noted her birth and date but said nothing about the life she lived between those dates or the time she and Powell had spent together. Or how it was she came to die and who was responsible.

He had visited Nora's grave every day after she died. He had no idea how to live without her and felt that if he sat by her grave day after day they were somehow still together. She had even reached beyond the grave and appeared to him when was most troubled, which had led Powell to think that they were still bound to each other, man and wife, forever. But when Nora stopped appearing to him, he felt as if she was telling him that she no longer needed to watch over him. He could let her go and move on with his life. But Powell knew no other life and so he continued visiting her grave, hoping he might one day see her again. But he never did, and over time he came less often.

Powell ran his hand through his hair and looked around the cemetery. The sun was lighting up the tombstones and monuments. He could see mourners placing flowers on the graves of their loved ones. He had attended Helen's funeral and now he was visiting Nora's grave. And somewhere out there Emma was still waiting to be found. Would he ever be done with the dead, Powell wondered. Not as long as he was alive.

He glanced at Nora's headstone and smiled. "Hey, baby," he said. "It's me. I guess you probably already knew that, didn't you? I guess I should've brought you flowers, huh? I'll bring you flowers next time, okay? Remember when I brought you flowers, baby? You remember?"

Powell reached into his pocket and took out the pint of Stoli he'd picked up on the way over. He wasn't much for drinking in the middle of the day, but he always liked to have a drink with Nora. He unscrewed the top and took a swig. Then, using both hands, he hiked his chair closer to the grave.

"I wanted to let you know that I'm back on the case. Gonna find out what happened to Emma Mayfield. You probably think I'm crazy, huh, how I can't let go of it. But I saw her, honey, just like I saw you. And I'm working with this reporter, and she saw her too. And you know what? I told her I saw you. Never told anybody, but I told her." Powell smiled sadly. "Wish I could see you again, baby." He sighed, then said, "Can you hear me, baby? Want me to get closer?"

Powell took another swig of vodka and tried to hike the chair even closer to the grave. But he lost his balance on the slope and the chair collapsed, dumping him onto the grass. The open pint fell out of his hands and spilled vodka on the grave. As he got to his feet, he saw a golf cart pull over and park. Two uniformed security guards got out of the cart and approached him.

"Alcoholic beverages are not permitted on cemetery grounds," the first guard said as he and his partner came up to Powell.

"Sorry," Powell said as he picked up the chair.

"You a family member?" the second guard said.

"She's my wife," Powell said, nodding at the grave.

The guards exchanged glances, then the first one said, "You're gonna need to leave."

"Sure, no problem, I understand," Powell said.

"Next time leave the bottle at home," the second guard said.

Powell nodded, then looked up at the guards. "You guys married?"

The guards looked from one to the other. "Yeah, why?" the first guard said.

"You're lucky," Powell said and walked away, the folding chair under his arm.

CHAPTER 28

Tana wasn't sure what her parents believed as she stood on the sidewalk and watched the Uber that would take them to SFO pull away from the curb. She had stayed up half the night with them, doing her best to convince them that Mimi had confused a nightmare with the real thing. She knew they were worried about her and maybe afraid for her, and she wanted nothing more than to set their minds at rest before they flew home to Montana. And yet lying her way out of something that seemed so profound to her made Tana feel ashamed. She wanted to tell them the truth, and she wondered if maybe in the end they did know the truth but decided to keep it to themselves.

Her cellphone rang as the Uber disappeared in traffic. Tana glanced at the screen and saw it was Mimi. She let whatever she had to say go to voicemail. Mimi could leave another message if she wanted, though Tana hardly saw the point, seeing as how she'd already left three messages since she confronted her at *Falseta*. What could she say that would be different? Hadn't she said it all the first time? They would talk eventually, but for now Tana felt as they were on opposite shores of some dark and ghostly sea. They could see each other but could not find a way to cross such treacherous waters.

Tana hailed a cab and headed south of Market to *The Bugle*. This week's dead were waiting for her, and she didn't want to be late.

"Bunch of lucky stiffs, if you ask me," her father had said when Tana phoned her parents to tell them she'd landed a job at *The Bugle* as an obituary writer.

"Um, how are they lucky, Dad?" Tana had replied. "They're like dead."

"They've got you to remember 'em. Not everybody gets someone to remember 'em."

Was she remembering the deceased she wrote about, Tana wondered. Or was she just faking it in return for a paycheck? The question was irrelevant, she realized, because Helen Mayfield had changed her life forever. She had showed Tana how a mother's love could reach beyond the grave and take command of the living. Now she would always wonder if the deceased whose lives she memorialized were not truly dead and would reach out to her again one day to finish what was left undone at the time of their passing.

First on the list of those to be remembered was Raymond Treadway, who had died of a heart attack while riding a Powell Street cable car on his 75th birthday. Treadway was a retired supermarket executive who was famous for having founded the Golden Gate SuperSave chain. According to the background materials in the manila folder that JD had dropped with a thud on Tana's desk, Treadway had started out with a single mom-and-pop store in the Marina. From there he built a retail grocery empire that blanketed the Bay Area with stores.

There were pictures of Treadway standing proudly in front of the first store. They contrasted with other photos, taken later, of Treadway standing in front of one of his supermarkets. He looked older, but just as proud. Tana scanned the file and jotted down some notes, then reached out to Treadway's widow, Louise. Background materials were useful, but as Tana had learned during her time on the obituary desk, family and friends could help celebrate a person's life in ways that documents never could. And that, of course, was the point of an obituary—to bring to life a life that was lost.

"Hello, Mrs. Treadway," Tana said, after Treadway's widow picked up. "This is Tana Grant from *The Bay Area Bugle*. I'm working on your husband's obituary."

"Oh yes. Hello, Tana, I suppose you want to talk about Raymond."

From the sound of her voice Tana guessed she was close to Treadway's age.

"Yes, if you don't mind."

"No, I don't mind. But please call me Louise."

"Sure, no problem," Tana said. "I know this is a difficult time. I'm sorry for your loss, and I appreciate you taking my call."

Tana began every call with survivors this way, hoping that her expression of sympathy and respect would encourage the friend or relative to talk openly about the deceased. But the more she did so, the more she worried about coming off as a phony, apologizing for a loss that meant nothing more to her than a deadline. And yet, what else was there to say?

"What would you like to know?" Louise said.

"What do you think would be the best words to describe your husband?"

Tana heard Louise chuckle. "Well, he was very ambitious. You could see that right from the start when he opened the first store."

"That was in the Marina, right?"

"Yes, that's right. It's still open, by the way."

"Yes, I know."

"Well, as soon as he opened the store, he was thinking about the next one, and the one after that. He wanted to build an empire."

"Well, he succeeded, didn't he?" Tana said.

"Yes, he did. He was quite proud of that. Of course, he wasn't quite so proud of the Hector Vargas business."

Tana sat up straight and leaned into the call. She could feel her heart pick up the beat. What did Hector Vargas have to do with a supermarket chain? Had he tried to rob one of the stores?

"Did you say Hector Vargas?"

"Yes. Ever heard of him?"

"Yes, I have."

"I'm surprised."

"Why?"

"Well, you sound quite young. This was before your time, I'm sure."

"What happened? Would you mind telling me?"

"Well, I suppose it doesn't matter now that Raymond's gone." Then Tana heard Louise's voice turn cold. "It had to do with that Flowers woman..."

"Carmen Flowers?"

"Yes, that's the one. You know about her?"

"I know she was supposed to be a witness at the Vargas trial. But then she recanted."

"She worked for Raymond; she was a checker at one of his stores. Unfortunately, she was wearing a Treadway uniform when she went into that convenience store. Raymond liked everyone wearing a uniform. I suppose it made him feel important."

Suddenly Tana realized what Louise was telling her.

"Is that how they found her?"

"Found who?"

"Carmen. She was supposed to testify about the shooting and then she changed her mind. I was just wondering if Vargas was able to trace her because of the uniform."

"Carmen?"

"Yes."

"I suppose it could've happened that way," Louise said, in a tone of voice that made Tana think there was more to the story.

"Do you think Raymond had anything to do with it?"

Louise fell silent. Tana wondered if she had gone too far. Writing an obituary was one thing; accused the deceased of a crime was another. Then Louise broke the silence.

"Are you sure you're a reporter, Tana? You sound more like a detective."

"I think a good reporter has to be a little of both."

"I suppose," Louise said. "But I think I've said quite enough about my husband. More than I should have, perhaps."

"Sorry, I didn't mean to pry," Tana said.

Louise chuckled. "Of course you did. That's your job. Good day."

The line went dead. Something was off, Tana thought. Louise knew more about Carmen Flowers than she was letting on. And she didn't want any of it to appear in her late husband's obituary. Why, Tana wondered. What was she hiding?

She punched in a number on her cellphone, waited for a moment, then said, "I have news."

"Great," Powell said. "So do I. You free for lunch?"

CHAPTER 29

OF COURSE TANA WAS FREE FOR LUNCH. AND IF SHE hadn't been she would've cleared her calendar. Not that there was much chance of that. She was always on deadline with the dead, and usually just grabbed a salad and ate at her desk. But today was different. Powell had news to share and so did she, and Tana couldn't wait to find out what he knew and tell him what she'd learned. The case was moving forward, and she and Powell were moving with it. Tana had just gathered her things and signed out when Ricky swung by her cubicle.

"Hola, chica, you want to grab a bite?"

"Can't, Ricky, sorry."

Ricky's face sagged with disappointment. "What, you got a date or something?"

"Something," Tana as she swept past him and headed to the elevator.

How could she ever explain it to him, she thought. She could barely explain it to herself.

"You got a new boyfriend, you got no more time for me?" Ricky said, tagging along with her.

"I've always got time for you, honey," Tana said as she

pushed the button and waited for the elevator. "Just not right now, okay?"

Ricky smiled sadly. "When?"

"Soon, I promise."

The elevator doors opened, revealing a crowded car. Tana hesitated as the claustrophobia welled up inside her. Should she wait for next car? It could be just as bad. After all, it was lunchtime, when everyone in the building jammed the elevators in a rush to escape their cubicles, if only for an hour. Tana tamped down her fears and squeezed her way inside. After stopping at every floor to take on even more bodies, the elevator reached the ground floor. Tana waved to the bored security guard as she crossed the lobby, then pushed the door open and stepped out into streets filled with office workers heading to lunch.

A double-decker tour bus packed with sightseers rolled past the building. Tana couldn't help wondering if Emma was onboard. But then she remembered that Emma had already seen the sights, and they were filled with horror. Then Tana heard a horn honk. She looked out at the traffic, expecting to see Powell's Ford Bronco. Her face fell when instead of the Bronco she saw her ex-boyfriend Justin's tricked-out silver Subaru WRX pull up and double-park in front of her.

"Oh great," Tana muttered under her breath. "Just what I needed."

The door opened on the driver's side and Justin got out of the car. He was in his late twenties, and he was wearing a hoodie, jeans, and sunglasses. He looked over at Tana and flashed the smile that always worked for him.

"Hey babe, thought I'd surprise you."

"Yeah, I'm surprised, Justin," Tana said flatly. "Totally."

"So I just thought I'd come by and take you to lunch, and we could talk."

"Talk? Talk about what?"

"Us."

"Us?" Tana shook her head. "Get a clue, Justin. There is no us, okay?"

Justin screwed up his face. "Why you got to keep saying that?"

"Because it's true, Justin, that's why. You cheated on me, remember?"

"It just happened, okay? It don't mean we're done."

Tana said nothing. He didn't get it, and she knew he never would. What was it with guys, anyway? Why did they always think they could get away with it? She looked out at the street. Drivers were honking their horns as they tried to get around Justin's Subaru.

"You better go, Justin. You're blocking traffic."

Just then Tana saw Powell's Bronco slam to a halt behind the Subaru. She watched as he climbed out of the Bronco, his face twisted with annoyance, and looked over at Justin.

"Hey, asshole. You want to move the car?"

Justin whipped around to Powell. "What's your problem, man?"

"Right now, you're my problem," Powell said.

"Bounce," Justin said dismissively, and turned back to Tana. "You coming or what?"

"What'd you say?" Powell said, coming up to Justin. "Bounce? Is that what you said to me?"

"Yeah, bounce," Justin said.

Tana's face tightened with alarm. "It's okay, Bud, he's just leaving."

Powell gave Justin a hard shove that slammed him back against the Subaru.

"How about you bounce, like right now?"

Justin shrank back against the car, a stunned, fearful look in his eyes, as if Powell's sudden move had taken him by surprise and left him too scared to fight back.

Powell looked at Tana. "You ready?"

Justin looked up at Tana with surprised expression on his face. "You know this guy?"

Tana ignored the question.

"Yeah, I'm ready. Let's get out of here."

"Who's that, your new boyfriend?" Justin called out as he watched Tana and Powell walk to the Bronco. "Looks like a perv."

Tana flipped off Justin without turning around. Just then Ricky and Sheila came out of the building and saw Tana climb into the Bronco.

"Tana? What's up, girl?" Sheila said.

"No date, huh, chica?" Ricky said, a resentful look on his face.

"I gotta go, guys, sorry," Tana said, as she slammed the door.

She wasn't exactly sure what she was sorry about, but it was the only thing she could think of to say as Powell pulled out into traffic. Justin could've picked another time to surprise her, and she could have done without Ricky and Sheila seeing her with Powell, because now they would ask questions she would never be able to answer. So maybe she was sorry about that. Then again, how long did she think she could keep the most profound thing that ever happened to her a secret? Tana glanced in the side mirror and saw Justin, Sheila, and Ricky standing on the sidewalk. They were getting smaller and smaller as the Bronco faded into a haze of cars, trucks, and buses, but she could still see the puzzled expressions on their faces.

Powell glanced at Tana. "Who was that? Your ex?"

Tana nodded. "Sorry about that, he just showed up."

"Some guys can't take no for an answer."

Tana shrugged. "He will, soon as he finds a new girlfriend. He always does, even when he already has a girlfriend."

"The worst kind of boyfriend, huh?"

"Yeah, I guess so. I think you scared him."

"Yeah?"

Tana nodded.

Powell grinned. "Guess I haven't lost my touch."

Tana looked at him. "Is that like a guy thing?"

"Maybe a cop thing."

Tana paused and looked out the window. "I saw her again last night," she said quietly.

"Emma?"

Tana nodded. "Do you think she's watching us?"

Powell glanced at her. "Watching us?"

"Yeah, like maybe the dead watch over the living...the way your wife watched over you."

Powell seemed to flinch, and Tana immediately regretted bringing up his late wife.

"Sorry, I shouldn't have said that."

"No problem," Powell said. "Maybe you're right. Where'd you see her?"

"She was on a Muni bus."

"Last time we saw her she was on a Greyhound."

Tana looked at Powell. "What does that mean?"

"The bus?"

Tana nodded. "It's got to mean something, right?"

Powell shrugged. "I don't know what it means, Tana. Maybe it means that's where we'll find her."

"We're gonna find her on a bus? Seriously? Is that what she's trying to tell us?"

"That's what we have to find out."

"But how? How is it even possible to find out anything?" Tana shook her head. "I don't understand..."

Powell glanced at her. "Yeah, you do."

Tana looked at him.

"She chose you," Powell said. "You understand that, don't you?"

Tana nodded. "And then I chose you."

Powell and Tana locked eyes for a fleeting moment that, in Tana's mind, seemed to last forever.

"You said you had news. Was that it, that you saw her again?"

Tana shook her head. "There's more."

CHAPTER 30

They were heading down Fell toward the Avenues. It was late afternoon, and the sun was slanting over the city, making the old Victorians look even older. As they passed Panhandle Park on the edge of the Haight, Tana could see moms with strollers packing up after having picnics on the grass. Kids from the neighborhood were shooting hoops in the basketball courts. Joggers and cyclists were doing laps in the hope of eternal life through exercise Tana figured that none of them was thinking about being dead. But why was she even thinking that, she wondered. Was that what happened when you got paid to write wrote about the dead? Or was it that Helen and Emma had shown her that there was more to being dead than she could have ever imagined?

"I think I know how they got to Carmen Flowers," she said.

Powell kept his eyes on the road. "I'm listening."

While Powell rolled west on Fell, Tana filled him on the late Raymond Treadway and her phone interview with his widow, Louise Treadway. She explained how the fact that Carmen Flowers was wearing a Golden Gate SuperSave uniform when she walked into the convenience store just before the shooting meant that Hector Vargas knew where she worked, which would have made it easy for him to find her.

"So he knew where she worked," Powell said. "How'd he find out the rest?"

"The rest?"

"Where'd she live? When did she go to bed at night? What time did she get up in the morning? Did she need money? Was she lonely? The rest, okay? You don't take a bribe for no reason."

"I think she told him."

The Bronco caught a light. Powell turned and looked at Tana.

"Treadway? Is that what his wife told you?"

"His widow," Tana said.

"Whatever," Powell said, annoyed at being corrected.

Tana shook her head. "It's what she didn't tell me that makes me think she's hiding something. I think Treadway was how they got to Carmen, but I don't know why." She looked at Powell. "Did you interview him?"

"Yeah, sure we interviewed him. But we had no reason to consider him a person of interest. We knew Flowers worked at the store, but that was all we knew. We didn't find a connection between that and the fact that she recanted her testimony."

Tana looked out the window as Powell hung a left on Stanyan by Kezar Stadium and drove along Golden Gate Park. The neighborhood was known as 9th and Irving, and it billed itself as the heartbeat of the Inner Sunset. Shops, market, cafes, bars and restaurants were clustered around the intersection like it was some small-town Main Street. Sure, the old Victorians had been turned into flats, then converted to condos, but they still had charm and the architecture still had character.

"Where we going anyway?" she said. "I have to get back to the office and finish Treadway's obit."

"What's the rush? He's not going anywhere."

"My editor. He's the rush. The obit's supposed to go live online at midnight."

"We're heading out to the Sunset," Powell said as the Bronco approached the fogbound stretch of San Francisco where damp skies hung over gray streets and you could feel the mist seeping into your bones.

Tana made a face. "The Sunset?"

"Yeah, you ever been there?"

"Not if I can help it."

"That bad, huh?"

Tana gave a dismissive shrug. "The weather sucks and the houses all look alike."

"Yeah, they do. You know why?"

"I got a feeling you're gonna tell me."

"The houses were built by developers who used a basic floor plan to mass-produce thousands of homes, sometimes up to two a day."

Tana reacted with disbelief. "Two a day? How is that even possible?"

"They made it possible. Packed 'em in on twenty-five-foot lots and gave buyers two bedrooms, one bath and a garage. Even threw in a lawn out front."

"How come you know so much about it?"

"I lived here out here for a while when I moved to the city. Had a one-bedroom apartment on the corner of 24th and Noriega. I thought about buying a place, then I changed my mind and moved to the east bay." He glanced at Tana and smiled. "Guess I didn't like the weather much either."

"It doesn't even look like the city out here."

Powell nodded. "Yeah, I know what you mean. You don't see too many tour buses out here, or tourists taking selfies. But the houses made it possible for thousands of people who thought home ownership was only a dream to buy a house."

"Not my kind of dream."

"Maybe you're just a snob."

Tana gave herself a moment to think about it, then said, "Sometimes I think everybody's a snob in San Francisco."

Powell grinned. "I guess that's why I live in Oakland."

He turned down a side street, then pulled up in front of gray, row-house style home with a barrel-front stucco façade that was embellished with Mediterranean Revival ornamentation. An Asian kid in his twenties wearing jeans and a hoodie was washing his BMW in the driveway of the house next door.

"We're here," Powell said, and killed the engine.

Tana looked out at the house. A Paine Properties For Sale sign was planted in the lawn.

"You're buying a house?" she said with a puzzled expression. Then it hit her. She turned to Powell. "You found out about the plate, didn't you?"

Powell nodded. "Yeah, I found out about the plate."

Tana noticed that the sign included a photo of the realtor. A caption identified her as Allison Paine. Tana saw the photo and her eyes widened.

"Oh my God, it's her!"

"Who?" Powell said.

"The woman I saw with the rose at Helen's funeral. Allison Paine. It's her."

"You sure?"

"Totally. It's her. Funny coincidence, huh?"

"Yeah, funny coincidence," Powell said, looking at the sign.

"What?" Tana said, sensing that there was something about Allison Paine that had registered with Powell. "You know her?"

Powell shook his head. "Nope, can't say as I do."

"So what is it?"

"I don't know, something. Just can't place it right now."

"Maybe it'll come to you."

Powell shrugged. "Yeah, maybe."

He pulled out cellphone and snapped a pic of the sign, then opened the door and climbed out of the Bronco. Tana climbed out as well and followed him up the walkway toward the front door. She paused for a moment as they passed the For Sale sign and looked again at Allison Paine's photo. She looked happier than she did at the funeral, Tana thought. Maybe because she was selling houses instead of paying her respects. But why was she paying her respects, Tana wondered. And what did any of it have to do with Emma Mayfield's disappearance?

Powell rang the doorbell. The chimes jolted Tana out of her thoughts. She stepped up to the door and waited for someone to answer it.

CHAPTER 31

But no one did. Powell rang the doorbell a second time. Still no answer.

"Looks like nobody's home," Tana said.

Then Powell noticed the realtor's lock box attached the doorknob. "Nobody's gonna be home," he said, nodding at the lock box.

"You're too late," the Asian kid called out. "The open house was last weekend. Realtor told me they got a bunch of offers."

Powell and Tana turned and looked at the Asian kid. "Arthur Kim live here?" Powell said, glancing at his notepad.

The Asian kid nodded. "Not anymore. Died two weeks ago."

Tana and Powell exchanged glances, then walked over to the kid.

"You mind if I ask you a couple of questions?" Powell said.

"About Arthur?" the kid said, sounding confused.

Powell nodded.

"You a friend of his or something?"

"Or something," Powell said.

The kid paused as a knowing smile spread across his face. "You're not here about the house, are you?"

Powell shook his head. "We're here about the Escalade."

The Asian kid scoffed. "The Escalade? Man, you too?"

Tana and Powell exchanged glances.

"What do you mean?" Tana said.

"Got stolen two weeks after he bought it. Arthur never got over it. Lost the car ten years ago and he still couldn't stop talking about it." The kid shook his head. "Get a new one, I told him. But he never did. Just kept talking about the one that got boosted. Go figure, right?"

"Did he say whether he reported it?"

"Yeah, sure, he reported it. But the cops never found it."

"How well did you know him?" Powell said.

The Asian kid shrugged. "He was the guy who lived next door. That was about it."

"He ever mention a little girl named Emma Mayfield?" Tana said.

The kid made a face. "Arthur? No way. He hated kids."

"Any particular reason why?"

"He told me they got on his nerves." The kid paused and looked at Tana and Powell. "So how come you're asking so many questions about him?"

"I guess 'cause you keep answering 'em," Powell said. Then he smiled and said, "Thanks for your time."

"No problem," the kid said, and went back to washing his car.

"Now what?" Tana said as they walked back to the Bronco.

"I want to follow up on the car. If Kim reported it stolen there's gonna be a record."

"Yeah, but so what? I mean, how does that help us? If the car was stolen, then Kim wasn't driving it when Emma was kidnapped."

"We don't know that yet."

Tana looked at him. "What do you mean?"

"We won't know for sure until we compare the date Emma was abducted with the date Kim reported the car stolen."

Tana shrugged. "It'd be a real bummer if it was him, seeing how he's dead." She stopped and snapped a pic of the For Sale sign with her cellphone, then turned to Powell. "I'm gonna follow up too."

CHAPTER 32
TUESDAY, JUNE 8, 2010

Helen closes *The Baby Tree* and glances at Emma, who's just now fallen asleep. Her sweet round face is framed by her blonde curls and her head is nestled against her pillow. She could look at her daughter forever, but now it's time to turn off the light and let Emma drift off into her dreams. *The Baby Tree* is one of Emma's favorite books. Helen's read it so many times she could probably recite it from memory. But Emma never tires of it. And so Helen reads it again and again.

She remembers the time when Emma wanted to know how she got in Helen's belly. It was a big question and at first Helen wasn't quite sure how to answer it. Then she found *The Baby Tree*. In the book, a boy who's wondering where babies come from asks his babysitter, teacher, mail carrier, grandfather and parents until he finds the right answer. It was the right answer for Emma too, and now Helen imagines her reading it years later when she's a mother with children of her own.

She turns off the light and slips quietly out of Emma's bedroom, gently closing the door behind her. She's tired, the way she always is this time of night. Nine hours on her feet at the DMV really take it out of her. And then she has to deal with a four-year-old child who wants so much from her. Not that she's have it any other way. Emma was the miracle that grew inside her and lit up her life. Nothing could ever be more important. And though it's too early to go to bed, Helen wishes she could curl up next to Emma and they could drift away to dreamland together.

She goes into the kitchen and takes a bottle of white wine out of the refrigerator and pours herself a glass. Then she walks into the living room and settles on the sofa to watch some TV. That and the wine will help her sleep. She's surfing channels, deciding what to watch, when the phone rings. Helen glances at the phone as a flicker of annoyance crosses her face. Who's calling now, she wonders. She doesn't want to talk to anyone right now. She spent the whole day talking as one person after another stepped up to her window wanting to register a vehicle, renew their driver's license or transfer ownership. Now she wants no one to talk to. She just wants to drink her wine and watch TV and fall asleep.

But she worries that the sound of the phone ringing might wake Emma, so she sets the wine glass on the coffee table and mutes the TV, then stands and walks over to the phone and answers it.

"Hello?"

There's a pause, but Helen can hear someone breathing on the other end.

"Hey, it's me."

"Frank?" Helen says as she feels her body stiffen.

"Yeah. Remember me?"

"Yes, I remember," Helen says, "though I'd rather not."

"Don't talk that way, okay? I don't like it. You got no right to talk to me like that."

"Why do we have to talk at all?"

"Because I want to see her, that's why. I want to see Emma."

"Why now?"

"I'm in town for a couple of weeks before I have to head back out again. I'm gonna be stuck on an offshore rig in the Gulf of Mexico for a couple months, and I was hoping to see her before I left."

"I don't think that would be a good idea."

"Why not?"

"You think you can just breeze into her life and be a father whenever you want?"

"You won't let me be a father, Helen. Does she even know she has a father?"

Helen feels her eyes flooding with tears. "That's not my fault. You could've been her father—"

"I still am her father!"

Helen wipes her eyes. She doesn't want Frank to hear her cry. Not now, not ever. She walks over to the coffee table and picks up her wine glass and takes a sip. "It's been a long day, Frank." She throws a glance at Emma's bedroom door. "I don't want Emma to hear us fighting."

"You can't stop punishing me, can you?"

"You've punished yourself, Frank. Don't blame me."

Helen hangs up. She waits for a moment by the phone, as if expecting Frank to call back. But he doesn't. She takes a deep breath, then lets it out slowly. He'll call again, she tells herself, before he heads to the Gulf of Mexico, but it won't change anything. He says he's her father, but he's not, not really, not anymore. Emma doesn't have a father; she only has Helen. All she needs. Helen gulps the rest of her wine, then settles back on the sofa, picks up the remote and looks for something to watch. But the tears won't stop. She drops the remote and buries her face in her hands and, over the sound of TV noise, she weeps.

CHAPTER 33

JD was waiting for Tana when she breezed into the office. In fact, he wasn't just waiting for her—he was in her cubicle, sitting at her desk like it was his. And in a way it was, given that as managing editor he ruled over everyone and everything in the newsroom, and could sit wherever he damn well pleased.

He swung around and looked up at Tana. She noticed that her Aeron chair was a bit too small for him.

"Montana! How nice of you to drop by."

"Sorry I'm late, JD."

"How was lunch?" he said, faking a smile.

As if he really cared, Tana thought. "Fine," she said, hoping that would be enough and that JD wouldn't interrogate her about where she went and why she was late.

JD glanced at his watch. "Long too, I'd say." He looked up at Tana. "Would you say that too, Mon-ta-na? That it was a *long* lunch?"

Tana nodded. There was no point in fighting it. She could feel the color rushing into her face. She was working on the biggest story of her life, the scoop of the century, and if JD had a clue, it would've blown him away. Get the fuck out of my office, I'm busy, she wanted to tell him. Instead, she said, "Sorry, JD... I guess I lost track of the time."

JD paused to consider it, then looked up at her. "But you won't lose track of it again, will you?"

Tana shook her head.

"Because when you lose track of time, then we lose track of you, and if we lose track of you then one day you don't have a job anymore, do you?"

"You're not gonna fire me, are you, JD?"

JD smiled broadly. "I hope not." He stood, then edged his way past Tana out of the cubicle. "I'm so glad we had this little talk. Aren't you?"

Tana nodded.

"Well then, I suppose you'd like to get back to work now."

"Yeah, that'd be great," Tana said.

"Excellent. Where are we on Treadway's obit?"

"I'll file it today."

JD locked eyes with Tana. "Yeah, you will." Then he turned and walked away.

Tana took a deep breath, then sat down. She would have to be more careful, she reminded herself. She couldn't afford to lose her job, not with everything else that was going on in her life. Still, it seemed to her that being careful was the last thing she needed to be now that she was on the case. And she doubted that Emma would let her, even if she tried.

She tapped a key on her MacBook and the screen blossomed into an ocean. It was dotted with Word doc icons that looked like gravestones floating in an open sea. Which of course they were since every doc was an obituary. She was about to open Treadway's obituary, when she heard a familiar voice.

"So who's the hunk, girlfriend?"

Then another familiar voice. "You holding out on us, chica?"

Tana spun around to see Sheila and Ricky standing by her cubicle. They were looking at her with knowing smiles on their faces, waiting expectantly for Tana to spill all the juicy details.

"I can't talk now, guys, "Tana said. "JD almost fired me."

Sheila and Ricky threw disappointed glances. "That's it?" Sheila said.

"That's not fair, muchacha," Ricky said. "You got to come clean."

"So who is he?"

"And how come he's so old?"

Tana looked up sharply, her eyes flashing with annoyance. "He's not old, okay?"

Sheila and Ricky traded teasing glances. "Ooh, she likes him," Sheila said

"Umm hmm."

"I didn't know she was into older men."

"Me neither. She never said a word."

"Excuse me, I'm like right here, okay?" Tana said.

"Yeah, but you're not telling us anything, chica."

"Can we please talk about this later?" Tana said, sound exasperated, "when I'm not on deadline?"

"Promise?" Sheila said.

"Yeah, promise," Tana said, and turned back to her screen.

She had no idea what she would tell them. What she did know was that she had just made a promise she had no intention of keeping. Because there was no way she could ever tell them the truth.

Tana filed Treadway's obit a little after six, then picked up her iPhone and entered a number.

It rang three times, then a woman picked up.

"Paine Properties," she said. "How may I direct your call?"

"Allison Paine, please," Tana said.

CHAPTER 34

I⊤ WAS A FEW MINUTES AFTER SIX AND THE DAY WAS fading out when Tana's Uber driver pulled up in front of the Paine Properties building on West Portal Avenue. The driver, a pregnant Asian woman in her late twenties wearing cat eye sunglasses and way too much eyeliner, glanced at Tana as she opened the door.

"You buy house?" she said, startling Tana.

She turned and saw the sunglasses in the rearview. Ever since that first night, when her Uber driver turned into Helen Mayfield, she had feared that it might happen again, and wondered if she should switch to Lyft or start taking cabs. But she liked riding Uber and finding a cab in the city when she needed one wasn't easy. And she doubted that it would make any difference whether she was in an Uber, a Lyft, a cab, a bus, or even a car of her own. The spirits knew where to find her. Lucky me, she thought.

"Yeah, right," Tana said in a sarcastic tone of voice as she climbed out of the car and closed the door. As if anyone other than the tech bros who had ruined the city for everyone else could afford to buy a house or a condo in San Francisco.

The ground-floor windows of the Paine Properties

building were papered with color photos of houses and condos for sale. Tana lingered on the sidewalk by the entrance as she looked at the photos, then opened the door and went inside. There was no one at the receptionist desk and the lights were out in most of the offices. For a moment she wondered whether Allison Paine had forgotten about her. Then the door opened behind her. Tana turned and saw Paine step into the office.

"Sorry," Allison said, "I had to step out for a moment."

"No problem," Tana said.

"Tana Grant, right?"

Tana nodded. "Yes, right."

Allison stuck out her hand. "I'm Allison Paine."

She wore a navy blue blazer and jeans, and the grief Tana had seen in her eyes at Helen's funeral was hidden by a smile.

"Thanks for meeting with me," Tana said as they shook hands.

"We can talk in the conference room. Right this way."

Allison walked into the conference room ahead of Tana. She turned the lights on, then took a seat at the head of the table.

"Have a seat," she said, indicating the chair closest to her.

"Thanks," Tana said, and sat down across from the floor to ceiling windows that looked out on a darkening sky.

"So you said on the phone that you were a reporter and you wanted to talk about Helen Mayfield."

Tana nodded. "Yes, that's right. I wrote her obituary for *The Bugle*."

A shadow fell across Allison's face. "So you didn't know her, did you?"

Tana shook her head. "No, I didn't." She paused. "I never do—I just get the assignment."

"I see. So what's so special about this assignment? I mean, if you've already written her obituary, why do you want to talk to me?"

"It's important, I just can't tell you why."

Allison's eyes narrowed with suspicion. "Why not?"

"Because you'll never believe me."

Allison gave Tana a skeptical look. "So I'm supposed to trust you, is that it?"

"I get it if you don't want to talk to me. I just hoped that you would."

"Off the record?"

Tana nodded. "Off the record."

Allison gave herself a moment to think about it, then said, "How'd you find me anyway?"

"I saw you at the funeral. And then I saw your pic on a for-sale sign."

Allison looked up, surprised. "You were at Helen's funeral?"

Tana nodded. "You had a rose."

Allison gave a sad smile. "Helen loved roses...I wanted her to have one." Then the smile faded, and she looked at Tana with a puzzled expression. "But why were you there if you didn't know her?"

Tana paused. How could she reply to a question that could never be answered? "It's a long story," she said.

"But you want to know why I was there, don't you? And you want to know where I fit in your long story. Next you'll ask me what Helen meant to me."

She was miles ahead of her, Tana thought. Could she even keep up?

"I'll tell you what she meant to me, okay?" Allison said suddenly, her eyes filling with tears. "Everything, that's what she meant to me."

The room fell silent. Tana noticed that the sky had gone

black. Shadows lengthened, and she wondered if Helen and Emma were there as well, listening in on their conversation from the comfort of night.

"I'm sorry," Allison said as she reached for a tissue and wiped her eyes. "It's hard for me to talk about Helen without getting emotional and embarrassing myself in front of strangers."

"It's okay, I understand," Tana said, stunned that Allison had revealed her innermost feelings to her.

"I thought we would always be together...then she got sick....and well, you know the rest."

"How did you meet?"

Allison gave a sad, ironic smile. "We met at the DMV. I mean, who meets at the DMV, right? But I had to renew my license, and there she was..."

Her voice trailed off and Tana knew that in her mind's eye she was back in line at the DMV, waiting to step up to Helen's window, waiting for her life to change forever.

"Did you know her daughter?"

"Emma? Of course. She was a darling little girl...and then she was gone. Now they're both gone."

"Do you have any idea who could have kidnapped her?"

"The rumor was that Hector Vargas took her because of what happened at the trial. But he wasn't only one who was angry at Helen."

Tana looked up at her. "What do you mean?"

"Helen and I both had angry husbands who didn't like the idea of us together. Jerry was furious—"

"Jerry?"

"Jerry Paine, my ex. He went nuts when he found out about Helen and me. Leaving him for another man would have been bad enough. But leaving him for another woman, well, that was way worse."

"Is he still around, your ex?"

Allison nodded. "He's the sales manager at a Honda dealership in the city. Or at least he used to be. That's how we met. He sold me a car." She smiled bitterly. "Sold me on a lot of other stuff that didn't turn out to be true."

"Do you think he could have kidnapped Emma?"

Allison shrugged. "I don't know...I suppose he could have. Or maybe it was Frank."

"Frank Aiken? Helen's husband?"

Allison nodded. "But I can't imagine what either one of them would've done with a four-old-girl once they got over being angry."

"Maybe they never did."

"For all I know they could still be pissed."

"Did they know each other?"

Allison looked at Tana. "Jerry and Frank?"

Tana nodded.

"Yeah, they did. Not at first, of course. They sort of found out about each other when Helen and I got together. Gave 'em each a shoulder to cry on, I suppose." She smiled sadly. "Doesn't matter much now, does it? Helen's gone and so is Emma."

No, Tana wanted to say, they're not gone. They'll never be gone until I find out what happened to Emma. Paine had told her everything and Tana had told her nothing. But there was no way she could tell her anything.

Allison glanced at her watch. "Was there anything else? I have to show a house to a prospective buyer who wants to see what it's like at night before he makes an offer." She shook her head wearily. "Clients."

"Thanks again for your time," Tana said. "I appreciate it."

Allison stood, then looked at Tana and their eyes met. "Did you get what you came for, Tana?"

Tana held her gaze. "When I saw you at the funeral, I wanted to know who you were, and why Helen mattered to you. So yeah, I guess I did get what I came for."

"Good," Allison said. "Perhaps someday you'll tell me why Helen mattered to you."

They shook hands at the door, then Tana stepped out onto West Portal Avenue. The night had turned cool, and she pulled her coat tightly around her to ward off the chill. The story of Helen and Emma had taken another turn and was no longer only about whether Hector Vargas had taken out his anger at Helen by kidnapping her child. It was also about two women in love, and they price they may have paid for that love. Was that the truth, Tana wondered. Or was there another truth yet to be discovered?

She looked up and down the busy street. What did she expect to see? A glimpse of Emma in the headlights flashing past her? Her mind raced with questions as she watched the rush of traffic. Then a silver Lexus sedan that looked as if it had just been driven off the showroom floor sped past her, and Tana smiled. Of course, she thought, and reached for her iPhone.

CHAPTER 35

Twenty minutes later Tana found herself sitting in the passenger seat of a brand-new Honda CR-V. The Honda was parked in the lot behind the showroom at San Francisco Honda, and a salesman with a soul patch and way too much aftershave was sitting next to her. His name was Jerry Paine and, in addition to being a salesman, he was also Allison Paine's ex. Paine was tall, thin, and pushing fifty, and he wore a suit that was shiny from too many trips to the cleaners. He looked hungry, Tana thought, but she figured it probably came with the territory of being a salesman and having to sell to live. She thought of Allison Paine and wondered what she saw in him.

Tana had tried her best to pretend that she was actually interested in buying the car and had nodded appropriately at what she hoped were the right moments as Paine went over the car's features and functions. Now it was time to actually drive the car. the last thing she wanted to do. But she was a reporter, as she reminded herself in the cab ride to the dealership, and reporters did what they needed to do to get the story.

"So...you ready to go for a ride?" Paine said.

Tana gave a casual smile, as if she went on test drives every day of the week. The truth was she had never test-driven a car or even considered buying one. She had a driver's license, but never had a reason to use it. She was a city girl, and city girls didn't drive.

"Yeah, sure."

"Great. I'll drive it off the lot and then you can take over. How's that sound?"

"Sounds good," Tana said, trying to go with the flow.

Paine smiled, then started the engine and pulled out of the lot. He hung a right and headed down Van Ness Avenue. Tana heard a click as the doors locked automatically, and suddenly felt her body tense, though she wasn't sure why. Perhaps because she was faking it, Tana thought. She wondered if Paine knew it too.

"How's it feel so far?" Paine said.

"Great," Tana said, not sure what else she should say. It felt like a car. Was she missing something?

"Well, you can't go wrong with Honda, right?" Paine said.

Tana smiled. "Right."

"Ever owned a Honda?"

Tana shook her head.

"What are you driving now? I noticed a cab dropped you off at the dealership. I guess you need a car, huh?"

Tana imagined Paine watching her through the windows, waiting for her to step inside the showroom so he could pounce.

"I'm not driving anything," Tana said. "Don't really need a car in the city."

"Wow. So this'd be your first car, huh?"

Tana nodded. "Yeah, I guess so."

"So why now?"

Tana shrugged. "I don't know, just thought it was time I got a car. Everybody else has one, right?"

"Well, you know, you caught me just in time. I was about to call it a night when you called me. Most people like to come by during the day."

Tana smiled politely.

"You come straight from work?"

Tana nodded. "Yeah, I did."

"You're a reporter, right?" Paine said, glancing at Tana. "You write obituaries for *The Bay Area Bugle*."

Tana felt her stomach tighten. She hadn't told Paine what she did for a living.

"Yeah, how'd you know?" she said, taken by surprise.

Paine gave a cold smile as the car rolled down the street. "I'll tell you what else I know. You didn't call me because you want to buy a car."

"Oh yeah? So why did I call you?" Tana said, feeling a stab of fear.

Paine suddenly swerved into the right lane, then turned sharply down a side street lined with shuttered factories and warehouses.

"Where you going?" Tana said, as she tried to control the fear building inside of her.

Paine lurched over to the curb and slammed to a stop. Tana looked around, saw nothing but shadows. Paine turned the engine off, then locked eyes with her.

"What's going on?" she said. "Why are you stopping? I want to go back."

"I'll bet you do," Paine said. "You know, Frank Aiken told me all about you. Told me you were asking questions about Emma Mayfield."

So that was how he knew, Tana thought. She felt like a fool for not having anticipated that Aiken might have warned Paine in advance. So much for the charade of pretending to buy a car.

"You ought to stick to the dead, Tana. The living can cause you all kinds of problems."

What did they know, Tana wondered. What were they hiding?

"Is that a threat?" Tana said.

"Just some friendly advice."

"Friendly advice, huh? Frank gave me some friendly advice too. You guys double-teaming me?"

"Just looking out for your welfare, Tana."

"Yeah, I'll bet you are. What do you know about Emma Mayfield?"

"What makes you think I know anything about Emma Mayfield?"

"I talked to your ex-wife. She told me—"

Paine scowled. His face reddened. "I don't give a shit what that dyke told you!" he said, raising his voice. "If it wasn't for her and Helen—"

"Emma wouldn't have disappeared? Is that what you were about to say?"

Paine paused, and Tana wondered if she had gone too far. She was strapped into a car parked in the dark on a deserted street with the doors locked. What was she thinking?

Paine leaned across the seat toward Tana and put his hand on the back of her seat. Tana stiffened. She could feel the heat of his rage coming off him in waves. He would never get over what happened between Allison and Helen, she thought. And now she worried about what might happen next.

"You think Helen's some kind of saint because of what happened to her? Is that what you think?"

Tana wasn't sure if Helen was a saint, but she had traveled from the realm of the spirits, and wasn't that where saints lived?

"She stole my wife, okay!"

"She was in love."

"She should've been in love with me!"

Tana decided it was time to ditch and run. She reached down and tried to unlatch her seatbelt, but Paine latched it again. He looked down out through the windshield, down the empty street.

"You ever want to hurt somebody, Tana?" Paine said, still staring at nothing. "Hurt 'em so bad they never forget it?" He spoke calmly, as if he'd given himself time to think about it, which frightened Tana more than if he'd been screaming at her.

"I don't know, maybe."

"I guess everybody feels that way at one time or another. I know I did. Frank did too."

"Are you going to hurt me?"

Paine looked at Tana and smiled. "You're scared, aren't you? I can tell you're scared. You figured you'd pretend like you wanted to buy a car and I'd tell you what you wanted to hear."

"I don't know what I want to hear."

"Sure you do. You want me to tell you that we kidnapped Emma, me and Frank, so we could get back at Helen and Allison. Isn't that what you want to hear?"

"I want to know what happened to her."

"And you thought I might have had something to do with it, me and Frank, right?"

Tana nodded.

"What if we did? What are you gonna do about it? Call the cops? Tell 'em I confessed?"

Tana said nothing. She could feel herself trembling as she watched Paine.

"You know I wouldn't let you do that, Tana."

"Did you do it?"

"You're the reporter," Paine said. "You figure it out."

Paine reached down and unlatched Tana's seatbelt, then sat back and unlocked the doors. Tana grabbed the door handle and jumped out of the car. She was breathing fast and her heart was pounding, and she was still standing alone on the sidewalk long after Paine had driven away.

Then her cellphone rang, startling her. Tana glanced at the screen and her eyes widened with surprise.

CHAPTER 36

IT WAS SOMETIME AFTER TEN WHEN DARYL MAYWEATHER rapped on the window of Powell's Bronco. Powell looked over at Daryl and noticed that he was carrying a manila folder. He leaned across the seat and unlocked the door. Mayweather climbed into the car and pulled the door shut. He was black and in his fifties with a beard and buzzed salt and pepper hair. Mayweather was a lifer who had started out as a beat cop and now worked cold case homicides for the SFPD. He was also Powell's last partner before he retired.

"What the fuck you doin' out here, Powell?" Mayweather said. He nodded at the bar across the street. "Lookin' for some trim?"

"I'm working a case."

"Still doin' the PI thing, huh?"

Powell shrugged. "Part time, divorce work, mostly."

"What you got goin' tonight?"

"The usual. A husband who thinks he can get away with it, a wife who wants to nail his dick to the wall."

Mayweather chuckled. "Same old, same old, right?"

Powell nodded. "Human nature, Daryl. Keeps guys like me in business."

"I guess the bowling ain't enough, huh?" Mayweather said.

Powell smiled. "Can't bowl all the time, Daryl."

"I heard that."

"How's the family?"

"Family's doin' good. Fuckin' college tuition's killing me, but Chantal and Dion are keeping their grades up, so I can't complain. How about you? You seeing anybody?"

Powell shook his head. "Not yet."

Mayweather made a face. "Ain't no way to live, man. You gonna carry a torch for the rest of your life?"

"I don't know, maybe," Powell said, feeling defensive.

"One of these days it's gonna be too late, Bud."

"I'll keep that in mind, Daryl," Powell said, wanting to change the conversation.

Mayweather put up his hands in acknowledgement.

"Okay, I get it, none of my business, right?"

Powell smiled.

"Right."

"So how come you're looking into an Escalade that got boosted ten years ago?"

Powell paused. "I'm back on the Mayfield case."

Mayweather's eyes widened. He stared at Powell. "Emma Mayfield?"

Powell nodded.

"You're kidding me."

Powell said nothing.

"The department know about this?"

Powell shook his head. "No. It's on the down low and I'd like to keep it that way."

"Why now? You got a new lead?"

"Maybe."

"This got something to do with it?" Mayweather said, holding up the manila folder.

"I don't know yet. Too early to tell."

Mayweather gave Powell a knowing smile.

"You're not gonna tell me about it, are you, partner?"

"You wouldn't believe me if I did, Daryl."

"I'll tell you what I can't believe. I can't believe you're chasing this again."

"Yeah, I know."

"You think we missed something last time around?"

"Just want to take another look, Daryl."

"You can't let it go, can you?"

"Maybe not." Powell nodded at the manila folder. "Thanks for the file. Where'd you find it?"

"Got lost in the shuffle when the department updated their computer systems. The IT guys dug it up for me."

"Thanks, Daryl. I owe you one."

"I hope you know what you're doing."

"Yeah, me too." Powell looked up and saw a couple emerge from the bar. A middle-aged corporate suit with a woman who appeared to be half his age. "Showtime," he said.

Mayweather followed his line of sight and saw the couple. "That the lucky guy?"

Powell nodded. He pulled out his iPhone and began snapping pics as the couple embraced and kissed in the pool of light under a streetlamp.

"Ever feel like a peeping tom?" Mayweather said.

"All the time."

"So now what? You follow 'em to the no-tell motel for the X-rated stuff?"

Powell shook his head. "This is all I need," he said, holding up his phone. "I send 'em to the missus along with a bill and the rest is up to her." He nodded at the manila folder. "Thanks again, Daryl. I appreciate it."

They shook hands and Mayweather opened the door. "I'd say keep me posted, but you won't, will you?"

"I will if I can," Powell said.

"Take care, Powell. Good to see you."

"You too."

Mayweather climbed out of the Bronco and headed down the street. Powell leaned over and locked the door. Then he opened the manila folder and turned on the Bronco's interior light. A photo of the Escalade was clipped to the first page of the report, which was dated three days before Emma was abducted from the daycare center. The photo showed a young Asian man whom Powell assumed was Arthur Kim standing in front of the vehicle with a proud smile on his face.

As he reviewed the file, Powell tried to imagine Emma in the back seat, scared and crying as she was swept away to oblivion. Who was behind the wheel, he wondered. Then Powell thought of Hector Vargas, and he felt his face get hot. Drive like hell, motherfucker, he thought. I'm coming. He turned off the light and started the engine. The night was young, and Powell had one more stop to make before last call.

CHAPTER 37

Twenty minutes later Powell nosed the Bronco into the crowded parking lot of an East Oakland Latin club called Bahia. He circled the lot until found a space in the back, then killed the engine and looked up at the blazing neon marquee:

Live Onstage! Adelita Santos, La Soldadera!

Powell had no idea who she was, but figured she was some kind of star. There was a life-size cutout of Adelita Santos by the door in case anyone missed the marquee. It depicted a voluptuous, middle-aged Latina woman with glossy black hair and dark eyes. She wore a colorful peasant blouse and a long black dress. Ammo belts were slung across her breasts, and she wore pistols in holsters on her hips.

She reminded Powell of the pictures he had seen in a magazine of the female soldiers, or *soldaderas*, who fought with Pancho Villa and Emilio Zapata in the Mexican Revolution. The revolution ended a hundred years ago, but Powell figured that the look was part of Santos's act, just as it was for the kids he saw on the street wearing camouflage and combat boots.

They'd never seen a battlefield or faced enemy fire, but they liked the style, if not the blood and bullets.

He rolled down the window and looked out at the club. A door opened and mariachi music rushed out into the lot. Powell remembered the night he and Nora had gone dancing at a Latin club in the Mission. He wasn't much of a dancer, but she loved it and that was enough for him. Anything she wanted was enough for him. He glanced at the empty passenger seat and imagined her sitting next to him. She would've been wearing a dress that showed off her curves, and the Bronco would've been filled with the scent of her favorite perfume.

"You ready, baby?" she would've said with a smile.

He was always ready, Powell thought, as a knife opened somewhere inside. But the one thing he wasn't ready for was losing her. What was he ready for tonight? He hadn't been to a Latin club or listened to Latin music in years, not since Nora was killed. So what was he doing here? It wasn't for the music. He was here because five years later he still couldn't let go of the case that had haunted him for a decade. Or the man he believed was the culprit.

Powell climbed out of the Bronco and walked across the lot to the entrance. A uniformed black security guard gave Powell a sidelong glance as he opened the door, as if to determine whether or not he might be trouble. Powell had done the same when he was on the force, but it felt strange to be on the receiving end of that assessment.

He stood by the door and looked around. Cocktail tables filled with fans waiting for the show to start dotted the room. Cute young barmaids in tank tops and cleavage balanced trays filled with drinks as they made their way through the room. Powell could hear the roar of conversation, the tinkle of glasses. A Latina singer on the sound system, whom he assumed was Adelita Santos, rode the energy in the room.

A stocky Mexican doorman wearing a mustache and a burgundy tuxedo approached him.

"Welcome to Bahia, señor. You have a reservation?"

Just then, a spotlight lit up the stage, and the crowd erupted in cheers, wolf whistles, and applause. A group of musicians, presumably La Soldadera's band, took the stage. Powell turned to the doorman.

"No reservation," he said, "just thought I'd stop by and catch the show."

The doorman offered an apologetic smile. "Lo siento, señor, but there are no tables available. "La Soldadera, she is very popular."

Powell looked around the club, then spotted an empty stool at the bar.

"Mind if I sit at the bar?"

The doorman nodded. "Si, señor." He extended his arm in the direction of the bar. "Enjoy the show."

"Thanks," Powell said, and headed over to the bar.

He slid onto the stool and ordered a beer. Moments later, an MC in a sparkly pink dinner jacket bounded onto the stage and grabbed the microphone.

"Good evening, ladies and gentlemen, welcome to Bahia. Please give a warm welcome to the great Adelita Santos, La Soldadera!"

There was another round of applause, then the band started playing. Moments later, Adelita emerged from the wings. The audience roared as she swaggered across the stage, pistols on her hips. She gave a warm smile, then moved to the microphone and began singing a romantic mariachi ballad. The audience quieted down as her sultry voice took over the room. Couples were getting up from their tables, slipping into each other arms and slow dancing to the song. Suddenly, Powell wanted to dance, wanted Nora in his arms. He would've danced with her ghost if he could have, but instead all he could do was let the song wash over him. The lyrics were in Spanish, but Powell didn't need to speak the language to understand it. The music told him what the lyrics meant, and so did the ache in his heart.

He sipped his beer and wondered what he was doing there. He got his answer three beers later, at the end of Adelita's second set. The crowd had begun to thin out as couples headed for the door. That was when Powell saw them. Hector Vargas and his date, a top-heavy bottle blonde in a skintight miniskirt who looked like a stripper. He watched as Vargas and his date stood, then went up the stairs and headed backstage. What did he want, an autograph? Powell wondered. He slid off the stool and stepped to the door.

CHAPTER 38

THE GUARD GLANCED AT POWELL AGAIN WHEN HE emerged from the club, and Powell wondered if he checked out everybody twice, just to make sure nobody sneaked past him. Being a security guard was boring duty and standing outside a club night after night wearing a uniform that never quite fit while everybody else was inside having fun had to weigh on a man.

Powell nodded at the guard, who returned the favor, then waited until the guard had lost sight of him in the crush of fans emerging from the club and walking to their cars. He looked around, as if to get his bearings, then walked around the building until he found the stage door. He checked his watch, then hung back in the shadows and waited for the door to open.

Thirty minutes later, Vargas and his date stepped out into the pool of light created by the lantern mounted above the door. Then Adelita joined them. She was still wearing the guns and ammo belts. Powell wondered if she slept with them, an angel of the revolution, ready at a moment's notice to take up the fight. He watched as Adelita and Hector warmly embraced and kissed each other on the cheek. They seemed to know each other, Powell thought. But what was the connection? There was obviously more to it than just an autograph. Adelita turned to Hector's date and kissed her as well, then went back inside. Powell watched as Hector and the blonde headed toward the parking lot, then stepped out from the shadows.

"You get your autograph, Hector?" he said.

Vargas looked up at Powell. The surprised look on his face hardened into a scowl.

"What the fuck you doing here?"

"Came to see the show."

"Yeah, well now you saw it so fuck off."

"Didn't figure you for a music fan, Hector." Powell nodded at the stage door. "You a fan?"

Vargas's face darkened with resentment. "No, I'm a son, pendejo. Adelita Santos is my mother."

Powell stared at Vargas, taken by surprise. "Your mother?"

"Yeah, my mother, okay?"

Powell let the news sink in. He never imagined that a thug like Vargas could have a mother, or even a mother that loved him. It was as if he believed that thugs like Vargas emerged fully formed, with no connection to anything other than the evil that shaped them. But then his natural suspiciousness kicked in. If Adelita Santos was his mother, Powell thought, what did she know about Emma's disappearance? And what did she think about a son who'd escaped justice only because the eyewitness recanted? Or did a mother love her child no matter what he or she did, simply because they were her son or daughter?

"What's going on, baby?" the blonde said. "Who is this guy?"

Powell reached for his wallet, pulled out a pair of twenties and handed them to the blonde.

"Get out of here," he said.

"What?" the blonde said, a puzzled look on her face.

She glanced at Vargas, as if for clarification, but he was too busy staring bullets at Powell.

"Don't look at him," Powell said. "Look at me." He nodded toward the street in front of the club. "Grab a cab, get the hell out of here."

Vargas grabbed the twenties out of the blonde's hand, crumpled them in his fist and tossed them on the pavement.

"The only one who's goin' anywhere is you," he said, glaring at Powell, "so get the fuck out of here." He turned to the blonde. "Let's go."

The blonde hesitated, her eyes brimming with fear and confusion as they darted from Vargas to Powell.

"I said let's go!" Vargas said.

He grabbed the blonde by the arm and pushed her toward the parking lot. "You're hurting me!" she said, trying to wrestle free of Vargas's grip.

"Let her go, Hector."

"Shut the fuck up!"

The blonde wrestled free of Vargas's grip, hesitated for a moment, then crouched down and picked up the crumpled twenties.

"Call me later, okay?" she said, looking up at Vargas with a nervous smile.

Then she kicked off her heels, picked them up with one hand and ran barefoot toward the street, no doubt hoping there would be a cab waiting at the curb when she got there.

"Hey! Where the fuck do you think you're going? I paid for you, bitch!"

Vargas started to go after her, but Powell blocked his way.

"Where is she, Hector? Where's Emma? Does your mother know about her?"

"You leave my mother out of it. Who the fuck are you to be talking about my mother?"

"Did you tell her all about it, how you snatched her from daycare?"

"You're fucking crazy, you know that, Powell? You think you can just go around harassing people? My lawyer's gonna sue your ass for this. Who the fuck do you think you are? It's against the law, asshole!"

"I'm not harassing you, Hector," Powell said calmly. "I'm just talking to you. Just tell me where she is."

"I don't know where she is, okay?"

"I think you do."

"I don't give a fuck what you think! Get outta my face!"

"I'm not gonna stop, Hector. Just so you know. I'm not gonna stop."

"Yeah, we gonna see about that. Maybe somebody stop you."

"You think you're the one to do it, Hector?"

Vargas gave a cold smile. "Be my pleasure."

Just then the security guard came up to Powell and Hector. Powell had figured the guard had forgotten about him, but he realized that the only way the man could do his job was not to forget about anybody.

"Everything okay here?"

"Yeah, everything's fine," Powell said.

Then he pushed past Vargas and the guard and walked back to the Bronco. He climbed in behind the wheel and watched as Hector climbed into a black Lincoln SUV. It wasn't an Escalade, but it was still an SUV, and ever since Powell had learned that an SUV was used to abduct Emma, the sight of one always made him think of her. And since most people drove SUVs, the child was always in his thoughts. He was haunted by her and haunted by his failure to discover what had happened to her. He could feel the rage burning inside, a helpless rage that threatened to consume Aloysius Powell and no one else.

A familiar scent filled the Bronco. Powell looked around the car but saw no one. He rolled down the window and scanned the parking lot. But all he saw were music fans walking to their cars. He wondered if any of the women were wearing the perfume he knew so well. Had it drifted across the lot on an evening breeze? But the night was still, as if the air itself has stopped.

Powell sensed a presence. He turned and saw her sitting next to him.

Nora.

She wore a black dress, the one she liked to wear with the string of pearls he had given her for her birthday. Powell stared at her as love and loss and sorrow welled up inside him. He reached out to touch her, but all he felt was a cold mist on his fingers. Nora smiled sadly, as if to say there was no way to bridge the great divide between the living and the dead, there were only memories, and the apparitions of memories.

Then she was gone. The scent of her perfume lingered for a few moments, as if it too was a memory Powell could never forget.

CHAPTER 39

THE BAR WAS CALLED THE MISSOURI LOUNGE. TANA HAD never been there. She'd never been to Missouri either. The place was on Post Street, not far from the St. Francis Hotel and the tourist attractions that drew visitors from around the world to Union Square. But it seemed to belong to another time in the city and reminded Tana of the bars she saw in the old movies she watched on TCM late at night when she couldn't sleep. The crowd was older too—the men in suits and bowties, the women in pearls. As she stood by the door and looked around, Tana wondered if it was seniors night, or if it was that way every night at The Missouri Lounge. A jukebox was playing a song by some crooner who, like everything else about the bar, seemed lost in the past.

Then she saw a thin, birdlike woman in her seventies sitting alone at a corner table. She was wearing an elegant navy blue suit and hat, and she was nursing a dry martini. The woman waved at Tana, and she walked over to her table.

"Tana?" the woman said, looking up at her with an inquisitive gaze that had not dulled with age. She had sharp blue eyes that despite her years still had a spark of the woman she once was.

"Yes," Tana said. "Louise?"

Louise smiled. She nodded at the empty chair across from her. "Won't you join me?"

Tana smiled politely and sat down.

"My, you are young, aren't you?" Louise said as she studied Tana. "I suppose you must be wondering what you're doing here with all us old fogies."

"Actually, I was wondering why you called me," Tana said.

"Yes, I can see why. I hung up on you last time, didn't I?"

Tana nodded. "Yeah, you did." She gave a rueful smile. "Happens a lot to us reporters."

"Well, let me make it up to you," Louise said. "What are you drinking?"

"Just a glass of white wine," Tana said, passing on the lemon drop martinis that went straight to her head.

Louise flagged a passing waiter, who seemed as old as everyone else in the bar. He was tall and thin, with silvery hair that that seemed to shine under the lights. Tana wondered if he once had been an actor. When he came up to the table Louise ordered for Tana.

"A glass of Chardonnay for my friend, Walter, if you please."

"Of course, Louise." He paused, then looked at Louise with a mournful expression. "I was very sorry to hear of Raymond's passing. We shall miss him."

"Thank you, Walter. I shall miss him too."

Walter nodded and moved away from the table. Family was where you found it, Tana thought, and Louise and Raymond Treadway had found their family at The Missouri Lounge.

"I hope you don't mind that I ordered for you," Louise said.

"No problem," Tana said. "But you still haven't told me what I'm doing here or why you called me."

"No, I haven't, have I?" Louise paused to sip her martini,

then looked at Tana. "Well, I suppose I called you because you were Raymond's biographer. In a way, you're everybody's biographer, aren't you? The only one most people will ever get to tell their life stories."

A biographer? Tana wasn't so sure about that. Biographers spent years writing books that ran to hundreds of pages. She had eight hundred words and a few hours to sum up a life before it was forgotten.

"Did you have something you wanted to add to his obituary?"

Louise shook her head. "Not to his obituary. To his story."

Tana reacted with surprise.

"I don't understand. What's the difference?"

Louise gave an enigmatic smile that turned sad as she looked around the bar.

"Raymond and I used to come here," Louise said. "I guess you could say we were regulars, just like everybody else. We used to come with my brother and his wife, a double date, I suppose you'd call it. After they passed away it was just the two of us. Now...well, now it's just me, and I hate drinking alone."

Walter returned with Tana's Chardonnay and set the glass down in front of her.

"Thank you, Walter," Louise said.

Walter nodded and moved away.

Louise raised her glass in a toast. "Cheers."

"Cheers," Tana said, raising her glass.

They clinked glasses and sipped their drinks, then Louise set her glass down and looked at Tana.

"I had a change of heart after we spoke on the phone," she said. "I don't know why, exactly, but I got to thinking about that business with Carmen Flowers and that poor woman's daughter being kidnapped—"

"You remember all that?"

Louise looked sharply at Tana. "Of course I remember it," she said in an indignant tone of voice. "I'm not senile!"

"Sorry, I didn't mean it that way," Tana said.

"No, of course you didn't. You're just young and think anyone my age must be a doddering old fool with dementia or something."

Tana felt chastened. She lowered her eyes. Louise was probably right. She wrote about the dead every day for *The Bugle*, and most of them were old. But then she thought of Helen Mayfield, who was far from old when she passed away. And who, in her afterlife, had become a part of Tana's life. Then, for reasons she couldn't explain, Tana flashed on her unborn child, who never had a life or even a name, or someone to write her obituary.

"Tana?" Louise said, jolting Tana out of her thoughts.

She looked up and saw Louise staring at her with a concerned look on her face.

"Are you okay? Is something wrong?"

Tana shook her head. "I'm fine," she said. She wondered if, in the bar's dim light, Louise could see the tears in her eyes.

"Good. So I got to wondering about what you asked me, about whether Raymond was somehow involved in what happened."

"Do you think he was?"

Louise paused to let her face harden. "They were involved," she said.

"Who was involved?"

"Raymond and Carmen Flowers. They were having an affair."

Tana stared at Louise, stunned by the news. "Raymond and Carmen?"

Louise nodded.

"But he was so much older—"

"Yes, of course he was. That was the whole point, I suppose. That a woman half his age would want to sleep with him." Louise smiled bitterly and sipped her drink." "He should've been embarrassed by what he was doing. Such a cliché, isn't it? The older man and the younger woman."

"Did you know?"

Louise shook her head. "I only found out after he passed. And then it was too late. I wanted him to still be alive so I could confront him. So I could scream at him, do something, I don't know. Can you imagine grieving the death of your husband of forty years and at the same time being furious with him because he cheated on you?"

Tana shook her head. "No, I can't."

Louise fell silent. Her lower lip was trembling.

"How did you find out?" Tana said, breaking the silence.

"It was on his phone. There were emails, pictures—selfies, I suppose you'd call them. You'd think he would've deleted it all but maybe he wanted me to find it. Maybe he wanted to brag about it. But it doesn't matter how I found out. What matters is what it had to do with the trial." Louise looked sharply at Tana. "That's what you want to know, isn't it?"

"If you want to tell me."

"Well, I suppose I do want to tell you, or I wouldn't have asked you meet me." Louise sipped her drink, then locked eyes with Tana. "You have to promise me that none of this will appear in his obituary."

Tana shook her head. "No worries, it went to press."

"And you won't publish an updated version?"

"I promise," Tana said, even though she had no authority to do so.

Louise paused to collect her thoughts. "She didn't want to take the bribe."

"Carmen?"

Louise nodded. "She was afraid if she lied, she would go to jail. So she turned them down."

"She didn't take the bribe?" Tana said, surprised.

"Not at first, but then Raymond talked her into it."

"Raymond knew about the bribe?" Tana said, shocked by the news that Raymond Treadway was complicit in Carmen Flowers perjuring herself and obstructing justice.

"Vargas's lawyer, Jimmy something—"

"Jimmy LaSalle."

"He made Raymond an offer he couldn't refuse. Persuade Carmen to take the bribe, or they would expose his affair with her."

"So he did it."

Louise nodded. "He did it." She paused to sip her drink. "And helped set a killer free." She looked up at Tana. Her eyes were blazing. "He killed two people, and Raymond set him free! My Raymond!"

"I'm so sorry," Tana said.

"You live with a man forty years and you think you know him. But you don't. Why do you have to wait until he's dead to find out what he's really made of? Can you tell me that?"

Tana shook her head. "I can't."

"Didn't think so."

"Did you tell the police what you discovered?"

Louise shook her head.

"But it proves that Carmen took the bribe. She could be prosecuted for bribery and obstruction of justice."

"Why should I tell them? So they can drag Raymond's name—and mine—through the mud?"

"They could retry Vargas. She would have to testify."

"Ten years is a long time, Tana. What's done is done."

"There's no statute of limitations on murder, Louise."

Louise shrugged. "Perhaps not, but I suppose I have my own statute of limitations."

"Then why tell me?" Tana said.

"I had to tell someone, Tana, and you were his biographer." Louise picked her up her glass, but her hands were shaking, and the liquor ran down her chin and spilled on her suit as she gulped the rest of her martini. She gathered her things and stood. "I have to go now."

"Wait a minute," Tana said, "where are you going?"

But Louise wasn't listening. She motioned to Walter.

"Walter, would you be so kind as to call me a cab?"

"Of course, Louise."

"I'll wait outside," she said. Then she turned to Tana. "Sometimes the less you know the better," she said, and turned toward the door.

"Louise, wait..." Tana said as she stood and pulled on her jacket.

But Louise ignored her and walked out of the bar. Tana stood and pulled on her jacket and was about to go after Louise when Walter came up to her.

"I'm worried about her," Walter said, trading glances with Tana. "But I don't know how to help her. So all I do is worry. That's how it is with family, isn't it?"

Tana nodded. "Yeah, I guess so," she said, remembering the child they cut out of her. He or she was family too, she thought, feeling the sting of tears in her eyes.

"But you're not part of her family, are you?" Walter said.

Tana shook her head. "No, I'm not."

"So why are you here?"

Tana shrugged.

"She told me she didn't like drinking alone. I said I didn't either."

She went outside, dodging an older couple all dressed up

for an evening at The Missouri Lounge. But Louise was nowhere in sight. As if she'd vanished into the night. Who could blame her, Tana thought. Raymond had reached beyond the grave and cursed her with the terrible knowledge that the husband whose death she mourned had cheated on her and helped a killer go free.

CHAPTER 40

"That used to be me," Tana said as she looked out at the crowd of mostly young white-collar professionals like herself.

She and Powell were seated at a window table at Drexel, the downtown dive that was packed with a happy hour crowd knocking back shots after a hard day at the office.

Tana could hear the beat of hip hop-flavored R&B percolating on the sound system. She flashed on Justin, remembering how they used to lay in bed and listen to music in the dark. Just the two of them, like they were the only people left in the world and all they wanted was the rush of each other's bodies. She thought then that that would be enough. But it was never enough with Justin, who also wanted the rush of other women's bodies, not just hers.

The memory lingered, then Tana pushed it out of her mind. Justin was gone, and so was that life. She had a new life now. Trouble was, she had no idea how to make sense of it or long it would last.

"You miss it?"

Tana gave a wistful smile. "Doesn't matter, it's gone."

"For now."

"Forever." Then it hit her. "You know what? I think this is where me and Sheila were sitting the night it happened."

Powell looked up at her. "The night you saw Helen?"

Tana nodded. "The night my life got turned upside down." She sipped her beer. "One minute everything's totally normal and then next minute…" Her voice trailed off and she ran her hand through her hair.

"Normal's overrated," Powell said.

"I wouldn't know anymore."

Powell looked at her with concern. "You okay?"

Tana shrugged. "Maybe we should've gone somewhere else."

"Doesn't matter where we go, Tana."

"She's always gonna be with me, right? Is that what you were gonna tell me?"

Powell smiled, as if to say, *you know the answer to that one. What are you asking me for?* Then he changed the subject.

"So what were you thinking, pretending to buy a car just so you could talk to the guy?"

Tana had braced Powell on her encounter with Jerry Paine, and it was clear from his reaction that he thought it was a reckless move that could have put her in serious danger.

Tana shrugged. "I don't know, I just ran with it."

"You just ran with it, huh?"

Tana looked up at Powell, her eyes blazing with defiance. "What, you never followed your gut?"

"Yeah, all the time, but usually I was armed."

Tana looked away. "I wanted to see if I could find out anything."

"So what did you find out?"

"That he'll never get over what happened." She paused, then said, "They were lovers."

Powell reacted with surprise. "Helen and Allison?"

Tana nodded. "Allison wanted to spend the rest of her life with Helen."

"I guess Paine didn't much like the idea."

"Allison said he went ballistic when he found out. He sure went ballistic on me when I brought it up."

Powell nodded. "Losing her to another man would been bad enough, but a woman..." He shook his head. "That's got to hurt. But what's that got to do with Emma?"

Tana looked up at Powell and their eyes met.

"I don't know. He was pretty pissed," Tana said. "Maybe he wanted to get back at her."

"So he kidnaps her girlfriend's kid?"

"I don't know. He wouldn't tell me one way or the other."

"You didn't expect him to cop to it, did you?"

Tana's eyes narrowed. "Duh. Of course not. I expected him to tell me he had nothing to do with Emma's abduction, like Vargas did when we saw him at Helen's funeral. But here's the thing: He wasn't the only one who freaked out when he found out about Helen and Allison."

A knowing smile spread across Powell's face. "Frank Aiken."

Tana nodded. "They knew each other. Paine told me that Aiken had called him and warned him that I asking questions about the case. What if they were in on it together?"

Powell was skeptical. "Next you're gonna tell me the two of 'em snatched her."

"I don't know. Maybe."

Powell scoffed. "Yeah, maybe they all went on double dates together."

Tana felt her face flush. "You don't have to make fun of me, okay? Just because you've convinced yourself it was Hector Vargas, and you can't let go of it."

Powell's face hardened. "It was Vargas, okay? It was him ten years ago and it's still him today."

"Maybe it was and maybe it wasn't. But until we know for sure I think we should keep an open mind. Isn't that how it's supposed to work in an investigation?"

Powell gave a mocking smile. "What, you're an expert all of a sudden?"

Just then, the barmaid came up to the table. She was a few years younger than Tana, a pale blonde with pierced lips and colorful tattoos that illustrated her arms. Tana noticed that her head was shaved on one side. On the other side, a curtain of pink hair fell to her shoulders.

"You guys ready for another round?"

Tana and Powell exchanged glances, then Powell said, "Sure."

"You got it," the barmaid said. She started to walk away, then turned and looked at Tana. "You were here the other night, right? When we had all that lightning and stuff?"

"Yeah, right," Tana said.

"I thought it was you. Weird weather, huh?"

"Yeah, for sure," Tana said.

The barmaid smiled and moved away from the table.

"At least she didn't ask me if I was the one who saw a ghost," Tana said as she watched the barmaid make her way through the crowd.

"Yeah, but you were the one," Powell said. "Just like I was."

Powell took a sip of his drink and looked at Tana. "What else you got?"

Tana sipped her beer, then braced Powell on what she'd learned from Louise Treadway.

"Okay, so you interviewed her for her husband's obit and then she called you back?"

Tana nodded.

Why?"

"He knew."

Powell looked at her. "What do you mean, he knew?"

"Treadway. He knew about the bribe. He made Carmen take it."

CHAPTER 41

Powell jaw dropped. He exhaled, floored by the news, and stared at Tana. "He was in on it?"

"Louise was going through his stuff after he died when she found out about it."

Powell shook his head in disgust. "That must've hurt. So what happened?"

"Treadway and Carmen were having an affair."

Powell reacted with disbelief. "Treadway and Carmen?"

"Yeah. And then Jimmy LaSalle found out about it—"

Powell scowled. "Jimmy LaSalle?"

"Yeah. "Jimmy LaSalle," Tana said.

The barmaid returned with a round of beers. She set the mugs down on the table, then moved away.

"So you were saying that Jimmy LaSalle found out about Treadway's affair."

Tana sipped her drink, then nodded. "Yeah, according to Louise, he pressured Carmen to take the bribe and when she turned him down—"

"Why'd she turn him down?"

"Louise figures she was scared."

"Or maybe smart."

"So when Carmen turned him down, he leaned on Tread-way. Threatened to expose his affair if he didn't persuade Carmen to take the bribe."

"So he did it."

Tana nodded. "Yeah, he did it. If Jimmy had gone public with his affair, he would've lost his job and maybe his marriage, too."

"So instead, all he lost was his conscience."

They fell silent. She could hear the sounds of club life around her, the ripple of laughter and conversation as it surfed around the room, the tinkle of glasses, the bass-heavy beat of the music. Everybody was having a good time, and nobody was thinking about being dead. Except maybe Tana, who thought about it for a living.

"Is that it?" Powell said, breaking the silence.

Tana nodded. She tapped the manila folder that Powell had brought with him to the bar.

"So what's this?"

"I want to show you something." He opened the manila folder and took out some documents. "I got hold of the stolen car report."

"How'd you do that?"

Powell shrugged. "Ex-partner of mine dug it up. Take a look."

Tana looked at the docs and the first thing that caught her eye was a faded color photo of an Asian man standing next to a Cadillac Escalade and smiling at the camera.

"Arthur Kim?"

Powell nodded. "He must've supplied the pic when he filed the report. But take a look at this." He shuffled through the papers, then pulled out a series of fuzzy black and white screen grabs.

"What's this?"

"Turns out Kim went to the movies the night the Escalade got boosted. These are screen grabs from the security cameras in the theater parking lot." He pointed at a vehicle. "There's the Escalade."

"Oh yeah, there it is. Funny seeing it just sitting there, huh?"

Powell shuffled to another image. "Remember him?" he said, pointing to a white man with an afro in the crowded parking lot.

Tana looked at the image, then at Powell. "Is that Jimmy LaSalle?"

Powell nodded.

"Wow, he looks so much younger."

"Ten years on the clock'll do that to you," Powell said

"Looks like he's walking over to the Escalade."

Powell shuffled to another image. "Here's another one, taken later."

Tana studied the image. "The Escalade's gone."

"Stolen's more like it," Powell said. "Jimmy's gone too."

Tana's eyes widened. "You think he stole it?"

"I wouldn't put anything past Jimmy LaSalle. But all this proves is that Jimmy went to the movies the same night Arthur Kim did. We don't see him climbing in behind the wheel and driving the Escalade out of the lot."

Tana took a closer look at the image of the empty parking space.

"Wait a minute, there's something there..."

"Where?" Powell said, looking at the image.

"There," Tana said, pointing at what appeared to be a crumpled sheet of paper on the ground.

"Just trash," Powell said. "The lot's littered with it."

Tana shook her head. "No, I've seen it before...I just can't place it. Wish we could blow it up..." She studied the image for a few moments longer, then it hit her, and she gasped.

"What is it?"

"Picture day."

"What?"

She pointed at the image. "See right there, where it says 'Picture'?"

"Yeah..."

"It was picture day at the daycare center the day Emma was kidnapped. There was a big banner at the school about it. I saw it the night Helen showed me what happened."

"You sure?"

Tana nodded.

Powell smiled at her. "Good work, detective."

Tana beamed. "So it can't just be a coincidence, right? The Escalade, LaSalle and a flyer for photo day."

Powell gave himself time to think about it. "That would be one helluva coincidence."

"So it was LaSalle."

"Maybe. But not just LaSalle."

"He did it for Vargas?"

Powell nodded. "Shoots your theory about Aiken and Paine all to hell, doesn't it?"

Tana shook her head. "Not yet it doesn't. We still have to prove it, one way or the other."

"We need to find out who drove the Escalade out of the lot."

"How we gonna do that?"

Powell said nothing. He knocked back the rest of his drink, then scowled as his eyes dropped to the image of the crumpled photo flyer.

CHAPTER 42
WEDNESDAY, JUNE 9, 2010

Emma says, "Mommy, I don't want to go home."

Helen sighs. She's just picked Emma up from daycare after a long day at the DMV. She went without lunch because one of her coworkers is out sick and there was no one to cover for her. All she wants to do now is go home and put her feet up before she has to make dinner and give Emma her bath. But she doesn't let Emma see that she's tired and worn out. Instead, she glances in the rearview and smiles at her daughter.

"Where do you want to go?" she says.

"I want to go to the playground!"

"The playground?" Helen says with mock-surprise. "Really?"

"Yes!"

"What are we gonna do at the playground?"

"You're gonna push me on the swings!"

"I am?"

"Yes! 'cause that's what mommies do."

"Okay then, I guess we have to go to the playground."

"Yay!" Emma yells as Helen pulls away from the curb.

When she pulls up in front of the playground Helen notices that it's nearly deserted. She's not surprised. Kids are supposed to be home by now. She wishes she was home too. But at least there aren't reporters waiting for her to get out of the car so they can ask her more questions about the trial. Maybe they've given up by now, she thinks. The news is always changing the subject.

"C'mon, mommy!" Emma yells, jolting Helen out of her thoughts. "I wanna go play!"

Of course you do, Helen thinks, glancing at her daughter, who's fidgeting in her car seat. She gets out of the car, opens the back door, and unstraps Emma. She bolts from the car and runs across the playground to the slide. She runs up the ramp, then waves to Helen.

"Watch me, mommy!" she yells.

I'm always watching you, Helen thinks as she walks across the playground. I'll spend the rest of my life watching you. What else would I look at when I have a daughter like you?

"Here I go!" Emma shouts as she goes down the slide. She laughs out loud when she reaches the bottom, and then runs back up the ramp to do it all over again.

"Don't you wish it was that easy? If all it took to be happy was to go down a slide on the seat of our pants?"

Helen turns and sees a mother around her age sitting on a bench. She's wearing sunglasses and yoga pants and watching a little boy hanging by his arms on the monkey bars. Helen notices that the woman isn't wearing a ring.

"All the time," Helen says.

The two women share a smile.

"You single too?" the woman says.

Helen nods. "Does it show?"

The woman shrugs. "Maybe it's just me, but I think people just look at me and know I'm a single mom."

"There are worse things to be," Helen says. "We've got our kids."

"Ever miss having a man?"

Helen's face hardens with bitterness. "I had a man."

The woman takes off her sunglasses and looks at Helen.

"Hey, wait a minute...I know you...I saw your picture in the paper..."

Helen is startled. She turns away from the woman and rushes over to the slide.

"We have go, Emma," she says, and grabs her by the hand.

"I don't wanna go," Emma wails. "I wanna play!"

"Now, I said!"

"I hate you!"

"Tough."

Emma cries as Helen drags her across the playground to the car.

"You're mean!" Emma screams.

I know, Helen thinks, I know. She straps Emma into her car seat. Her face is red and streaked with tears.

"I'm sorry, honey," she says as she wipes Emma's tears.

"No, you're not. You're mean."

Helen smiles. "What if we go get ice cream instead?"

Emma brightens. A smile spreads across her face. "Okay!" she says.

Helen kisses her, then goes around to the driver's side and gets in behind the wheel. As she starts the engine and buckles her seat belt, Helen notices that the woman is still looking at her. I made her day, Helen thinks. Now she can tell her friends about how she saw that woman whose picture was in the paper. Maybe Emma and I should move away, Helen thinks as she merges into traffic. Go someplace where no one will recognize me, where I can stop being famous for all the wrong reasons. But where? Helen has no idea. She has a job, a child, a life. It'll never end, she thinks, no matter where she goes. Why couldn't have just gone along with all the other jurors? Why did she have to be a hero? Did she think it would make a difference? Her mind races with the questions she's asked herself over and over ever since the trial.

"Ice cream!" Emma shouts, pointing out the window at the ice cream parlor on the corner.

Helen glances in the rearview and smiles at Emma.

"I love you, munchkin," she says.

"You're the munchkin," Emma replies.

As she pulls into a parking space, Helen wonders if someone in the ice cream parlor will recognize her.

Suddenly, she's afraid to get out of the car and go inside.

CHAPTER 43

TWENTY MINUTES AFTER LAST CALL, POWELL NOSED THE Bronco into the loading zone in front of Tana's building. It was long past two in the morning and Tana had no idea how she going to drag herself into the office a few hours later. She had closed down bars before, hanging out with friends until 2 a.m. but never because she was working on a case with a man twice her age who had yet to come on to her. She was buzzed by what she had discovered in the screen grabs from the security cameras in the theater parking lot, especially since Powell never saw it.

But, of course, there was no way he could have seen it. You had to be there, Tana thought. Just as she was there, courtesy of Helen Mayfield. She had shown Tana what no one had seen, and now she could never forget it. Had LaSalle crumpled the flyer and dropped it on the ground so that Tana could discover it ten years later? Had he stolen the Escalade and then stolen the child? Was it as simple as that? Her mind raced with questions as she stood on the sidewalk in front of her building and watched the Bronco pull away. She waited until it had disappeared in traffic, then turned to go inside.

But she never got there.

A gray sedan braked to a stop in front of her. The doors flew open and two men jumped out of the car. They grabbed Tana and pushed her toward the car.

"Hey! What are you doing? Let go of me! Help!" Tana yelled as she tried to fight off her attackers and free herself.

But there was no one around to hear her or come to her rescue. The men overpowered her and shoved her into the back seat. Doors slammed and the car peeled away.

Then somebody threw a hood over her head. Tana went blind as the dark closed in around her, black as a grave. She broke out in a cold sweat. Panic climbed into her throat. She tried to breathe but the fabric of the hood was sticking to the sweat on her face. She felt as if she was suffocating.

"I can't breathe," she said. Her voice sounded muffled inside the hood and her breath was hot.

She heard a man chuckle. "Then I guess you're gonna die, eh?"

A man laughed. Then she felt the man sitting next to her in the back seat grab her by the back of her neck. He clamped a hand tightly against her nose and mouth.

"How about now, chica?" the man said. "Can you breathe now?"

Tana tried to scream. She could feel the panic strangling her. She shook her head from side to side, trying to free herself. Then the man let go of her.

"You asshole!" she said, gasping for air. "You think that's funny?"

"For you, not so much. For us, yeah, pretty funny."

"Who are you? What do you want?"

A man laughed. "You don't want to know, chica."

"Where are you taking me? Is this about Hector Vargas?"

"Too many questions, chica."

"I'm a reporter. That's what I do. I ask questions for a living."

"Maybe you stop living, eh?"

The car fell silent. Tana could feel her heart pounding. Her mind raced with questions as they rolled through the night. Who besides Powell knew that she was looking into the Vargas case and Emma's abduction? Who, besides Powell and the ghosts of Helen and Emma?

Tana could hear the rush of the traffic around them. She strained to hear anything that might indicate where they were or where they were going. But she heard nothing and may as well have been deaf as well as blind. The car kept stopping at what Tana assumed were stoplights, which told her they were still in stop-and-go traffic on surface streets. Then the car picked up speed and Tana figured they were on a freeway. But which freeway? And what was their destination? And what was going to happen to her when they got there?

The car slowed and Tana figured that they were back on city streets somewhere. She could hear the sounds of cars, trucks, and motorcycles. Different from the hum of the freeway. Somebody lowered a window and the sounds of salsa and mariachi music drifted into the car. Where were they, she wondered? South of the border? Not likely. They hadn't been driving long enough to cross a border. And how exactly would they have gotten past the guards when they looked in the car and saw a woman in the back seat wearing a hood? It could have been worse, Tana thought. They could have thrown her in the trunk. Then again, maybe they still would.

"Please...don't do this," Tana said, fighting back tears. "Just let me go and I'll forget this ever happened."

"We gonna let you go, chica," the man sitting next to her said. "Soon as we're done."

They couldn't be serious, Tana told herself. Then she realized they were. She hated being scared, and yet she was scared. More scared than she had ever been in her life. Was this why Helen had reached out to her from beyond the grave? So that she could end up at the hands of a couple of thugs whose job it was to dispose of her before she asked any more questions?

"So what's the plan?" Tana said, trying to push past her fear as the car pulled out of the lot. "You gotta have a plan, right?"

Then one of the men pulled the hood off and Tana saw they were rolling past strip malls, convenience stores, liquor stores, food trucks, bars. Then the lights died out and were replaced by blocks of abandoned buildings splashed with graffiti.

"Over there," the man sitting next to her said. He pointed to a deserted warehouse shrouded in darkness.

They turned off the main drag and drove down a side street riddled with potholes.

"Pull inside, kill the lights."

The driver drove into the warehouse. He turned off the lights and got out of the car. He opened the back door and they pulled Tana out of the car. She noticed that one of them had a tattoo on his neck of what looked like a Mexican sombrero resting on top of a bloody knife. The two men traded glances, then pulled out 9mm Glock semiautomatics. Tana gasped at the sight of the guns. She tried to back away but the men pushed her to her knees.

"Sorry, chica," one of the men said.

Tana was shaking. She felt herself going into shock. The men pointed the guns at her at point blank range. But then, just as they were about to open fire, the Glocks turned hot and began to glow a deep, dark red. The men started screaming. They shook their hands as they tried to drop the guns. But the weapons were fused to their hands and they were unable to let go of them. The color changed from red to orange as the guns got hotter and hotter. Tana could smell burning flesh. The men collapsed on the ground, writhing, and screaming in pain as the guns glowed white as molten steel.

Tana stared at them, stunned by what she was seeing. The guns were melting and their hands were turning to ashes. The men looked up at her in agony, pleading for her help. The same men who moments ago were ready to kill her and drive away. But they were beyond help. It was time for Tana to help herself. She jumped in the car, then started the engine and turned on the lights.

That was when she saw it. A message she'd seen before. Scrawled in bright red crayon on the windshield, as if by a child.

Find me.

CHAPTER 44

TANA DROVE ACROSS TOWN IN A DAZE. SHE HAD NO IDEA where she was going. But it didn't matter. She was on the move in a stolen car and not lying dead on the floor of some abandoned warehouse. She was alive. But she could still hear their screams as their hands burned down to ashes. Still see them twisting in agony. Still smell their burning flesh. She suddenly pulled over, threw open the door, and vomited on the pavement. Then she wiped her mouth, pulled out her phone, and figured out where she was going and how to get there. She was too scared to go home, and needed to be with Powell, wherever he was.

An hour later she was rolling past a shuttered wholesale produce market north of the Amtrak station and blocks from Oakland's Jack London square. The lights of the square had faded as the night closed in around the empty buildings and factories that hugged both sides of the tracks. Tana glanced at the railway and imagined Amtrak trains and freights and big rigs stacked with containers from halfway around the world. But now it was late and the only signs of life on the streets were the homeless who lived there.

It was raining and with the window down Tana could hear

it clattering on the tattered stalls and rusted awnings of the produce market, which seemed like a relic from another time. She didn't know the town, she was a city girl without a car, and rarely traveled to the east bay. Now, in the middle of the night, alone and scared, when even the dark itself seemed like a threat, she was relying on her iPhone's GPS to guide her to her destination. Another time she might've felt like a tourist. But not tonight. Not after what happened, when the only tour she was on was a murder tour.

Powell had told her he had place down by the water with a view of the bay, and according to her phone, she was almost there. The rain was coming down harder now, gray sheets blurring the streets, and Tana wanted to get out of the car, which felt like a hearse that had very nearly transported her to her death. Two blocks later her phone's automated GPS voice informed Tana that she had reached her destination. She pulled over, parked, and peered through the rain at Powell's building, which looked as if it once had been a warehouse that was converted to lofts. She could hear the rain tapping on the windshield as if it wanted to be let in. Tana remembered that it was raining the night she saw Helen and Emma, the night her life changed forever. She wondered if the rain would always remind of that night. Then she jumped out of the car and ran to the entrance as the rain soaked her to the bone.

"They tried to kill me," Tana said when Powell opened the door. Then she collapsed in his arms in tears.

Powell clenched with alarm. "Who tried to kill you?"

"These guys...they tried to kill me...if it wasn't for Emma, I'd be dead."

Powell looked at her. "Emma?"

Tana nodded. "You saw her again?"

"Not exactly...I saw what she did."

Powell looked at Tana, shivering in her wet clothes. "You

better change before you come down with pneumonia, then you can start from the beginning and tell me what happened."

Tana gave an awkward smile. "I don't have a change of clothes...this is all I have."

"Yeah, I know," Powell said with an understanding smile.

She watched as Powell stepped across his loft to a dresser by the bed and pulled out a pair of sweats. He looked back at Tana, who was still standing by the door.

"It's okay, you can come in," he said.

"I'm dripping wet." Tana said. She looked down at the water pooling on the hardwood floor and gave an embarrassed smile. "Sorry."

"Don't worry about it," Powell said as he handed her the sweats. "It's just water, right?" He cocked his head toward the other end of the loft. "Bathroom's down the hall on the left."

"Thanks," Tana said with a grateful smile.

Then she walked down the hall to the bathroom, passing what seemed like an entire wall of vinyl records. A high-end system consisting of a tube amplifier, preamp, turntable, and speakers sat across the from the records. There were two lounge chairs in front of the speakers, and as she walked into the bathroom Tana imagined Powell turning it up, then sitting back and letting the music wash over him.

She closed the door, then noticed three photographs mounted on the wall. Two were of a woman Tana assumed was Nora, and the third was of Nora and Powell together. They were on a beach somewhere and looked like they were on vacation. Nora was wearing a bathing suit and smiling at the camera, unaware that somewhere in the future her killer was waiting for her. Tana turned away from the photos, wishing in a way that she'd never seen them. She towel-dried her hair, then changed into the gray sweats that Powell had given her. She smiled when she looked in her mirror and saw that she was wearing a San Francisco P.D. sweatshirt.

When she came out Powell was sitting on the sofa with his feet up on the coffee table.

"Better?" he said.

Tana nodded. "Yeah, thanks."

Tana nodded at the records. "I guess you're into vinyl, huh?"

Powell nodded. "Ever since I was a kid."

"Looks like you've got the rig to play 'em," Tana said, indicating the sound system.

"Thanks, you know about this stuff?"

"My dad's into it, built his own tube amp and preamp."

Powell smiled, then changed the subject. "So what happened?"

"You won't believe it."

Powell scoffed. "I'm probably the only one who will believe it."

Tana curled up on the sofa next to Powell and braced him on what had happened.

"They took me out to some warehouse...they were gonna shoot me...and then this weird thing happened. I don't know how to explain it."

"Try."

Tana took a moment to gather her thoughts, to find a way to put into words something that was beyond words, beyond explanation. Then she looked up at Powell and filled him in on what happened at the warehouse, which now seemed to her like a scene out of a horror movie. Except that the movie was her life.

"She saved my life, Bud."

"Emma?"

Tana nodded.

"How did she know this was going to happen?"

Powell shrugged. "I don't know...it was like that with Nora too. She just seemed to know when I needed her." He smiled sadly. "Trouble is, I still need her. Always will."

Tana paused, as if she wasn't sure what to say. She hadn't lived long enough to lose anyone, and Justin didn't count.

"You recognize either one of the guys that grabbed you?"

Tana shook her head. "I never saw either one of 'em before, but one guy had this weird tattoo on his neck."

Powell looked sharply at Tana, as if she'd gotten his attention. "What kind of tattoo?"

"It was a Mexican sombrero resting on top of a bloody knife."

"Nuestra Familia," Powell said.

Tana looked puzzled. "Nuestra what?"

"It's a Mexican-American prison gang. Started up in Soledad back in the late sixties, then it spread to other prisons in northern California, including San Quentin. That's their logo—a sombrero on top of a bloody knife."

"So they were ex-cons?"

"My guess is that they were part of Hector's crew. He did a stretch or two over the past ten years, which would have given him chance to join up. See if you can turn up a connection between Vargas and Nuestra Familia."

"The gang?"

Powell nodded.

Tana went quiet, then said, "They would've killed me if it wasn't for Emma."

"She melted the guns, huh?"

"Melted them too...I could smell them burning." Tana shuddered at the memory. "Made me puke."

"Helluva way to go," Powell said.

"You think Vargas sent them?"

Powell shrugged his shoulders. "He's not used to women humiliating him—"

"Aiken and Paine didn't like being humiliated either."

"Yeah, but you're not the one who humiliated them. Their ex-wives humiliated them, and maybe you're right, maybe Emma paid the price for that. Either way, it's got nothing to do with you."

"So this is payback for what happened at the funeral?"

"You slapped him, Tana, in front of other people. You think he's gonna forget that? A guy like Hector? No way."

Tana was dismayed. "He was gonna kill me for that?"

"People kill people for all kinds of reasons, Tana. And thugs like Vargas don't need much of a reason to pull the trigger."

Tana buried her face in her hands. "So what am I gonna do?" she said, as the panic rose in her throat. "They know where I live."

"You're gonna stay here tonight. We'll figure out the rest tomorrow."

Tana looked up at Powell. "You want me stay here?"

"You got a problem with that?"

Tana shook her head. "Thanks," she said with a grateful smile. "I don't think I could drive across the bridge right now."

Powell looked surprised. "You drove here?"

"Yeah."

"I thought you didn't have a car."

"I don't. I stole their car."

"The guys who were gonna clip you?"

Tana nodded.

Powell gave a grim smile. "I guess they weren't gonna need it, right?" He looked around the loft. "You take the bed. I'll take the sofa."

"You sure?"

Powell nodded. "Sorry, there's not much privacy, you know how it is in a loft."

"It's okay."

Powell retrieved an extra comforter and pillow from the laundry room and made up a bed for himself on the sofa. Then he turned to Tana.

"You ready to call it a night?"

Tana nodded. "Totally."

Powell smiled. "See you in the morning. Then he turned off the lights, plunging the loft into darkness.

Tana looked out the loft's factory windows. In the distance she could the lights of the container terminals at the Port of Oakland, the cranes lit up like birds of prey. Then she crawled into Powell's bed and pulled the comforter up around her. She was out of town, alone in another man's bed, and yet somehow it felt like home. She didn't have a boyfriend anymore to save her. But she did have Aloysius Powell. A bowler twice her age.

"Can I ask you a question?" she said in the dark.

"Shoot."

"Is your name really Aloysius?"

There was a pause, then Powell said, "Is yours Montana?"

Tana laughed out loud. "Okay, got it," she said.

"Smart girl," Powell said.

They came for her in the middle of the night. The two of them, still burning, their hands engulfed in flames. They reached out and grabbed Tana, and as they did so she caught fire, the flames shooting up her arms and igniting her face and her hair.

She woke suddenly, gasping for air and screaming.

Powell heard her and went to the bed. She sat up and threw her arms around him.

"I was in flames...they set me on fire...I was burning up...my hair, everything" the words rushing out of her as she tried to catch her breath.

"It's okay, you had a nightmare. It's over now."

"It seemed so real..."

"Yeah, I know. They always do."

Tana looked up at him. "You mind sleeping with me?"

Powell looked at her. "You want me to sleep with you?"

Tana nodded. "Please?"

Powell smiled. "Sure, no problem."

He crawled into bed beside her. Tana turned to him so he could hold her.

They lay in silence for a few moments, then Tana said, "Is this weird?"

"It's okay."

"Are you gonna come on to me?"

Powell chuckled. "Maybe later. It's past my bedtime."

CHAPTER 45

Tana could smell the coffee brewing as she awakened, slipping out of a dream she could barely remember. She loved the smell of coffee first thing in the morning and liked it even better when she didn't have to make it. She took a moment to let the aroma fill her nostrils, then looked over at Powell, who was in the kitchen pouring two mugs of coffee. He was wearing olive drab cargo pants and a black T-shirt, which, together with his buzz cut and his tattoos, made him look like a soldier on leave. Tana had no idea whether Powell had ever been in the Army, but he had been a cop, which was close enough.

"Smells good," she said.

Powell looked over at her and smiled. "I guess that means you want a cup."

"Yeah, I do."

Tana threw back the covers and climbed out of bed, then joined Powell in the kitchen.

"You sleep okay?" he said.

"Yeah, I did."

Tana was surprised that she had slept as well as she had in

another man's bed. But she was scared, and Powell had made her feel safe. She knew that if she'd stayed alone in her apartment she would have been strung out and sleep-deprived the next morning.

"Here you go," Powell said, handing her a mug.

"Thanks," Tana said, as she climbed onto one of the stools facing the counter.

"Cheers," Powell said, and took a sip.

Tana smiled. It felt like the morning after, Tana thought. But the morning after what, she wondered. Powell had not come on to her—did she want him to? What would she have done if he had come on to her? She wasn't sure. She missed a man's touch and drifting off to sleep in Powell's arms came close. But he never crossed the line, and she didn't either.

It felt different with him. Maybe because he wasn't trying to fuck her. Did he want to, Tana wondered. Had he thought about it? He was a man, after all, and weren't all men attracted to women half their age? She knew that Justin would be more than ready to touch her, but the problem was that he liked to touch other women too, which made Tana feel something less than special.

Then she heard the rumble of a train somewhere beyond Powell's loft and remembered that she still had a job.

"What time is it?" she said.

Powell glanced at the clock on the wall above the sink. "A little after seven."

"Shit. I gotta get to work," Tana said, gulping her coffee. She set the mug down a little harder than she needed to, spilling coffee on the counter. "Sorry."

"No problem," Powell said. He grabbed a sponge and wiped up the coffee. "I'll take you home."

"What about the car?"

"The one you stole?"

Tana nodded.

"I'll take care of it."

Tana became alarmed. "My prints and DNA all over it."

"It'll get wiped," Powell said. "Don't worry about it."

Tana nodded. "I guess we should go, huh?"

CHAPTER 46

Tana's cellphone beeped, alerting to a text as they rolled across the Bay Bridge and the San Francisco skyline came into view. She glanced at the screen, saw it was Mimi, and ignored it.

"I hope it wasn't too weird last night," she said.

Powell glanced at her. "Which part?"

"You know, us sleeping together."

"I've done it before, you know," Powell said.

Tana gave an embarrassed smile. "Yeah, I figured." She paused, then looked at Powell and said, "Thanks."

"Anytime," he said as he took the Fremont Street exit off the bridge and headed down Pine.

Tana's cellphone rang. She glanced at the screen and saw it was Mimi. Give it up, girl, she thought. We're so done. Ten minutes later Bud pulled up in front of her building.

"Thanks for the ride," she said.

Powell nodded.

"So where do we go from here?" Tana said.

Powell reached across Tana, opened the glove, and took out a Glock 9mm.

"We go upstairs," he said, shoving the gun in his waistband.

Tana sucked in her breath at the sight of the Glock. She looked at Powell. "With a gun? Seriously?"

"Yeah, with a gun," Powell said. "Let's go."

He opened the door and climbed out of the Bronco. Tana followed suit and they went up to her apartment.

But as they walked down the corridor to her apartment Tana saw at once that something was wrong. The door was ajar, as if someone had forced it open. Were they still inside, she wondered. She knew that break-ins were a common occurrence in the city. Residents shrugged, took inventory of what had been stolen, then changed the locks and went on with their lives. But getting ripped off was anything but common for Tana.

She threw a glance at Powell as the fear that began in the pit of her stomach climbed into her throat. He put his index finger to his lips. He looked up and down the corridor, then pulled the Glock out of his waistband. He indicated to Tana that he would go first, then moved closer to the door. He cautiously pushed it open and stepped into the apartment. Tana's heart was pounding as she watched Powell enter the apartment. She took a deep breath, then followed him inside.

What she saw made Tana gasp. The place was a shambles, as if a hurricane had blown through her apartment. Books had been thrown out of the bookcase and hurled across the room. Drapes had been torn from the windows. Curtain rods were left dangling. Most of the chairs had been upended along with her desk and the coffee table, and the Crate and Barrel sofa she bought on sale was resting on its side. The cushions were slashed and lay on the floor by the windows.

Powell turned to Tana and signaled for her to wait while he checked out the rest of the apartment. Then he went down the hall to the bedroom and the bathroom. Tana could feel herself trembling as she surveyed the damage. Who did this, she wondered. And why? What were they looking for? The rage with which everything had been torn apart terrified her. She felt as if they would have torn her apart if she had been there.

Then the sound of a loud thud made her jump. Tana froze for a moment, as if deciding whether she should run out the door and scream for help. Then she ran toward the sound and found Bud face down on the floor in the bedroom. The Glock was on the floor beside him.

Standing over him with the remains of a shattered bedside lamp in her hand was Mimi.

"Hey girl," she said. "You get my messages?"

CHAPTER 47

TANA STOPPED COLD AND STARED AT MIMI. THIS WASN'T happening, she told herself. Her legs went rubbery, and she felt as if she was losing her balance. She reached out and grabbed the door to support herself, then rushed over to Powell and crouched down beside him.

"Bud! Bud, please...please be okay...please don't be dead..." She swiveled to Mimi. "What the fuck, Mimi! What did you do? What are you doing here?"

Mimi looked stricken. "You wouldn't take my calls, so I just came over—"

"What, and bashed him on the head? What if you killed him?"

"You know this guy?" Mimi said with a stunned expression.

"Yeah, I know him."

Mimi's face crumpled with remorse. "I'm sorry—"

Tana's face twisted with anger. "Yeah, you're always sorry, aren't you, Mimi?"

Powell began moaning and Tana turned to him, relieved that he was showing signs of life.

"Bud, can you hear me?"

Bud slowly rolled over. He tried to sit up, then fell back down again.

"Don't move," Tana said. "Just take it easy, okay?"

"What the hell happened?" Powell said. He rubbed the back of his head, then looked at his hand. It was covered with blood.

"Oh shit!" Tana said at the sight of the blood. "I'll be right back." She jumped up and ran into the bathroom, then returned a moment later with tissues and a wet washcloth and began treating Powell's wound.

"This doesn't look good, Bud," Tana said. "Maybe we should call 911."

"I'll live. Is somebody gonna tell what the hell happened?"

"I happened," Mimi said.

Powell looked up at her. "Who are you?"

Tana scowled. "She used to be a friend of mine."

"Tana, don't say that, please."

"Why not? It's the truth, isn't it?"

"I'm not following...": Powell said, starting to sit up.

"Don't move, something might be broken." Tana said.

"I'm okay," Powell said, leaning back against the wall.

"Maybe he should go to the ER," Mimi said.

"Yeah, thanks to you," Tana said, her voice dripping with contempt.

Powell shook his head. "No 911 and no ER, okay? But maybe somebody could tell me why your friend here tried to bash my head in."

Tana looked up at Mimi.

"The floor's all yours, Mimi."

Mimi sighed. "You wouldn't talk to me, so I decided to just come over and try to see you before you went to work."

Then it hit Tana. "Oh shit! I have to go to work!"

She jumped to her feet, then looked at Powell, at the blood

on her hands and her sweatshirt. Suddenly, she felt torn between caring for him and keeping her job.

"Call in sick," Mimi said. "They don't care."

Tana shook her head. "You don't know JD. He'll fire my ass for sure."

"Go to work," Powell said. "I'll be okay, and you don't need to lose your job."

"I don't want to leave you like this."

"I've been through worse," Powell said.

"I'll try to come home at lunch and check up on you, okay/"

Powell gave a wry smile. "Yeah, that'd be great."

"I'll drive you," Mimi said. "We need to talk."

"Yeah? About what?" Tana said.

"About why somebody tore up your apartment, for starters. What were they looking for?"

"Maybe they were looking for her," Powell said, nodding at Tana.

"What?" Mimi said, a stunned expression on her face. "Why?"

Powell ignored Mimi's question. Tana tensed as the fear grabbed hold of her. She threw a glance at Powell, then at Mimi.

"What are you talking about?" she said.

"You weren't here, so instead of tearing you apart, they tore your place apart."

"You really know how to scare a girl, you know that?" Tana said.

"It's better that way," Powell said. "They won't catch you off guard."

"This is really scary," Mimi said. "Would somebody please tell me what's going on?"

"Trust me, the less you know the better," Powell said.

"How'd they get into the building?" Mimi said. "Did somebody let 'em in?"

Tana looked at her. "How'd *you* get into the building?"

"The UPS guy left the door open. And then when I got to your apartment, I saw the door was open and the place was turned upside down." She looked down at Powell. "And then you came in with the gun and..." Her voice trailed off.

"And you figured I was the bad guy."

Mimi nodded. "Yeah, something like that."

"Sorry."

Powell nodded. "That makes two of us."

Tana took a quick shower, threw on some clothes, and then let Mimi drive her to work. They did need to talk, but would the outcome be any different? She and Bud had seen what Mimi would never see, and that wasn't about to change anytime soon. Still, Tana hoped that despite the gulf between them, they could find a way to still be friends. But was there a middle ground between this life and the afterlife?

CHAPTER 48

Mɪᴍɪ ᴛʜʀᴇᴡ ᴀ ɢʟᴀɴᴄᴇ ᴀᴛ Tᴀɴᴀ ᴀs sʜᴇ ᴘᴜʟʟᴇᴅ ᴀᴡᴀʏ from the curb and merged her Subaru Outback into rush hour traffic. "So what's up with your apartment?"

Tana shrugged. "You heard him. They tore the place apart instead of me."

"But why?"

Tana did have an idea why. First, they tried to kill her. Then her apartment was tossed. The two had to be connected. It wasn't just some random break-in. That would have been bad enough, but it would've been better than the truth. But the thought of having to explain it all to Mimi made her dizzy. So she just shook her head.

"Maybe you should move."

"Right, like back to Montana."

"That's not what I meant, okay?"

"Sorry."

"They take anything?"

"I don't know…I haven't had time to check."

"Kinda weird if they didn't, huh?"

Tana nodded.

"Check your underwear drawer."

Tana looked at Mimi. "What?"

"A server at the restaurant got broken into and the only thing they took was her underwear."

"I'll be sure to check," Tana said.

"Lots of pervs out there, you know."

Yeah, and killers too, Tana thought.

"So what's the story with Bud? Is that his name?"

"Yeah, that's his name."

"So what's going on?"

Tana sighed and looked out the window.

"Come on Tana, don't do this, okay? Talk to me."

"He's helping me find Emma."

"The ghost you said you saw?"

"I did see her, Mimi," Tana said sharply. "I didn't just say I saw her."

"Sorry. So he believes you?"

"Yeah, he believes me. It happened to him, too."

"He saw a ghost?"

"His wife, after she died."

Mimi shuddered. "That's really scary, okay, Tana. I mean seriously."

Mimi fell silent as the Subaru crawled through heavy morning traffic. Tana looked at her. She was her best friend and she desperately wanted Mimi to understand. But how could she expect understanding when she could barely understand it herself?

"Look, I know you don't believe me, Mimi..."

"It's not that I don't believe you...it's that I don't know how to believe you. You know what I mean?"

Tana smiled. "Yeah, I know."

"I've never seen a ghost, never had any kind of paranormal experience. I don't know how to talk to you about it, I don't know how to understand it. I'm a cook, okay? The only visions I have are of entrees and appetizers."

The two shared a smile.

"So how'd you hook up with Bud?"

"He's an ex-cop. He led the search for Emma until the case went cold."

"And now he's back on the case, huh?"

Tana nodded.

"He's cute."

"He's old enough to be my dad, Mimi."

Mimi shrugged it off. "So? What's the big deal?"

"It's not like that, okay?"

"What's gonna happen when you find Emma?"

"I don't know. I'm scared to find her, and yet I have to find her."

Mimi hung a right on Mission and pulled into the loading zone in front of *The Bay Area Bugle*. She flipped on her emergency flashers and turned to Tana.

"Here you go, ghost girl. Door to door service."

"Very funny."

Mimi shrugged. "I don't think it's funny. I think it's true."

"So you do believe me?"

"I'm working on it," Mimi said with a wry smile. "We're still best buddies, right, no matter what?"

Tana nodded. "No matter what."

"Sorry about the lamp."

Tana chuckled. "Yeah, so's Bud," she said as she opened the door and started to get out of the Subaru.

"Geez, Tana could you just wait a sec?"

Tana sighed, then turned to her.

"What? I'm late."

Mimi paused, a contrite expression on her face, then said, "I'm sorry, okay?"

"Yeah, I know. You already told me."

"I didn't mean to hurt him, I was just worried about you."

"Don't stress about it, I'm sure he understands. But I really gotta go."

"Call me, girlfriend. I want to know you're okay."

"I promise."

Tana waved at Mimi as she drove away, then walked to the entrance. The dead were waiting for her to give them their due before they disappeared forever, and if she didn't deliver they might start appearing to her as well. Tana shuddered at the thought. But a portal had opened, and what if Emma and Helen were only the beginning?

CHAPTER 49

Powell sat on the floor with his back against the wall as the hammering in his head worked overtime to pound him into submission. The shattered, blood-stained lamp that Mimi had used to take the back of his head off lay on the floor beside him. He waited until the room stopped spinning like a carousel, then slowly got to his feet, staggered into the bathroom, and turned on the faucet in the bathroom sink. He rinsed out the bloody washcloth that Tana had used to clean the wound, then picked up where she left off. But what he really needed besides a triple dose of ibuprofen was Polysporin, hydrogen peroxide and a bandage. Powell hoped he didn't also need stitches, but if he did Tana would have to drive him to the nearest ER. He could scarcely stand, let alone climb in behind the wheel of the Bronco.

He found a bottle of Advil in the medicine cabinet and downed three tablets, but the rest would have to wait until Tana came home at lunch. When he was finished cleaning the wound as best he could, given that he couldn't see it, only feel it, he went into the living room and surveyed the damage. But the more he looked at it, the more it seemed that whoever had tossed the apartment had done it out of anger and rage, and not because they were looking for anything in particular. Rage over what, he wondered. The fact that they had failed in their attempt to kill her? And who were they? Vargas's people? Had to be. Or was Tana right? Was he so certain that Vargas was guilty that he was blind to the possibility of other suspects besides him?

Powell turned a side chair right side up, then sank into it and buried his face in his hands as he waited for the Advil to kick in. Then, as the hammering in his head began to subside, he started putting the furniture back in place and generally straightening out the apartment as best he could. It wasn't perfect, but it least the place no longer looked as if a category 4 hurricane had blown in through the window. But nature's rage was nothing compared to the rage you could find in a human heart, Powell thought, and that was the part that worried him.

His cellphone rang. Powell pulled it out his pocket. His expression turned to surprise as he glanced at the screen and saw the caller ID.

CHAPTER 50

LIEUTENANT HARVEY PHELPS WAS A COP'S COP. HE HAD come up through the ranks, and unlike some of the department brass, he'd done his time on the beat and understood what it was like on the ground. What he didn't understand was the behavior of the retired cop who sat in front of him.

Powell shifted in his chair as Phelps studied him like he was some kind of specimen. Phelps underscored this impression by twisting a pencil in his fingers while he watched Powell, as if he were ready to jot down any insights into his behavior that might occur to him.

"Who are you, the lone fucking ranger?" Phelps finally asked.

"Sir?"

"I asked you a question."

"No sir, I'm not the lone fucking ranger," Powell replied.

Phelps's eyes narrowed. He glared at Powell. "Don't get fucking smart with me, Powell," Phelps snapped, breaking the pencil. "I got everybody up my ass over this."

Powell nodded. "I understand, sir. Things got out of hand."

Phelps looked at Powell in disbelief. "Things got out of hand? Is that what you call it?"

Phelps got up and started pacing back and forth in front of the windows overlooking 3rd Street. "I'll tell you what got out of hand, Powell," he said, turning to Powell and pointing a finger at him.

"You did. Vargas's lawyer is threatening a lawsuit. What the hell did you think you were doing out there? He was visiting his mother, for Christ's sake!"

Powell said nothing. He could hear the sounds of the squad room on the other side of the door. The world he used to live in. The cops who used to his brother officers.

"In case you forgot, you're not a cop anymore, Bud, and Vargas was acquitted."

Powell's eyes flashed with anger. "It wasn't an acquittal; it was a miscarriage of justice."

"According to you," Phelps said. "Unfortunately, it wasn't up to you. You're not judge, jury and executioner. You're a retired cop who apparently doesn't know what the hell to do with himself. That case went cold ten years ago, Bud. What the hell were you thinking?"

"I don't care when the hell it went cold. He did it. Simple as that."

"He did it, huh? Why, 'cause you say so?" Phelps shook his head. He sat down and looked into his hands for a moment, then looked up at Powell. "You know, you keep this shit up you're gonna find yourself facing assault charges. Is that what you want?"

Powell didn't answer. He thought it best to let Phelps vent. There was no way Phelps was going to approve of Powell strong-arming Vargas outside Bahia.

"This isn't just about you, Bud. It's about the department too. It makes us look bad with the community, and there's no fucking way I'm gonna stand for it. You hear me?"

Powell's face darkened. "Emma Mayfield was only four

years old. Her mother died without ever seeing her again. Was that good for the community?"

Lt. Phelps's face turned red. A vein on his forehead bulged out. Powell imagined it bursting and spraying blood all over his desk.

"You know what your problem is, Bud?"

"I got a feeling you're gonna tell me."

"You were a good cop, but you're a lousy ex-cop."

It was true, Powell thought. He often felt that way himself. But he didn't feel like an ex-cop anymore. He was back on the case, and it wasn't cold, it was burning hot. He looked up at Phelps and decided it was time to cut to the chase.

"Where we going with this, sir?"

"Where *you* going with it is the question. I see you in here again it won't be to warn you, it'll be because you've been arrested. And I won't be there to save you. We clear?"

"Clear," Powell said.

"I hope so," Phelps said. "Now get the fuck out of here. Go bowling or something."

His eyes dropped to the papers on his desk. *Nice to see you too*, Powell thought as he stood and walked to the door.

CHAPTER 51

Tana heard it the moment she stepped inside the lobby.

"Mon-ta-na!" a voice boomed across the lobby.

Tana looked up and saw JD grinning and holding the elevator for her.

She rolled her eyes, then walked over to the elevator. "Morning, JD," she said.

"It is still morning?" JD said, checking his watch with a theatrical flourish.

"Sorry, I'm late," Tana said as the elevator doors closed. "My apartment got broken into last night."

"Oh no," JD said as he faked a horrified expression. "That's terrible. They take much?"

"I don't know, haven't had time to check. Didn't want to be late. Or more late, anyway."

"Of course you didn't," JD said with a patronizing smile. The elevator stopped and the doors slid open. JD stepped out first. "The Healey file's on your desk," he said over his shoulder he walked away. "It's due at noon. Let me know if you have any questions."

Tana shook her head wearily, then headed for her cubicle.

Charles "Chuck" Healey was an ex-astronaut who had passed away in his sleep at 86. As she worked on his obituary, Tana couldn't help wondering if he had died dreaming of outer space. Healey never made it to the moon, but he went to Hollywood after he left NASA and became an actor. He made mostly sci-fi movies, where he played astronauts exploring planets he never got to see when he was in the space program.

Up to now Tana had assumed that she was in control of her subjects because, after all, they were totally dead. But Helen Mayfield had taught her that death was no obstacle. What next, she wondered. Would Chuck Healey suddenly appear, dressed in his space suit, and whisk her off to a faraway planet in some undiscovered galaxy?

She filed Healey's obituary just before noon, then pulled out her iPhone and called Powell to check in on him and tell him she couldn't get away.

"Where are you?" she said, surprised when he didn't pick up. "Are you okay? Call me. I'm worried about you."

Then she caught herself. When was the last time she told a man she was worried about him? Justin, of course. Tana let the thought linger for a moment, then signed out for morgue duty and took the elevator down to the basement. She hoped that somewhere in the paper's vast, windowless archives she could find a link between Hector Vargas and Nuestra Familia. She began her search by reviewing the news reports that covered the Vargas trial in 1999. She had researched the decade-old stories about the case when she was working on Helen Mayfield's obituary, but there was always the chance she had missed something that didn't seem relevant at the time. She wasn't looking for a link between Vargas and the gang the first around; this time she was.

Three hours later, having moved on from Hector Vargas to Nuestra Familia, she was still looking. But the search was taking its toll. Whether it was about Vargas or the gang, the stories she read were filled with savagery, brutality, and suffering. The violence behind prison walls mirrored the violence on the streets. It was as if there was no other way to live. Kill or be killed. In prison or out.

Tana stopped reading and rubbed her eyes. She'd been staring at text, either online or hardcopy, for hours, and all she wanted was to close her eyes and see nothing. One more hour, she told herself, and then she'd call it a day. Half an hour later, reading an obituary written by her predecessor and published in *The Bugle* in 2014, Tana found something that stopped her cold.

The deceased was a gangbanger named Tito Tavares, aka TNT. He was a member of Nuestra Familia and had founded the San Quentin Prison chapter of the gang. Tavares had died at San Quentin at the age of fifty-six, some ten years into a twenty-year sentence, after being slashed to death in a gang fight.

But what jumped out at Tana was not the fact that Tavares was a member of the gang; that was in the lede. It was what came in the close, which listed his survivors. Among them, a cousin named Hector Vargas. The same Hector Vargas who five years earlier had beat the rap for robbery and murder when the prosecution's star witness recanted her testimony.

Tana stared at Vargas's name as if she could scarcely believe what she was seeing. She could feel her heart pounding. "Yes!" she whispered, as a triumphant smile spread across her face. She had found it. She had done what investigative reporters did and found the connection between Vargas and the gang. He was not only a member, he was also a blood relative. And he had sent his loser thugs to kill her because she had embarrassed him at Helen's funeral. Or was it because she was asking questions about Emma's disappearance? Questions, Tana assumed, only Vargas could answer? She pulled out her cellphone to call Powell but still got his voicemail.

"Call me," she said, "I found something."

CHAPTER 52

DARYL MAYWEATHER WAS SITTING AT A BOOTH BY THE window, nursing a cup of coffee, when Powell walked into Tops Coffee Shop on Market. Back when Powell was on the force and he and Mayweather were working graveyard, they had rolled to the diner every morning after their shift. It was a tradition, a place where they celebrated surviving another night on the street. As he slid into the booth across from his old partner, the only one he ever really trusted, Powell felt the tug of the life.

A tiny Asian waitress came up to the table.

"Coffee?" she asked with a smile.

"That'd be great, thanks," Powell said.

Daryl looked around the diner. "Almost like the old days, eh, Bud?" he said with a nostalgic smile.

Powell nodded.

"You ever miss it?"

"Yeah, sometimes, but then I see you and I don't miss it so much," Powell said with a teasing smile.

Daryl laughed out loud. "Back at you, motherfucker," he said.

It was almost like the old days, Powell thought. The only thing missing were the bad guys, and the adrenaline rush that was like an addiction. But now he was back on the case that had haunted him for a decade and feeling the rush one more time.

The waitress returned with a pot of coffee and filled Powell's mug. He nodded his thanks.

"Let me know if you want to order," she said.

"Sure, will do."

The waitress smiled and moved away. Powell sipped his coffee. It was black and strong, and just as good as he remembered, which was more than you could say for most things.

"I heard Phelps reamed you a new one," Daryl said. He pointed at Powell's shirt. "You got blood on your collar, partner. He take a swing at you too?"

Powell looked down at the bloodstains on his shirt.

"I cut myself shaving," he said.

Daryl scoffed. "Yeah, right."

"I guess news travels fast," Powell said.

"Yeah, especially when it's about ex-cops playing Dirty Harry."

Powell smiled. "I always liked that movie."

"Yeah, I liked it too. But this ain't no fuckin' movie, Bud, and Phelps won't put up with that kinda shit. As far as he's concerned, that case is over and done with. Maybe Vargas got away with it, and maybe didn't—"

Powell face hardened.

"You know damn well he got away with it!"

Daryl put up his hands. "Hey, I'm not the enemy here, okay? We gave it our best shot until it went cold, but it you think he's guilty, then prove it. Just don't take yourself and the department down along with him."

Powell nodded, then changed the subject. "You said on the phone you found something," he said.

Daryl nodded. "Found some more screen grabs from the stolen car report you were asking about."

"From the parking lot?" Powell said, suddenly interested.

"Looks like they slipped through the cracks. Not sure if the guys in auto theft ever saw 'em." He reached into his briefcase and pulled out a manila folder and handed it to Powell. "Thought maybe you'd want to take a look at 'em."

"Thanks, partner," Powell said.

Daryl nodded. "I ain't gonna ask you how it's going, 'cause you probably won't tell me, but I think you're takin' a chance doin' this on the down low."

"So how come you're helping me?"

Daryl shrugged.

"I guess I'm getting homesick in my old age. We had a good run, me and you."

Powell nodded. "Yeah, we did."

Daryl indicated the manila folder.

"But whatever happens, you didn't get that from me."

"Got it," Powell said. He pulled out his cellphone, then pulled up the pic of the Paine Properties sign and showed it to Daryl. "This mean anything to you?"

Daryl studied the pic, then locked eyes with Powell. A moment later, his cellphone beeped with a text. He read it, then held up his hands.

"Yeah, I know," Powell said. "Duty calls."

"Send it to me," Daryl said, nodding at the pic of the Paine Properties sign. Then he stood up to leave. Stuck out his hand.

"Thanks, partner," Powell said, shaking hands.

Daryl nodded. "Be careful out there," he said, "and stay the fuck off Phelps's radar."

Powell smiled to himself as Daryl headed for the door. If he was being careful, he would've stuck to bowling. He sent Daryl the pic, then dropped the phone in his pocket. The tiny Asian waitress came up to the table and offered a smile as she topped off his coffee. Powell took a sip and opened the manila folder.

CHAPTER 53
THURSDAY, JUNE 10, 2010

Emma's in the tub and Helen's trying to give her a bath. But Emma's splashing so much water on her that it seems as if Helen's the one taking a bath. Helen doesn't mind. This happens every time she gives Emma a bath. They give each other baths, mother and daughter. She loves this time alone with her daughter, just the two of them, happy in the world that Helen's made for them. It all she needs, all she'll ever need. She doesn't need a husband; she had one and look what happened. She just needs her daughter.

But she knows that it won't always be just the two of them. Emma will grow up to have her own life. Maybe even a family. Helen will be alone then. But that won't happen for a while. The future's still far off. Emma's only four. She's not going anywhere. All she needs now is her mother, and all Helen needs is her daughter. Why worry about any of that now, Helen wonders, as she watches Emma play with her pink and yellow rubber ducks. Enjoy this moment, she tells herself. Why worry about what hasn't happened?

But she does worry. She's worried every day since the trial about what might happen. Why couldn't have she just gone along with the others? Wouldn't it have been easier that way?

Why did she have to draw attention to herself by hanging the jury? Was it worth it to be afraid every day?

"Picture day!" Emma says, jolting Helen out of her thoughts.

Helen smiles at her daughter. "Are you excited?"

"Yay!" Emma screams.

"You're the prettiest girl in the world," Helen says. "I can't wait to see your picture. And you know what?"

"What?"

"We're going shopping tomorrow for a new outfit for picture day."

"Yay! Can I have ice cream too?"

Helen smiles. "Of course."

You can have anything you want, sweet child, Helen thinks, as she leans in to give her daughter a kiss.

CHAPTER 54

THERE WAS NO SIGN OF BUD WHEN TANA GOT HOME, which only made her more worried. She hadn't heard from him all day, and now she imagined him lying on a gurney at the nearest ER waiting for medical attention before he bled out from his head wound. But she was surprised to discover that despite his injury he had done his best to put her apartment back together before he left or got wheeled out by the EMTs. Tana smiled to herself as she looked around, touched by Powell's gesture.

And yet, at the same time, it made her feel lonely. She was pushing thirty and had yet to find a man she could call her own who would do something like that for her. Then again, she wondered if perhaps she had found him and didn't realize it. But seriously? An ex-cop who was twice her age? Who liked to bowl and carried a torch for his murdered wife? That was the last thing she would have expected. So how did she feel about Powell? And how did he feel about her?

Tana wasn't sure. She knew she couldn't have come this far without him. But what if she had never met him? Could she have done this on her own? She needed him and maybe he needed her too. It had been his case before it was hers, and now it belonged to both of them. But it was more than that. They had been granted glimpses of the afterlife, had traveled from the world of the living to the world of the dead, and that had bound Tana more deeply to him than to anyone she could think of.

And yet, did that mean that she could never be close with anyone else because she could not share the secret she shared with Powell? Was that the price she would pay for having seen what most people would never see? She thought of Mimi and what had happened when she tried to tell her about how Helen and Emma had appeared to her. Of course Mimi didn't believe her. Who would? Only Aloysius "Bud" Powell. Whatever their relationship was, whatever it would become, only time would tell.

Tana was about to call him again when her intercom buzzed. She walked over to the panel and pressed the button and was flooded with relief when she heard his voice.

"Where have you been? Why didn't you call me?" she said when she opened and door and saw Powell standing there, a manila folder in his hand.

"Sorry, got tied up," Powell replied.

He walked into the apartment and Tana closed the door. "Well, you could've called me, okay? I was worried."

Powell nodded. "You're right, I should've called you."

"Are you okay? There's blood on your shirt."

"Nothing a few Advil won't cure."

"I got some in the medicine cabinet," Tana said, and went to the bathroom.

"Maybe we should go to the ER," she called out.

Powell shook his head. "I'll be all right."

Tana returned with a glass of water and dropped three Advil tablets into Powell's palm. He popped them into the mouth, then chased them with a sip of water.

"Thanks," he said, handing her the glass.

Tana set the glass down on the coffee table, then looked at Powell.

"You didn't have to put the place back together, you know."

Powell slumped on the sofa. "How we gonna sit down otherwise?"

Tana smiled. "It was really sweet."

"Hey, I'm a sweet guy."

"Yeah, I know," Tana said.

Powell looked up at her and their eyes met. They held each other's gaze for what seemed to Tana like forever. Then she looked away and said, "I got news."

"Me too," Powell said. "You first."

"Does the name Tito Tavares mean anything to you?"

Powell thought about it, then shook his head.

"Never heard of him. Who is he?"

"A gangbanger who was doing time at San Quentin. Got killed in a knife fight."

"Okay..." Powell said, as if he wasn't sure where the story was going.

"But before that happened, he founded the San Quentin chapter of Nuestra Familia."

Powell leaned into the story. Now he was interested.

"Is that right?" he said.

Tana nodded. "And guess who went to his funeral?"

Powell shrugged.

"His mother?"

"His cousin Hector Vargas," Tana said with a triumphant smile.

"No shit," Powell said. "All in the family, huh?"

"Which pretty much proves that the guys who tried to kill me were part of Hector's crew. Probably sent some other losers to tear my place apart."

Powell nodded, impressed. "Good work, detective."

"Thanks. So is that enough to turn 'em in again?"

Powell shook his head. "It's still circumstantial."

Tana's face fell. "Nothing is ever enough for you guys, right?"

"You want to explain to SFPD why they were after you, or why two of Vargas's thugs were found burned to death with melted guns in their hands?"

"No, I guess not," Tana said in a dejected tone of voice. "So we keep going, huh?"

Powell nodded. "We're closer than you think."

Tana looked at him. "What are you talking about?"

"I want to show you something," Powell said, and opened the manila folder. "Remember those screen grabs from the parking lot?"

"Yeah, we saw the Escalade and it looked like Jimmy LaSalle stole it out of the lot."

"Right," Powell said. "I got more." He spread out the screen grabs on the coffee table. "These are from a camera near the driveway leading in and out of the lot."

"Where'd you get these?"

"My ex-partner took pity on me," Powell said. "Take a look at this one."

Tana peered at the fuzzy image. "That's the Escalade driving out of the lot."

"Right. Take a look at who's behind the wheel."

Tana studied the image more closely.

"It's really fuzzy, but it looks like a woman."

"It is a woman," Powell said.

"Who is she?"

"Carmen Flowers," Powell said.

CHAPTER 55

Tana's eyes went wide. She stared at Powell. "That's Carmen Flowers?"

Powell nodded.

"Are you sure?"

"It's been a long time, but I sat through the trial, saw her on the stand. I'd recognize her anywhere."

"I don't understand..." Tana said with a puzzled expression.

"Neither do I, but it looks like she did more than just perjure herself."

"You think she kidnapped Emma?"

Powell shrugged. "She stole the car, maybe she stole the kid too."

"But where's Jimmy LaSalle? He was there too. We saw him."

Powell shook his head. "No idea. Maybe he didn't want to be caught on camera. Can't imagine Carmen would want to either, but maybe she didn't have any choice."

Tana looked at Powell. "What do you mean?"

"I don't know what I mean," Powell said. "All I do know is there she is, and I don't know why."

"I'm totally blown away," Tana said.

"Not yet you're not."

Tana looked up at him and waited for the rest of it. She could feel her heart beating rapidly. Whatever was coming, she was filled with expectation.

"Remember when we were at Arthur Kim's house?" Powell asked.

"Yeah, sure I do."

"I told you that there was something about the realtor that sounded familiar."

"Yeah, Allison Paine. What about her?"

"I found out why her name rang a bell."

"Okay, why?"

"You won't believe it."

Tana scoffed. "I became a believer the night Helen appeared to me."

"She and Helen Mayfield weren't just lovers," Powell said.

Tana looked at Powell. Her heart was pounding.

"What do you mean, they weren't just lovers?"

Powell paused for a beat, then said, "They were on the Vargas jury together."

CHAPTER 56

TANA'S BREATH CAUGHT IN HER THROAT. SHE SAT BACK, AS if slammed against the sofa by the sheer force of what she had learned. She knew she had to say something, but it was as if the simple task of forming words was, for a moment, beyond her.

"They were on the jury together?" she said finally, as if all she could do was repeat what Powell had just told her. "Helen and Allison?"

Powell nodded.

"She never told me..."

"Probably never told anybody else either."

"I can't believe it," Tana said. "It's like everything keeps turning into something else."

Powell smiled. "Yeah, I know what you mean."

"But why didn't she tell me?"

"Didn't want you to know is my guess."

"Why not? Helen's dead."

Powell gave Tana a sidelong glance. "Is she?" he said.

Tana locked eyes with Powell, then looked away.

"Okay, good point. But still, what does it matter now?"

"Matters to her, Tana. Maybe the fact that Helen passed gave her all the more reason to keep it to herself."

Tana let it sink in, then looked up at Powell. "We have to go talk to her."

"Yeah, we do."

"How'd you find out?"

"I showed my ex-partner the pic I took of the realtor's sign."

"You said there was something about it…"

Powell nodded. "Yeah, there was. He checked it out for me and then I remembered why there was something about her name, her face that rang a bell. I couldn't place it but when I showed it to Daryl, he put it all together." Powell gave a rueful smile. "Guess his memory's better than mine."

Tana shook her head in wonderment.

"I still can't believe it…Helen and Allison…" Then she looked at Powell. "We should go. Maybe we can catch her before she leaves the office."

Powell stood. "Let's roll."

Tana stood, then pointed at the bloodstains on Powell's shirt.

"What about that?"

"What about what?"

"The blood."

Powell looked down at the bloodstains. "Right. The blood."

"You can't show up like that, okay?"

"I don't think we have time for me to go home and change," Powell said.

Tana gave herself a moment to think about it, then said, "I got an idea."

She disappeared into the bedroom, then emerged holding a gray hoodie.

"Try this on," she said, handing to Powell. "Justin left it behind."

"You sure?"

Tana nodded. Powell took off his shirt and pulled on the hoodie. Tana stood back looked at him.

"It's weird..."

"You mean me in a hoodie, or me in Justin's hoodie."

"Yeah, it brings stuff up, you know?"

"You want me to take it off?"

Tana shook her head.

"I want to go."

A double-decker tour bus rumbled past Tana's building as she and Powell came out the door. She glanced at the tourists sitting in the upper deck waving their iPhones, and for some unaccountable reason wondered if any of them had ever photographed a ghost. The bus momentarily blocked her view of the row of cars parked across the street. Which would explain why Tana she failed to notice the man sitting in a black Chevy Tahoe and watching them as they headed down the street to the Bronco. The man waited until the Bronco pulled away from the curb, then started the engine and followed them.

CHAPTER 57

FORTY MINUTES LATER, AFTER FIGHTING RUSH HOUR traffic from one end of the city to the other, Powell pulled into a parking space a few doors down from Paine Properties. He killed the engine, then turned to Tana. The manila envelope containing the screen grabs lay on the seat between them.

"You ready?"

Tana shifted in her seat. "Yeah, sure," she said, a little too casually.

"You sure about that?"

Tana sighed. The truth was she wasn't so sure about it. She was about to confront Allison Paine about why she had failed to reveal that she and Helen were on the jury together. How would she react, Tana wondered. How would anyone react? Nobody liked being outed. Especially by someone who was sticking her nose into a private life that was none of her business. And yet, it was Tana's business. Helen and Emma had made it her business, for better or worse.

"She's not gonna be happy to see us," Tana said.

Powell chuckled. "You need to get used to that if you want to be a detective. Nobody's ever happy to see you."

Tana nodded. "Let's go," she said, and opened and door and climbed out of the Bronco.

Meanwhile, the man in the Tahoe, who had managed to tail Tana and Powell across town without losing them, pulled in across the street from the real estate office. He lit a cigarette and watched them walk toward the office.

The receptionist, who was still on duty and probably wanted to go home, looked up at Tana and Powell as they walked in the door.

"Hi, welcome to Paine Properties," she said, flashing a standard front-desk smile. "Can I help you?"

"We'd like to see Allison Paine," Tana said, "if she's still in the office."

"Do you have an appointment?"

Tana shook her head and gave an apologetic smile. "Sorry."

"Your name?"

"Tell her it's Tana Grant. She'll know."

The receptionist picked up the phone. "Hi Allison, Tana Grant is here to see you." She listened for a moment, then said, "Sure, no problem." She ended the call and looked up at Tana and Powell. "She'll be right out."

"Thanks," Tana said.

A moment later, Paine emerged from a back office. She was wearing a suit and a surprised look on her face.

"Hi Tana," she said. "Didn't expect to see you again so soon."

"Hi, sorry to bother you," Tana said.

Paine turned to Powell. "I see you brought reinforcements this time," she said. "Who's your friend?"

"Oh, sorry," Tana said. "This is Bud Powell. He's helping me out with something."

"Hi, Bud, I'm Allison Paine," she said, extending her hand.

"Pleasure," Powell said, shaking hands with her.

"So what's up?" Paine said, turning back to Tana.

"Can we talk in private?" Tana said, throwing a glance at the receptionist.

"Sure, right this way."

Paine led them back to the same conference room where Tana and Paine had met the first time around. Tana wondered if the ghosts of Helen and Emma would still be there.

Paine closed the door, then turned to Tana and Powell. "Have a seat," she said. "Anywhere you like."

They sat down, then Paine turned to Tana. "So what can I do for you?" she said. "You're not looking for a house, are you?"

Her eyes darted from Tana to Powell, and Tana wondered if perhaps Paine thought they were some kind of couple.

Tana paused, glanced at Powell, then jumped in headfirst. "Why didn't you tell me you were on the jury with Helen?"

Paine's face reddened and took on a shocked expression. Tana regretted ambushing her, but there was no other way around it.

Paine took a deep breath, then slowly exhaled. "Wow. Never saw that one coming," she said.

"Sorry," Tana said.

"How'd you find out?"

"Doesn't matter," Bud said. "We found out, that's all."

Paine looked at Bud. "You look like a cop."

"Ex-cop."

"I guess that's how you found out, huh?" Paine said.

Powell nodded.

"Why didn't you tell me?" Tana said.

Paine's eye's flashed with anger. "Maybe because it was none of your business. You ever think of that?"

Tana lowered her eyes and said nothing.

"You just barge into people's lives, invade their privacy—"

"It's not like that," Tana said.

"Oh, no? How is it, Tana? You want to know all about me and Helen, but you still haven't told me why."

"I'll tell you why," Powell said.

Tana shot Powell a warning glance. She had used the tenth anniversary of Emma's abduction as the cover story for her investigation, and now Powell was about to reveal the truth.

"We're trying to find out what happened to Emma," he said.

Paine looked at Powell, a stunned expression on her face. "Emma? All these years later?"

Powell nodded. "Better late than never."

Paine's face softened. She gave a sad smile.

"She was such a sweet child." She looked up at Tana and Powell. "You would've loved her."

"I'm sure we would have," Powell said.

"But the police never found her. Why do you think you can find her?"

"I can't go into detail," Powell said, "but we're working some new leads."

"Well, I hope you find her," Paine said.

"Could you tell us about when you and Helen were on the jury?" Tana said.

"We didn't want anybody to know," Paine said. "We were already together by then, and we thought if they found out they might throw us off the jury or arrest us or something, so we kept it a secret."

What was Helen like as a juror?"

"I thought she was great. Better than me, probably. She took it seriously. Not everybody was like that. Some of the other jurors just wanted to get it over with. Not Helen. She wanted to make sure they got it right."

"What was it like when the witness recanted?"

"It was a huge shock. None of us saw it coming. I don't think the D.A. saw it coming either."

"The rumor was she took a bribe to recant."

"Yeah, I know, but I'm not sure about that."

"Why?"

"I think maybe she was afraid to testify against Vargas. Terrified of facing him in court when she took the stand. I mean, she would've had to gone into witness protection or something after that. So maybe it wasn't about money. Maybe she was just scared."

"How did Helen react?"

"I think she felt betrayed. She was really angry with Flowers. She was convinced that Vargas was guilty and wanted Flowers to prove it. And when she didn't, Helen felt like Carmen had stabbed us all in the back."

"How'd the jury take it?"

"Well, the D.A.'s case had fallen apart, so by the time we started deliberating it was like, okay can we go home now? We took a vote, and everybody voted to acquit Vargas. Everybody except Helen, that is."

"You voted to acquit?"

Paine lowered her eyes. The room fell silent. Tana and Powell traded glances.

"Yes," Paine said quietly, breaking the silence.

"How did Helen react?" Tana said.

Paine looked up at her with a bitter smile. "How do you think she reacted? We had a big fight about it afterwards. I told her that without the eyewitness testimony we didn't have the evidence to convict. Her attitude was to hell with the evidence, I know he's guilty." Paine shrugged. "Maybe she was right, I don't know. It's just that, given what happened, I wish she'd gone along with the rest of the jury. Maybe then she wouldn't have lost her daughter and Helen wouldn't have died without ever seeing her again."

Powell opened the manila envelope and took out a screen grab. He pushed across the table to Paine.

"Is that Carmen Flowers?"

Paine studied the image, then nodded. "It's pretty fuzzy, but yeah, that's her." She looked up at Tana and Powell. "You know, it's the weirdest thing..."

Tana and Powell traded glances.

"What?" Tana said.

"She's a checker at the market where I buy groceries."

Tana and Powell exchanged shocked glances, then leaned in, stunned by the news.

"Carmen Flowers?" Tana said.

"Yeah, funny, huh? After all this time."

"How did you know it was her?" Powell said.

"I was in her line, and she was wearing a name tag that said 'Carmen,' but I would've recognized her anyway."

"After all this time?" Powell said.

Paine shrugged. "Some people you never forget. It was because of her that Helen hung the jury and Emma got kidnapped."

"You ever talk to her?"

"You mean like about the case?"

Tana nodded. Paine shook her head.

"What's the name of the market?"

"It's called Mondelo's Market. They're open twenty-four hours. She must work nights because that's when I saw her. I'll jot it down for you," Paine reached for a notepad, then scribbled a name. She tore off the note and handed it to Tana.

"Thanks, Tana said.

"Sure, no problem."

Tana paused, then said, "I'm sorry, Allison..."

"About what? Outing me and Helen?"

"Yeah, I guess so."

Paine smiled sadly. "It's okay. I guess it doesn't matter much now that she's gone." Paine looked out the window, staring into the dark as if there was something there. And maybe there was. "Not sure what does matter anymore."

Tana and Powell traded glances, then Powell said, "Thanks for your time. I know this wasn't easy."

Paine turned away from the window and looked at Bud. "You ever lose anybody you loved, Bud?"

Tana thought she saw Powell flinch.

"Yeah, I have."

"Then you know all about what's easy and what's not."

Powell nodded. "Yeah, I do."

Paine pushed back her chair and stood. "I hope you find out what happened to that sweet little girl," she said warmly. Then her voice turned cold. "But don't ever come back here. I went through it all once, and I don't need to do it again."

CHAPTER 58

POWELL PULLED INTO A PARKING SPACE IN FRONT OF AN all-night burger stand on Lakeshore called *Fat's*. Tables out front, a takeout window lit up like a beacon. Tana looked out at the sign, which spelled out the name in fat neon letters, then turned to Powell.

"What's up with the name?"

Powell shrugged. "I guess they want you to know what you're in for," he said. He looked at Tana. "You hungry?"

"Starved."

They climbed out of the Bronco and went inside. It was late and the place was filled with a crowd that was hooked on fast food grease. Tana and Powell placed their orders, then grabbed a table by the window. A pop tune rocking the sound-track caught Tana's ear and made her think of Justin. What was it about songs that they stuck with you even after the person who shared them with you was gone? But that was another life, Tana told herself. She had a new life now. Trouble was, she had no idea how long it would last.

"So what do we do now?" Tana said.

Powell looked at her. "We wait for our orders."

"I mean after we're done eating."

"Don't you have to go to work tomorrow?"

Tana shook her head. "I'm gonna call in sick."

"Can't stop now, can you?" Powell said.

Tana shrugged. "I guess not. Can you?"

Powell gave a rueful smile. "Emma wouldn't let us even if we wanted to."

Tana fell silent. She looked at Powell, then looked away.

"Something on your mind?" Powell said.

Tana paused, then looked up at him. "I feel bad about what happened with Allison Paine."

"Which part?"

"I don't know, it was like we ambushed her."

"Yeah, we did."

"Is that okay?"

"We got a line on Carmen Flowers," Powell said. "That's what matters."

"What about her feelings?"

"Collateral damage," Powell said.

"That's it? You just blow it off?"

Powell pulled out his car keys and slammed them on the table, startling Tana.

"You want to go back and apologize? I'll tell 'em to keep your burger warm. Then again, I might just eat it myself. I'm pretty hungry."

Tana frowned. A male server with a soul patch and his hair in a bun came up to the table with their orders.

"Two Fats with cheese and fries?" he said as he set their plates on the table.

"Thanks," Powell said.

"You guys need anything else?" the server said.

"We're good," Powell said.

But Tana wasn't good. "You know what?" she said, staring

hard at Powell. "I think I'll take mine to go." She looked up at the server. "You mind?"

The server's eyes darted from Tana to Powell and back again, as if he had picked on the vibe between them.

"No problem," the server said as he picked up Tana's burger and fries and headed back to the kitchen.

Powell's face hardened. "What the hell do you think you're doing?"

"What it's look like?"

"Grow up, Tana."

"Why? So I can be like you?"

"Yeah, you might learn something."

"I think I already have."

The server returned and handed Tana a bag containing her burger and fries. "Here you go."

"Thanks," she said, and walked outside.

There was a chill in the air, and as she pulled her coat tightly around her, Tana wondered if she had acted on impulse, without thinking it through. But there was no way she was going to walk back inside just because she was cold. She sat down at one of the outdoor tables and reached into the bag and took out her burger. She bit into it and watched as people pulled up, parked their cars, and went inside. Some of them gave her a sidelong glance, as if they were wondering what a reasonably attractive young woman was doing eating by herself at an outdoor table on a cold night.

Then she heard a voice she knew say, "Mind if I join you?"

She looked up and Powell standing by the table with a bag of burgers and fries.

"No, I don't mind," she said.

"Great," Powell said, and sat down beside her. He zipped up his jacket and looked around. "Kinda cold out here, huh?"

Tana nodded.

"We could go back inside," Powell said.

"That would be weird."

"You want to eat in the Bronco? I can turn the heat on."

Tana gave a grateful smile.

"Yeah, that would be great," she said as she popped her burger back into the bag.

They stood, and then Powell turned to her. He hesitated for a moment, then said, "Look, about what happened in there—"

"It's okay, don't worry about it. I'm sorry I walked out on you."

"The way I am," Powell said, "it just comes with the territory of the world I lived in, you know what I'm saying?"

Tana nodded. "Yeah, I understand."

"You're a woman, you got a softer touch."

Tana smiled. "So I guess that makes us a good team, huh?"

"Yeah, I guess so."

"Great. So can we eat now? I'm freezing my ass off out here."

Just then a red Corvette pulled into the lot and parked. Tana noticed that the front license plate holder read "Bowlers Have Bigger Balls." The driver's door opened and a guy in his early fifties with thinning blond hair and a middle-aged paunch got out of the car. He glanced at Tana and Powell and his face lit up with surprise.

"Hey, Bud!" he called out.

Powell looked up at him. The expression on his face told Tana that he was less than pleased to see him.

"Hey, Herb," he said.

Herb stepped over to Powell and stuck out his hand. "I'm surprised to see you, buddy." He glanced at Tana. "Where you been keeping yourself? The guys are wondering what happened to you."

"I been kinda busy, Herb. You know how it goes."

Herb threw Tana a leering smile. "Yeah, I can tell. Who's your friend?"

"Tana," Tana said.

"Pleasure, Tana," Herb said. He turned to Powell. "You ought to bring her by the bowling alley, Bud. The guys'd love to meet her."

"Sure, no problem," Powell said. He stood abruptly, then he picked up his bag of burger and fries and turned to Tana. "You ready?"

"Yeah, sure."

"Good to see you, Herb. Say hi to Linda."

"Yeah, well, good to see you too, Bud." He glanced at Tana with a leering smile. "I guess you guys are in kind of a hurry, huh?"

"Just cold out here, you know?" Tana said.

"Yeah, sure. Stay warm now."

Powell nodded, then and he and Tana walked to the Bronco.

"Who was that?" Tana said after they got in the car.

"Guy from the league."

"Guess you don't like him much, huh? Or maybe you just didn't like him seeing us together."

Powell paused to look out the window, then said, "He's got a big mouth. I just didn't want him getting the wrong idea, is all."

"Is that what we are, Bud?" Tana said with a teasing smile. "A wrong idea?"

Powell turned to her, and their eyes met. Tana held his gaze until he looked away. She realized suddenly that it bothered her that Powell had referred to them being seen together as somehow wrong. But did that mean she thought it was right?

CHAPTER 59

THE QUESTION LINGERED IN TANA'S MIND AS THEY DROVE to Mondelo's Market. But she sensed that Powell didn't want to talk about it, and so kept her thoughts to herself. And if he had wanted to talk about it, what would she say? Tana had no idea, and so they drove until Powell pulled into the lot. He chose a spot that gave him a clear view of the entrance, including the security guard standing by the door. The lot was crowded with cars, which explained why Tana failed to notice the black Chevy Tahoe that had tailed them throughout the night.

That was two hours ago. Now it was after nine, but the market was bustling with customers who liked to shop for groceries after dark. Neither Powell nor Tana knew whether Carmen Flowers still worked there, which days she worked, or which shift. But Allison Paine had seen her at night, and so they decided to start there. Now all they could do was wait.

Tana watched as shoppers pushed carts filled with groceries out to their cars. She often put off grocery shopping until the cupboards were bare, then found herself rolling a shopping cart down the aisles at midnight at the Safeway on Market Street, which was open 24 hours.

She spotted a little girl riding in a cart and wondered if

Helen let Emma ride in the cart when they went shopping. Then she remembered how she would beg her mother to let her ride in the cart when they went to the supermarket back in Billings. Kids were all the same, Tana thought, but some, like Emma, never got to be more than just kids.

But Tana was tired of watching and waiting. Tired of being cold. And tired of the greasy, nauseating smell of burgers and fries that filled the Bronco hours after they finished eating.

"This is seriously boring, Bud. How long are we supposed to wait?"

"All night if we have to. It's called a stakeout."

Tana made a face. "All night? Are you kidding me?"

Powell looked at her. "You want to call it?"

Tana sighed. "I want my life back."

"You want your life back?" Powell reached over and opened the door, then let it swing wide. "Go ahead. Nobody's stopping you, least of all me."

Tana locked eyes with Powell, then pulled the door shut. "You sound like my dad."

"That bad, huh?"

Tana smiled.

"It's just us, like you said," Powell said.

"Yeah, I know. I guess sometimes it scares me."

"Yeah, me too."

Suddenly, the Bronco's windshield began to glow. The glow grew brighter and brighter until the light filled the Bronco. Tana shivered as the fear ran through her. And yet, in a way, she knew what was coming. She had seen it before. She stared at the windshield, which now had become a screen for what could have been a movie, a video or even a hallucination.

Helen and Emma were walking hand in hand down a street in San Francisco, smiling as they passed shops and restaurants and paused to look in the windows. The sight of them happy together brought tears to Tana's eyes.

Tana nudged Powell.

"Bud," she whispered, as if afraid that Helen or Emma might hear her.

She glanced at him and saw that he was watching in rapt attention. They watched as Helen and Emma walked into a children's store that was filled with books, toys and clothing. Emma wanted to play with the toys, but Helen wanted her to look at the clothes. They walked hand in hand through the store, checking out dresses, tops, leggings, bodysuits, jackets. Tana wondered if they were there to buy an outfit for a special occasion. She and Powell watched as Helen would hold up an outfit, and Emma would either nod or shake her head as the smiling salesgirl looked on.

Helen paused to speak to the salesgirl about a pink top and gray leggings with pink stripes, and Tana suddenly remembered that she had seen that outfit before. Then Emma turned and looked at the camera. Tana's breath caught in her throat. She reached for Powell, and he took her hand.

"She's looking at us..." she said.

Powell nodded. "Yes, I know."

Then Emma said, "Find me," and Tana and Powell heard her voice for the first time.

The image faded out and the screen once again became a windshield looking out on a crowded grocery store parking lot late at night.

Tana and Powell looked from one to the other, but for the moment it seemed as if neither one of them could find the words to break the silence.

Then Tana said, "Sorry, I wasn't expecting that."

"Me neither," Powell said, his voice filled with awe.

"She spoke to us, Bud...we heard her voice. And seeing

them together, happy...the way she looked at us..." Her voice trailed off.

Powell pulled Tana into his arms and held her close as the tears ran down her cheeks. Then she wiped her eyes and looked up at him.

"That was the day before she was kidnapped. They were shopping for an outfit for picture day at the daycare center."

Powell looked at her. "How do you know?"

"That's what Emma was wearing when I saw her for the first time, the night that Helen appeared, and I saw them kidnap her. There was a big sign at the daycare center that said 'Picture Day.'"

"That's what she wearing the night she appeared in your apartment."

Tana nodded. "It's what she'll be wearing when we find her." She looked up at Powell. "She spoke to us, Bud. Why? Why now?"

Powell shrugged his shoulders. "Maybe she's tired of waiting to be found."

Tana sighed. "You never told me that was gonna happen on a stakeout."

Powell grinned.

Tana pulled out the screen grab of Carmen Flowers at the wheel of the SUV.

"She looks so young," Tana said, staring at the image of an attractive brunette who looked good even in a fuzzy security camera screen grab.

"She *was* young," Powell said.

"I wonder what she looks like now."

"Probably still looks like herself, just ten years older. Then again, some people change so much you can't recognize 'em."

"What about you?"

Powell looked at her.

"Do you look the same, just ten years older?" Tana said.

Powell shrugged. "Hell, I don't know. I always thought I was born old."

"Is that because you were a cop?"

"Maybe. The job takes the life out of you."

"So why do it?"

"It pulls you in, the rush of it, you can't let go. Then before you know it's twenty years later and you're out of a job."

"Is that what happened to you?"

"It's what happens to most cops," Powell said. He looked at Tana. "What's with all the questions?"

Tana shrugged. "I don't know, just killing time, I guess."

"Ever think you'd be killing time with an ex-cop who's old enough to be your father?"

Tana smiled.

"Never thought I'd be chasing ghosts with a guy who's old enough to be my dad."

Powell nodded. "Yeah, I guess we're a hell of a mismatch, huh?"

Tana looked out at the sky, as if expecting Emma to appear among the stars, then turned to Powell. "It's not a mismatch, it's just us," she said. "You and me. No matter what happens the rest of our lives, even if we never see each other again after this is all over, it'll always be just you and me. You know what I mean?"

Powell looked at her and their eyes met. Then Tana leaned across the seat and kissed him on the cheek.

He reacted with surprise. "What was that for?"

Tana smiled. "Does a girl need a reason?"

Powell offered a rueful smile. "Not at my age."

CHAPTER 60

"I WONDER IF EMMA IS HERE WITH US, WATCHING AND waiting."

Powell looked at her and waited for the rest of it.

"We can't see her right now," Tana continued, "because she only lets us see her when she wants to."

"Like when we saw her shopping with her mom, right?" Powell said.

Tana nodded. "I think maybe she's always with us." She looked at Powell. "I wonder if when we find her, we won't ever see her again after that."

"Will you miss her?" Powell said.

"Will I miss seeing a ghost? I was so scared at first when I saw her..."

"And now?"

"I'm not scared anymore..."

Just then a brunette in her late forties walked out of the cigarette. She exchanged smiles with the security guard, then stopped to light a cigarette. The flame lit up the years in her face.

"Look," Tana said, nudging Powell. "Is that her?"

Powell looked at the brunette. "Sure as hell looks like her.

But let's make sure." He climbed out of the Bronco. "Hey! Carmen!" he called out to the brunette.

The brunette turned in Powell's direction, her eyes searching for the face in the crowd that had called her name.

Powell looked back at Tana. "That's her, let's go."

Tana climbed out of the Bronco and followed Powell as he headed across the lot toward Carmen.

Suddenly, the Tahoe's headlights came on. The Tahoe that Bud and Tana had failed to notice. A door flew open and a big man wearing jeans and a hoodie jumped out of the vehicle and ran over to Carmen. He grabbed her and dragged her toward the SUV. She began kicking and screaming as she tried to fight him off.

"Hey!" Powell shouted, running now toward Carmen and her abductor.

"Let go of her!"

The man looked up at Powell, saw him coming, then shoved Carmen into the back seat and jumped in after her. The door slammed and the Tahoe roared out of the lot.

Powell stopped to catch his breath. Tana caught up to him. They traded stunned glances.

"He took her!" Tana said, stunned by Carmen's abduction. "Who was that?"

Powell ignored the question.

"Let's go," he said, and headed back to the Bronco.

"Where?" Tana said, bewildered, rushing to keep up with him.

"After them."

CHAPTER 61

Tana and Powell jumped into the Bronco.

"Grab a pic of the plate!" he shouted.

"What?"

"Now! Do it!"

"Okay, okay!" Tana said, pulling out her phone.

Powell turned the ignition key and when the engine fired, he reversed out of the parking space at speed, pitching Tana toward the windshield. She threw up her arms to protect herself and the phone fell out of her hands

"Shit!" she muttered, fumbling for the phone.

Powell glanced at her. His face creased with impatience. "Hurry up!"

"Wait a minute! I dropped my phone!"

"Find it!"

He threw the truck in Drive, then headed for the exit before Tana had a chance to close her door. It swung wide as Powell burned rubber out of the lot. Tana grabbed her phone, then leaned out and pulled the door closed, narrowly missing a woman in a Honda minivan who was turning into the lot.

"Look out!" Tana shouted.

"Shut up! You get the pics?"

"It's too dark out!"

"Just do it! Before we lose 'em!"

Tana held up the phone and snapped a few pics of the Tahoe racing away from them. Then she remembered to buckle her seat belt. She glanced at Powell. His eyes were on the Tahoe ahead of them, and his face was set.

"I don't understand," she said. "What the fuck just happened?"

"You saw what the fuck just happened."

"Yeah, no shit. But why?"

"I don't know why. But we're gonna find out."

"What's gonna happen then?"

Powell reached across Tana and opened the glove, revealing the Glock. The sight of it made her catch her breath. Then Powell closed the glove.

"We'll have a polite conversation about why it's not nice to kidnap people," he said.

"Maybe we should call the police," Tana said, fear beginning to stir inside her.

"The guard out front probably called 'em."

"Should we let them handle it?"

Powell gave Tana a sidelong glance. "You scared?"

Tana nodded.

"Yeah, I am."

"Good. It'll keep you on your toes."

The Tahoe drove west on Fell Street. Powell figured they were heading toward Oak Street, which would take them to Octavia, and from there they could jump on the Central Freeway. The traffic was heavy with rush-hour commuters and Powell had to weave in and out of the lanes to keep the Tahoe in sight. His tactics didn't exactly endear him to his fellow drivers, who responded by honking their horns and flipping him off.

But the fact was he and Tana had much more at stake than courteous driving or getting home on time.

As Powell expected, the Tahoe jumped on the Central Freeway, then merged into the left lanes and took the Interstate 80 exit toward Oakland.

"Where they going? Oakland?" Tana said.

Powell shrugged. "Hard to tell. East Bay for sure. That's all we know so far."

Tana could see the Tahoe up ahead as they rolled across the Bay Bridge, sailing through a sea of headlights and taillights. They were driving fast through the dark, but she wasn't sure if that was because they knew that she and Powell were tailing them, or if they were just in a hurry to reach their destination.

"Do you think they know we're following them?"

"They saw me running toward 'em when they grabbed Carmen. Just not sure if they saw us pull out after 'em. Carmen's probably screaming her head off right about now, which can make it hard to pay attention. We just can't lose sight of 'em, no matter what they do."

Tana gave an ironic smile. "You know what's funny?"

"Not until you tell me."

"We're following them, but what if they were following us?"

Powell glanced at her, waited for the rest of it.

"I mean, it's like they were waiting for Carmen, just like we were."

"Okay, I'll bite," Powell said. "Why were they following us?"

"Because they didn't know where Carmen was and needed us to lead them to her."

Powell nodded like he was impressed. "That's pretty good, detective. Might even be true."

"So why did they want to find her?"

"No good reason I can think of. That's why we need to get to her before they do."

Tana screwed up her face in dismay. "Excuse me? They've already got her, Bud."

Powell flashed a sly smile. "Didn't say it was gonna be easy, did I?"

Tana turned around and looked through the back window. But all she saw were headlights spearing the dark. Powell glanced at her.

"What, you see something?"

"Just worried about getting stopped for speeding or something."

Powell glanced in the rear-view. "We don't have time to get stopped," he said. "But if we do maybe you can sweet-talk him, show him a little skin, get us off the hook."

Tana's eyes narrowed. "I'm so sure," she deadpanned.

Powell took his eyes off the road for a moment, glanced at Tana and grinned.

And when he looked back the Tahoe was gone.

CHAPTER 62

"Shit!" Powell muttered.

Tana stiffened, looked at Powell. His face was hard and he was leaning forward, pushing against the seat belt, his eyes darting from car to car, as if he was looking for something. Or someone.

"What's wrong?"

"We lost 'em."

"What?" Tana said, scanning the bridge traffic for a sign of the Tahoe. "When?"

"Just now."

"You think they saw us following them?"

"Maybe."

"So what do we do now?" Tana said as a feeling of helplessness washed over her.

Powell glanced at her. "You got the plate, right?"

"I think so."

"You think so?" Powell said with a trace of annoyance.

"It's dark and it all happened so fast—"

"What is it?" Powell said, cutting her off.

Tana fumbled with her phone, then tapped the photo of the Tahoe's license plate.

"Hold it up so I can see it," Powell said, his eyes darting from the phone to the road.

Tana held up the phone. Powell glanced at the image.

"Can you make it bigger?" he said.

"Sure, no problem," Tana said, using her thumb and fore-finger to enlarge the image. "Better?"

"Too blurry, I can't make it out," Powell said, shaking his head. "Go back."

Tana shrank the image back to its original size. Powell checked his side mirror for oncoming traffic, then jumped into the fast lane, cutting off a BMW. Then he put the hammer down. Tana could feel the Bronco picking up speed as they raced across the bridge. It was as if he drove faster, he could catch up with the Tahoe, which had vanished out of sight.

"How's this?" she said holding up the phone.

Powell glanced at the image. "Hard to tell. Can you make it out?"

"Yeah, I think so."

"Okay, here's what we're gonna do."

He handed Tana his cellphone and gave her a number to call.

"It's ringing," she said, handing him the phone.

"Hey Daryl, it's me," Powell said when Mayweather picked up. "Yeah, I know what time it is. But I need a favor." Powell listened for a moment, then said, "I know what you said. Okay, yeah, last time, no problem." He paused to listen, then said, "No big deal, I just need you to run a plate for me." He paused to listen as his face tightened with frustration. "Yeah, I know you're not the fucking DMV, Daryl." He glanced at Tana. "Read me the number."

Tana looked down at the phone and read the number out loud, then Powell repeated it to Mayweather.

"Call me back when you've got it," Powell said, and ended the call.

"Who was that?" Tana said.

"My ex-partner. Daryl Mayweather."

"Didn't sound like he wanted to help you."

"Yeah, I know. He gives me a hard time because I won't act retired." Powell smiled. "Thinks I ought to spend more time bowling and less time playing detective."

"Maybe you will once this is all over."

Powell nodded. "Yeah, maybe I will. Guys must be wondering what happened to me."

"The Bowling Stones, right?"

Powell gave a sheepish smile. "Corny, right?"

"I don't know, I think it's kinda cute."

They were across the bridge, and into the flatlands, rolling past the cranes and container yards at the Port of Oakland when Mayweather called back.

"You're kidding," Powell said.

"You know her?" Mayweather said.

"Let's just say I caught her act." Powell paused. "Thanks, partner. I owe you one." He grinned. "Okay, maybe more than one." He ended the call and glanced at Tana. "We got a make on the plate," he said.

"Great. Who is it?"

"A daughter of the revolution," Powell said.

Huh?" Tana said, a puzzled look on her face.

CHAPTER 63

POWELL HEADED EAST FROM THE BAY BRIDGE TO Interstate 880, also known as the Nimitz Freeway, then drove south through Fruitvale and took the High Street exit to International Boulevard.

Tana rolled down the window. The smell of enchiladas from a taco truck filled the Bronco, then faded away.

"Where are we?" she said as the Bronco rolled past corner bars, strip joints, auto repair shops, Mexican restaurants, and nail salons.

"East Oakland, Powell said. "The heart of the shooting galleries."

Tana turned to Powell. "Shooting galleries?" she said, a puzzled expression on her face.

"That's what a cop I used to know called the high crime neighborhoods south of the interstate. He even gave 'em nicknames. Killing Fields, Murder Dubs, Ghost Town."

Tana shuddered. "That's weird."

Powell shrugged. "Which part?" he said. "Killing people or making jokes about it?"

Tana locked eyes with Powell, then looked away. What did she know about what it was like to work Oakland's meanest streets? She knew nothing, and yet here she was, working for the dead on a case that could mean her life. What if it did kill her, she wondered. Would Helen and Emma be there to greet her when she reached the other side? And what about her obituary? What would it say? She imagined the lede: 'Montana Grant, 26, wrote about the dead, who never wrote back. Until they did.'

"We're almost there," Powell said, jolting Tana out of her thoughts.

Tana peered out the window as they passed a string of tattered storefronts that had seen better days. It was a world that was far from her own, and if it wasn't for Emma Mayfield, she never would've found herself there, a stranger in ever-stranger territory.

Then she noticed the sign for a Latin club called Bahia. There was a garage behind the club that was surrounded with a chain link fence topped with barbed wire.

"I wonder if the Tahoe's in the garage," Tana said, nodding at the garage.

"Maybe. But the question is, where's Carmen?"

"I guess we're gonna find out, huh?" Tana said.

Powell looked at her and their eyes met. "You ready to find out?"

"Sure, I do this kind of stuff all the time," Tana said with a casual shrug.

Powell smiled. "Good to know, 'cause here we go."

Bahia's lights were on and the doorman out front was standing next to a life-size cutout of a buxom middle-age woman with long black hair wearing ammo belts and pistols.

"Is that her?"

"Yeah, that's her," Powell said, following Tana's line of sight.

Following Mayweather's call, Powell had explained that

the Tahoe was registered to a middle-age woman named Adelita Santos, a singer who performed at an East Oakland Latin club called Bahia. He also braced Tana on his visit to the club and his confrontation with Hector Vargas who, it turned out, was Adelita's son. Why Adelita would have put herself in legal jeopardy by allowing her vehicle to be used in a kidnapping puzzled Tana as much as it did Powell. Then again, maybe the fact that she was Hector's mother had something to do with it.

"What's up with the guns and stuff?"

"It's part of her act."

"Does she like shoot people, or something?"

Powell said nothing, but the look in his eyes told Tana that anything was possible.

The doorman opened the doors and the sounds of a live band playing mariachi music spilled out into the street. Tana remembered the night she and Justin went dancing at a Latin club in the Mission. She wasn't much of a salsa dancer, but she loved the music and hearing it live was a thrill. Hearing it again now reminded her of what she'd lost. How much more was she going to lose?

Powell pulled over and parked the Bronco. Then he reached across Tana, opened the glove, and took out the Glock. Tana drew back at the sight of the gun.

Powell looked at her. "You okay?"

"Yeah, sure."

"You ever shoot a gun?"

"Just shotguns when me and my dad went hunting."

Powell removed the magazine, then handed the gun to Tana, butt first.

"Go ahead, get the feel of it," he said.

Tana hesitated for a moment, then took the Glock. The gun scared her and yet she felt a thrill run through her as she held it.

"Will you teach me how to use it?" Tana said, surprising herself.

"Be glad to...if we get out of this alive."

Powell took the gun out of her hands and popped in the magazine. Then he reached behind his back, shoved the gun in his waistband and pulled his coat down over it. Then he opened the door and they climbed out of the Bronco.

CHAPTER 64

THE STOCKY MEXICAN DOORMAN WEARING A BURGUNDY tuxedo, wingtips and a mustache smiled at Tana and Powell as they approached the entrance to Bahia.

"Welcome to Bahia, señor y señorita." He nodded at the cutout by the door. "La Soldadera," he said approvingly. "A show you will never forget." He bowed and extended his arm to usher them into the club.

"Thanks," Tana said with a smile.

She suddenly felt as if she was Powell's date and took his arm. She was cool with the older man/younger woman thing, even if it was just an act. But what if it wasn't an act? What if they were becoming a couple, and she was the last to know?

The security guard posted by the door gave Powell a sidelong glance as they walked into the club, as if he'd seen him before, and wasn't happy to see him again. Tana looked up at Powell, and his expression seemed to return the favor.

"Let's grab a couple of stools at the bar," Powell said. "Cool with you?"

"Yeah, sure."

"The security guard looked like he wasn't happy to see you," Tana said as they walked to the bar.

"He's not."

"Because of what happened the last time you were here?"

Powell nodded. What's going to happen this time, Tana wondered as they slid onto a pair of stools at the end of the bar and ordered drinks. She looked around while they waited for the bartender to fill their orders. Cocktail tables filled with fans waiting for the show to start dotted the room. Cute young barmaids in tank tops and cleavage balanced trays filled with drinks as they made their way through the room. Tana could hear the roar of conversation, the tinkle of glasses. There was a Latin singer on the sound system, whom she assumed was Adelita Santos, aka La Soldadera, the woman whose cutout graced the entrance.

Just then, a spotlight lit up the stage, and the crowd erupted in cheers, wolf whistles and applause. A group of musicians, presumably Vargas's band, emerged from the wings and took the stage. An MC in a sparkly dinner jacket followed them onto the stage and grabbed the microphone.

"Ladies and gentlemen, welcome to Bahia. Tonight, our very special guest, La Soldadera, will be out very soon. Thank you for your patience."

There was another round of applause, then the band started playing.

"Great music, huh?" Tana said, her body moving to the salsa beat.

She watched as couples got up from their tables, moved into each other's arms and began to dance.

"Yeah, great music," Powell said, his voice flat, as if he hadn't heard a note of it.

Tana looked up at him and saw that his face had hardened, and he was staring at something or someone across the room. She followed his line of sight and saw Hector Vargas and Jimmy LaSalle and their dates sitting at a table near the stage.

"Hector's here," she said.

"Yeah, Hector's here," Powell said. "I guess it's friends and family night."

Tana watched as Vargas turned to catch a barmaid's eye, and as he did so, he saw Tana and Powell. He scowled, then nudged LaSalle. He turned around, saw Tana and Powell, then shrugged, as if to say, so what? Forget it, enjoy the show. But Vargas wasn't ready to forget it. Or let it go. He pushed back his chair and stood. LaSalle tried to stop him, but Hector shook him off and headed toward the bar.

"Now what?" Tana said.

"We're about to find out."

Vargas came up to Tana and Powell. She could smell the liquor on his breath and figured he'd had enough to start a fight.

"What the fuck you doin' here?" Vargas said, scowling at Tana and Powell.

"Hey, be polite, Hector," Powell said. "Show some class." He nodded at Tana. "There's a lady present."

"Fuck you and your lady," Vargas said, his eyes darting from Tana to Powell. "Like I said, what the fuck you doin' here?"

"We came to see your mom, Hector. We heard she's pretty good." Powell turned to Tana. "Isn't that right?"

"Yeah, that's right," Tana said.

Vargas glanced at Tana and gave a contemptuous laugh.

"Shut the bitch up!" he said to Powell, nodding at Tana.

Tana stiffened. "What did you say?" she said, glaring at Vargas.

"You heard me, bitch," Vargas said.

Tana had had enough. "Yeah, I heard you," she said. Then she suddenly reached under Powell's coat, pulled out the Glock and pointed it at Vargas. "You hear this, motherfucker?"

Vargas froze. His face turned a whiter shade of pale. Tana

could see the beads of sweat popping up on his skin as he stared down the barrel of a 9mm semiautomatic, which, at point blank range, would have taken a significant chunk of his head off.

A woman sitting at the bar saw the gun and screamed. Others abandoned their barstools as they scattered towards the exit.

Powell's face twisted with alarm. He stared at Tana in disbelief. "Jesus, Tana, what the fuck!"

Just then, the MC bounded across the stage and grabbed the microphone. "Señores y señoritas, La Soldadera!" he exclaimed.

The crowd roared as Adelita Santos emerged from the wings. She wore ammo belts and pistols on her hips. The audience cheered as she swaggered across the stage. She gave a warm smile, then moved to the microphone and began singing a sassy, upbeat salsa number.

But just then, as Powell wrestled the Glock out of Tana's hands, the gun went off. A round went wild and hit a chandelier, sending it crashing onto a cocktail table and the unlucky couple who happened to be sitting there. Panic spread through the crowd. Patrons screamed and trampled each other as they ran for cover.

Onstage, the band abandoned their instruments and ran at the sound of the gunshot, exiting stage right and stage left. But Adelita remained at center stage. She looked across the room, ignoring the chaos in front her, and saw the gun. Her face hardened. Apparently concluding that her son was in danger, she pulled her guns and began shooting in Tana and Powell's direction. Tana looked up at her. Now she understood what Powell meant when he called her a daughter of the revolution. That was what she looked like as she stood onstage, legs apart, blazing away, guns in both hands. But what cause was she fighting for, Tana wondered. Her killer of a son? She could hear the bullets whistling past her, shattering glasses and bottles in the bar, and slicing into the walls, turning chunks of plaster into shrapnel that ricocheted across the room.

"Get down!" Powell yelled, pushing her down out of the line of fire.

"Go!" he said, grabbing her arm and pulling her toward the door. 'Go!"

Tana looked back toward the stage and saw Jimmy LaSalle jump up and wave his arms, as if he was trying to stop the shooting. But all he did was turn himself into a target. He took two rounds and crumpled in front of the stage. So much for attorney-client privilege, Tana thought.

The security guard, having heard the gunfire, ran into the club just in time to take a round in the chest and collapse by the door. The audience, which by now was a terrified mob, trampled his body as they tried to run outside.

Powell pushed Tana out of the club. They ran through the crowd to the Bronco, which was parked on a side street adjacent to the club. Tana could hear the crashing sounds of cars slamming into each other in the parking lot as panicked drivers tried to escape. They jumped into the Bronco and tried to catch their breath. Then came the sounds of approaching sirens.

Powell waited until he could breathe, then looked at her. "You want to tell me what the fuck you were thinking back there?"

Tana shrugged. "He pissed me off. I hate guys like that."

"So you were gonna shoot him in front of a couple hundred witnesses?" Powell shook his head. "No wonder you can't hang on to a boyfriend. Probably scare 'em all half to death."

"He had it coming."

"He's got worse than that coming," Powell said.

"Tana looked out the window at the panicked crowd in front of the club, then turned to Powell.

"You were right."

"Yeah? About what?"

"Her guns. They really were part of her act."

Powell gave a weary smile. "You're gonna get us both killed, Montana."

Tana shook her head. "Not before we find Emma."

CHAPTER 65

POWELL TURNED THE KEY. TANA LOOKED AT HIM AS THE Bronco's 289-cubic-inch V8 rumbled into life.

"Where to now?"

"I want to go back inside."

Tana's jaw dropped. She stared at Powell. "What, you want to give her another chance to shoot us? Maybe this time she won't miss."

"I want to take a look at her dressing room."

"Why?"

"I want to know what's up with her and Hector."

"Besides the fact that they're mother and son?"

Powell nodded.

"I'm guessing we're not gonna use the front door," Tana said.

"Garbage trucks would need access, which means there must be an alley behind the club. Let's check it out."

Powell checked for traffic, then made a U-turn and drove down a dark alley filled with dumpsters. He pulled over and parked, then killed the engine and the lights. He took a Maglite out of the glove and they climbed out of the Bronco. They crept along the side of the club until they reached an alley behind the club that was shrouded in darkness. Powell switched on the flashlight and scanned the alley. Tana watched as the beam probed the darkness, then lit up a door.

"Bingo," Powell whispered.

Then they heard the sound of footsteps, someone running toward the door.

"Get back!" Powell whispered and pushed Tana into the shadows at the edge of the building.

They peered around the corner and saw the door fly open. Workers in kitchen whites who looked as if they were running for their lives stormed out of the building and ran down the alley in the opposite direction. Tana noticed that in their rush and panic to escape they had left the door open.

"Let's go," Powell said, and they slipped into Bahia and quietly closed the door.

Tana could hear the sound of chaos and confusion, people shouting, raised voices demanding answers as they moved down an empty hallway.

"This is crazy, Bud, they're gonna find us," Tana whispered.

But Powell ignored her and kept trying doors until he found one that was unlocked. They traded glances, then slipped inside and closed the door. Powell switched on the Maglite and swept the room. The beam fell across a makeup table, lighting up the headshots and promotional photos of Adelita Santos in performance that were taped to the mirror. A bottle of tequila and a glass with the club's logo on it were on the table.

"We're in her dressing room," Tana whispered as the flashlight's beam swept across a screen that she presumed Adelita used for costume changes.

Powell nodded. "Let's take a look around and see what turns up."

"What are we looking for, exactly?"

Powell shrugged. "Whatever we find." The beam fell across a desk on the other side of the room. "Let's start with the desk."

Tana nodded, and while Powell held the flashlight, she went through the drawers. They were filled with papers, photos and showbiz memorabilia that meant nothing to her.

"Anything?" Powell said.

"Not yet," Tana said as she continued rummaging through the desk. Then something caught her eye. "Hey, look at this."

She held up a slip of paper. Powell shone the flashlight on it, revealing a faded photograph of Emma's daycare center.

"What is it?" Powell said, shining the flashlight on the photograph.

"Looks like a daycare center."

"Emma's daycare center," Tana said. She pointed at the sign above the playground. "Picture Day."

Powell's face hardened. "Looks like it was a family affair."

Tana looked at Powell in dismay. "Hector's mother helped kidnap a four-year-old kid? How could she?"

Powell shook his head in disgust. "Makes you want to puke, doesn't it?"

Then Tana heard the sound of someone approaching the dressing room. Powell heard it too. He killed the flashlight and he and Tana ducked behind the screen.

The door opened and the MC stepped into the room. He flipped on the lights and looked around. Tana peered over the top of the screen and saw that the MC was still wearing his pinky ring and sparkly dinner jacket. But he was sweating profusely and there was a frantic look in his eyes. He sat down at the makeup table, picked up the bottle of tequila, and poured himself a triple shot. He knocked it back, then took a deep breath and poured himself another one. Tana watched as he knocked that one back as well. He ran his hands through his hair, then rushed out of the dressing room, slamming the door behind him.

"I guess he needed a drink," Tana said as they came out from behind the screen.

"Can't say as I blame him," Powell said. "But let's get out of here before anybody else stops by for a drink. I want to check out the garage before the cops show up and the whole place turns into a crime scene."

They slipped out of the club and drove out of the alley. Powell found a side street that ran parallel to the garage, then pulled over and looked out at the chain link fence and the padlocked gate.

"What about the fence?" Tana said.

"I got it covered," Powell said. He looked at her. "You ready?"

Tana nodded and they climbed out of the Bronco. Powell opened the trunk and took a pair of wire cutters.

"You always come prepared?" Tana said.

"Beats the alternative," Powell said, and they moved across the alley to the fence.

Powell looked around, then began cutting through the fence. Tana watched him with increasing anxiety. She looked up and down the alley with growing impatience, as if expecting someone to jump out of the dark and catch them red-handed. Then again, wasn't it a reporter's job to know as much as possible? To uncover the truth, no matter what? Then she remembered a story that had made the rounds in the newsroom about all the reporters who'd been killed for just doing their jobs.

Powell put down the wire cutters and bent back part of the fence. "Go ahead," he said, nodding at Tana. "You first."

Tana bent down and crawled through the opening. Powell looked up and down the alley one more time, then followed her. He dusted off his hands, then stood and looked at the garage.

"All we need now is the remote," Tana said, looking up at the garage door.

"There's a utility door over there," Powell said, nodding at a side door with a window. "We'll go in that way."

Powell used the wire cutters to cut the chain and padlock, then opened the door. They stepped inside and Powell closed the door behind them. It was cold and dark in the garage, and Tana shivered as she pulled her coat tightly around her. Then Powell felt for a wall switch and turned the lights on.

Tana had wondered if perhaps they would find the Tahoe in the garage. But instead they found a long black hearse.

"What's up with that?" she said, trading glances with Powell.

"Let's find out," Powell said, stepping over to the hearse. He opened the front door and looked inside. Then he turned back to Tana. "There's a casket in the back."

Tana shrank back from the hearse. "A casket?" she said, her eyes wide with fear.

Powell nodded, then walked around to the back of the hearse and opened the rear door.

"What are you doing?" Tana said.

"We need to open it. See what's inside."

"Are you kidding me? What if there's a body in there?"

"You scared?"

"Duh. Yeah, I am."

"You scared of the dead?"

Tana shrugged. "Yeah, I guess I am."

"But you write about the dead."

"Yeah, but I don't have to see them."

"Give me a hand, we're gonna pull it out."

Tana hesitated. "You know what, Bud? Maybe we should just go. The Tahoe's not here, right?"

Powell locked eyes with Tana. "We're not going anywhere until I see who or what's inside. Okay?"

Tana paused. "Do I have a choice?"

"Yeah, you do," Powell said, nodding at the casket. "You can take the right side or the left."

Tana rolled her eyes, then joined Powell and together they pulled the casket out of the hearse and set it on the floor.

That was when they heard it.

The sound of someone trying to get out.

CHAPTER 66

Tana forgot to breathe. Her eyes widened. She backed away from the casket as the fear swelled inside her. She looked over at Powell. He met her gaze but said nothing. The knocking sound continued, a beat from the afterlife. Powell looked around the garage, then ran to a workbench and sorted through various tools until he found a chisel and a hammer. Then he crouched down beside the casket and used the tools to rip open the lid.

That was when they saw her. Her face was pale and paralyzed with terror, her eyes wide enough to pop out of her head, gasping for breath but still alive.

Carmen Flowers.

Tana rushed over to Carmen and knelt down beside her. "Carmen?" she said.

Carmen nodded. She was trembling and her eyes were brimming with tears.

"Let's get her out of there," Powell said.

Tana nodded, and together they lifted Carmen out of the casket. She threw her arms around Tana and began to sob. Tana exchanged glances with Powell as she held her, a stranger in her arms.

"They were gonna kill me, bury me alive," Carmen said between gasping sobs. "I heard them talking..."

Her words rushed out of her, as if she was afraid that she would never get a chance to speak again. And if Tana and Powell hadn't found her, she wouldn't have.

Carmen drew back and looked from Tana to Powell. "Who are you? How did you know it was me? What are you doing here?"

"It's a long story," Tana said.

Who was gonna kill you?" Powell said.

"All of 'em," Carmen said. "Hector, Adelita, Jimmy..." She spat out their names. "I thought they would've forgotten about me after all this time."

"But they didn't, did they?" Powell said.

Carmen shook her head. "There were afraid I was gonna talk about what happened."

"With Emma?" Tana said.

Carmen nodded. "I guess they were looking for me...I don't know how they found me."

Tana and Powell exchanged glances.

"I do," Powell said.

"Where's Emma?" Tana said. "Do you know?"

The round came through the window in the door. Tana heard the glass shatter, then saw the blood spurting out of Carmen's chest. Carmen grunted, then fell back against the hearse.

Tana and Powell traded stunned looks, then crouched down behind the hearse.

Then the door opened.

Tana saw Hector and Adelita enter the garage, guns drawn.

"You're next," Hector called out. "You and the bitch."

"Temenos que matarlos," Adelita said.

Then they opened fire. Tana could hear the rounds tearing

into the car, slicing into the metal and shattering glass.

Tana didn't remember much from her high school Spanish class, but she was able to make out what Adelita had told her son.

"She just told him to kill us!" she whispered to Powell, the panic suffocating her.

Powell motioned to her to stay quiet, then pulled the Glock and shot out the fluorescent lights in the ceiling, plunging the space into darkness.

"You'll have to find us first, Hector."

"I'll find you motherfucker, I'll find both of you!"

"Not if I find you first," Powell said.

Then, suddenly, he stood and, using the flashlight, he speared Adelita and Hector with its beam. They froze, caught in the light. Which was all Powell needed. He fired twice and made both rounds good. He held Adelita and Hector in the flashlight's beam as they crumpled to the floor, then turned to Carmen. She was fading fast, but still alive.

"Where's Emma, Carmen? Do you know where she is?"

Carmen looked up at Powell and managed a faint, dying smile.

"Ace is the place," she said, as if it were a tagline.

"Ace? What do you mean, Ace?" Powell said, trying to hang on to her before death took her away.

But it was no use. Because a moment later the smile faded, and Carmen Flowers stopped breathing. She had been found alive and granted a reprieve, only to learn that the grave was where she belonged.

"Ace?" Powell said, his voice edged with frustration. "What the hell is Ace?"

Then the sirens got louder.

CHAPTER 67

THEY RAN TO THE BRONCO. POWELL KEYED THE IGNITION and when the engine fired, he hammered the throttle and they drove away, passing the black-and-whites racing past them in the opposite direction, sirens wailing, lights flashing. Tana turned around and looked at the police cars receding in the distance.

Powell glanced at her. "You okay?"

"I don't know. Never saw people get killed before. Never saw 'em trying to kill me." She looked at Powell. "They gonna find us, aren't they?"

Powell took his eyes off the road long enough to lock eyes with Tana. "The cops?"

"Yeah, I mean our DNA's got to be all over the place, right?"

Powell nodded.

"I don't want to go to jail, Bud..."

"Why are you gonna go to jail? You didn't shoot anybody."

"Yeah, but you did."

"It was self-defense. And like you said before, they had it coming."

"Is that gonna be our story, that they had it coming? Or that we were on a mission from the afterlife, and they got in the way?"

Powell grinned. "That's pretty good, Montana. A mission from the afterlife. I like that."

Tana was dismayed. "Jesus, Bud, aren't you worried?"

"We'll worry about it when we're done, and right now we're not done." He nodded at Tana's iPhone, which was resting on her lap. "Go online, see what you can find on "Ace.""

Tana stared at Powell. "Are you kidding me? We'll get a million hits."

"Then I guess the sooner you get started the better."

Two hours later, sitting across from Powell in all-night coffee shop off the interstate, Tana sighed. She put down her phone and rubbed her eyes.

"My head's killing me. I can't do this anymore," she said.

Powell nodded. "Give it a rest."

"'Ace' could mean anything, Bud."

"Yeah, I know. What we need to know is what it meant to Carmen."

"What if it didn't mean anything?"

"You want to give up?"

"I just want to crash for a while. I'm really tired."

"Sure, good idea," Powell said. "Your place or mine?"

"I don't care. Whichever's closer."

"Okay. Let's call it a night. We can pick it up tomorrow."

They stood and walked out to the Bronco. Powell figured that since they were in the East Bay, his place was closer, and he headed in that direction. Tana struggled to keep her eyes open as they rolled down the freeway. Still, her mind raced with questions. What was she going to do about work? What was she going to do about anything? She looked out the window. Everything looked like the middle of nowhere. She glanced at Bud.

"Are you okay to drive?"

Powell nodded. "I'm good. We don't have far to go."

Tana was nodding off when she saw it. The car carrier loaded with wrecked cars rumbling down the freeway in the slow lane, belching black exhaust into an even blacker sky. She noticed that the license plate holder read "Ace is the Place."

She snapped awake. Her eyes widened. "Holy shit!"

Powell gave her a sidelong glance. "What is it?"

"Look," Tana said, pointing at the license plate holder.

Powell saw it and read it aloud. "Ace is the place."

"Is that it?" Tana said. "Is that what she was talking about?"

Powell drove slowly past the car carrier. The sign on the door read "Ace Auto Wreckers San Leandro."

"Could be a coincidence. Like you said, a million hits."

"Only one way to find out, right?" Tana said. Then it hit her. "Oh my God! Remember when we saw Emma in the Escalade?"

"The movie on your bedroom wall?"

Yeah, and remember there was a truck just like this one—"

"A car carrier."

"Yeah, a car carrier. And it was loaded with wrecked cars."

"Just like this one."

"Yeah, just like this one."

"I said it was a clue..."

"Yeah, you did. But we didn't know what it meant."

"Maybe now we do," Powell said.

He moved the Bronco into the slow lane behind the car carrier and followed it into the dark.

CHAPTER 68

Tana's heart was pounding as they followed the car carrier south on Interstate 880. The driver took the Marina Boulevard exit for San Leandro, then rolled down surface streets to a junkyard on the outskirts of the city. The junkyard was ringed with lights that barely illuminated the acres of rusting hulks scattered across the lot. Tana saw a chain link fence topped with barb wire, and beyond it, dark mountains of dead metal. The sign posted on the front gate read "Ace Auto Wreckers." Another sign informed prospective customers that they could buy car and truck parts cheap.

Powell pulled over and turned off the lights. Tana looked around for signs of life, but all she saw were darkened factories with broken windows and warehouses with For Lease signs. She felt as if she had traveled to the end of the world, to the place where everything died.

Tana watched as the driver climbed down from the cab, unlocked the gate, then drove into the junkyard. She saw the lights go off and heard the diesel engine rattle into silence. The driver got out of the truck and walked over to a Dodge Charger that was parked by an office that appeared to be a repurposed shipping container. He climbed into the Charger, started the engine, turned on the lights, then pulled out of the lot. He stopped just beyond the gate to lock it, then drove away.

"You think he's done for the night?" Tana said.

Powell nodded. "I reckon we're good to go."

"You sure?"

Powell turned and looked at Tana, his face tight with annoyance.

"I just don't want to get caught, okay?" Tana said.

"Then wait in the truck and you won't get caught."

Powell grabbed the Maglite and climbed out of the Bronco, then went around back to open the tailgate. Tana frowned. But who was she angry with—Powell or herself? She got of the car and slammed the door shut.

"I didn't come all the way out here to wait in the truck, okay?" she said.

Powell smiled. "Didn't think so."

He took out the wire cutters and they walked up to the fence. Powell cut through it and they crawled onto the lot, then stood and looked around. The yard was a ghost town, filled with lane upon lane of dead cars, trucks, and buses. Some of the vehicles were impaled on front loaders, awaiting disposal. Other were stacked three and four deep or parked in neat rows, as if it mattered. Tires, wheels, and car parts littered the ground. The asphalt was riddled with potholes, as if the fact that none of the vehicles would ever run again made roads unnecessary.

A school bus lay on its side, eerily silent. A car crusher was mounted on a truck trailer. Tana wondered if the driver would be back in the morning to help load the cars he had brought to the yard into the crusher, which would turn them into steel bricks that could be trucked to a recycling facility.

A rat scampered across their path and disappeared under a truck that was resting on its brake drums. Tana saw a totaled

Dodge minivan with Raiders decals on the doors. Blood-streaked shards of glass pierced the seats. A trip to the game that turned into a trip to eternity.

A breeze whistled through the wreckage. Tana shuddered as she felt a chill.

"I feel like I'm in a graveyard," she said.

"You are."

"Is it Emma's graveyard?"

Powell turned to her, and their eyes met. "I don't know, but that's why we're here."

"But where do we even start?" she said, looking out at the yard, which seemed to go on forever. "It's pitch black out there."

Powell switched on the Maglite and swept the yard. But its beam was no match for the scale of the junkyard. Even so, a lane appeared, wide enough for a truck, and it seemed to run down the center of the lot.

"We'll start there," Powell said.

They began walking down the lane, the Maglite's beam bouncing off the vehicles piled up on both sides. But what were they expecting to see in all this wreckage, Tana wondered. What did any of it have to do with Emma? They had decided that this was what Carmen meant when she told them that "Ace is the place." But what if they were wrong? What if she meant something else? Or what if, because she was dying, she meant nothing at all?

They continued hiking through the junkyard. Tana felt as if they were walking through the bombed-out ruins of some dead city. And she didn't want to get stranded there.

"Let's not get lost in here, okay? I don't want 'em to find our bodies a year from now in one of these cars."

Powell looked up at the sky. "It'll be light soon. We'll need to be out of here before the sun comes up."

They walked on.

Then Tana saw what seemed at first to be a mirage. Something was glowing in the distance. Was it a car? And how was that even possible?

"Look," she said, "over there."

Powell followed her line of sight and saw what she saw. They traded glances, then moved toward it.

"Is it a car on fire?"

"Maybe. Could be homeless squatting in one of the cars started a fire to keep warm."

They moved toward the glowing light as if it were a beacon, passing the derelict, shadowy wrecks that rose up in silence around them. They got closer and Tana saw that wasn't a car fire after all.

But it was a car.

A car she had seen once before in what now seemed like a dream.

A Cadillac Escalade.

The windows were shattered and the front wheels were missing. The Escalade was pitched forward on its axle, as if it were sinking underground, into the grave. But the license plate matched the plate on the Escalade Tana had seen racing away from the daycare center the day Emma was abducted.

She and Powell stopped cold and looked at each other.

"It's the Escalade, Bud...we found it."

She moved closer to the car.

"Tana, wait..."

Tana looked over her shoulder at Powell and shook her head. "I can't. Not now."

She went up to the Escalade and was absorbed by the light. It enveloped her in its shimmering glow. Just as she was absorbed by the lightning storm the night she saw Helen for the first time. And yet she was not afraid. This was the moment she had been waiting for, even if she had not known it until now.

Tana opened the trunk and saw a shabby, dusty suitcase. She looked back at Powell and motioned for him to join her. He came up to her and he too was absorbed by the light. They traded glances at the sight of the suitcase, then Tana opened it, revealing the skeletal remains of a child wearing a ragged, faded pink top and torn gray leggings with pink stripes.

Tana's hand flew to her mouth. "It's her, it's Emma."

Bud nodded. He looked at what remained of Emma and his face crumpled with sadness.

Then, suddenly, Helen's ghost appeared above the Escalade. She wore the same shroud she wore the first time Tana saw her. But the pain she had seen in Helen's eyes that night had been replaced by a kind of sad joy.

Tana and Powell watched, awestruck, unable to move, as Helen reached out to touch her daughter's remains. As she did so, Emma's ghost rose up from her bones. She smiled and took her mother's hand.

Emma turned and looked at Tana. Then, hand in hand, mother and child walked through the ruins until they disappeared.

"They're gone," Tana said as she watched Emma and Helen vanish into nothing.

"They're home," Powell said.

Tana turned to him. Her eyes were filled with tears. She moved into his arms, and he held her close as dawn broke and the morning sun rose over the wreckage.

ABOUT THE AUTHOR

Robert Baty is the author of "The Blonde in the Lotus Elite" and "The Girl in the MGA," two mysteries set in the world of classic cars. He is also the author of "Murder Goes On Tour," published by Next Chapter in 2021. When he's not following his characters down the mean streets of his imagination, Bob's piloting his Alfa Romeo through the blind curves that lie just ahead.

———

To learn more about Robert Baty and discover more Next Chapter authors, visit our website at www.nextchapter.pub.

Printed in Great Britain
by Amazon